THE NIGHTS ARE HOT IN ATLANTA!

What the critics are saying...!

"Fascinating. A total subversion of the most fundamental dichotomies of Western literature, in particular good/bad; an autodeconstructing textual engine that poses but never answers the unposable (but in today's world, far too answerable) questions. A full on assault on the centricity of such dominating ideas as quality, consistency, coherence, and that dirty books ought to give me a stiffy." —*John Barnes*

"ATLANTA NIGHTS: I haven't been this stunned since my colonoscopy." — *Dennis L. McKiernan*

"Only a sequel could follow this!" —*Tina Kuzminski*

"That's so bad it makes my skin hurt." —*Raymond E. Feist*

"The skin of your back, Ray?" —*Dave Smeds*

"No, actually, just about all of it, 'cept maybe this little spot of callous on the ball of my left foot . . ." —*Raymond E. Feist*

"Unputupwithable!" —*M. V. Capobianco*

"ATLANTA NIGHTS: surely to be the Great American Naval!" —*Sherwood Smith*

"You'll be half-reduced to tears, one-quarter fully amazed, and one-quarter totally mired in these pages for as long as you can keep the book open." —*Ted Kuzminski*

"Don't fail to miss it if you can!" —*Jerry Pournelle*

"ATALANTA NITES might rival Tolkein with enough editing." —*Brook West*

"An unbelievable effort - incredible! Read it and your jaw will drop." —*Brenda Clough*

"Unbelievable! Incredible! A real jaw-dropper!" —*Tom Easton*

"ATLANTA NIGHTS ... An incredible, jaw-droppingly unbelievable effort ... read it and weep.... Words fail!" —*Andrew Burt*

"A young man's passion, a jaded siren's last chance for love, a world gone mad, cheap thrills, fast cars, expensive wines, the triumph of victory, the overthrow of ontologically incipient hegemony, and gum! I have no idea if this book has any of them! But I liked the part about the bunny." —*Esther Friesner*

"ATLANTA NIGHTS democratizes the practice of fiction. If this can get published, ANYTHING can." —*Susan Shwartz*

"Better than a poke in the eye with a sharp stick. On second thought, maybe not." —*Roby James*

"There is little doubt that it will be given all the consideration it deserves by deep-thinking critics and readers alike. It's sure to be an immediate benchmark of SOME kind for aspiring authors everywhere." —*Russell Davis*

"I can never read too much work of this quality. I couldn't wait to finish it." —*Brian Plante*

"ATLANTA NIGHTS, where the bobcats meow. . . heed the call of the Serengeti!" —*Vera Nazarian*

The world is full of bad books written by amateurs. But why settle for the merely regrettable? ATLANTA NIGHTS is a bad book written by experts. —*T. Nielsen Hayden*

"A must for aspiring authors!" —*Anonymous*

Atlanta Nights

by

Travis Tea

ATLANTA NIGHTS

www.lulu.com
ISBN: 1-4116-2298-7
January, 2005

First Lulu.com edition, with stock back cover, January 25, 2005
Second Lulu.com edition, with blurb quotes on back cover, January 28, 2005
Third Lulu.com edition, with ISBN on cover, January 30, 2005
Fourth Lulu.com edition, with reformatted text and afterword, February 3, 2005

Chapter 1

Pain.

Whispering voices.

Pain.

Pain. Pain. Pain.

Need pee—new pain—what are they sticking in me? . . .

Sleep.

Pain.

Whispering voices.

"As you know, Nurse Eastman, the government spooks controlling this hospital will not permit me to give this patient the care I think he needs."

"Yes, doctor." The voice was breathy, sweet, so sweet and sexy.

"We will therefore just monitor his sign's. Serious trauma like this patient suffered requires extra care, but the rich patsies controlling the hospital will make certain I cannot try any of my new treatments on him."

"Yes, doctor." That voice was soooo sexy!

Bruce didn't care about treatments. He cared about pain, and he cared about that voice, because when he heard the voice, the pain went away, just for a few seconds, like.

"Report to me if there is any change," the man's voice said.

"Yes, Dr. Nance," said the sexy voice.

A door closed, and Bruce heard breathing, and smelled the enticing smell of shampoo, and perfume. It was Chanel Number 5.``

He opened his eyes.

All he saw was the roundest, firmest pair of tittles he'd ever seen in his life, all enclosed in a crisp white nurse's uniform.

I'm in heaven, he said. No, he tried to say, but his voice wouldn't work, his mouth was dry, and there was some terrible tube thing in his nose— and hey, what's that thing in his dick? It hurts!

The tits bounced like Aunt Alice's molded jello back at home, and then moved away. Oh. She was just straightening the covers on the bed.

Bed.

Bruce realized he laid in a bed, his left arm being strapped down, with something sticking an up-a tube—on the top of his hand.

Bruce looked up. The tits belonged to a beautiful face carved out of ice and whipped cream, with a pair of glowing emerald eyes. Around that perfect face was brown hair like one of those super models, all puffed up.

"Oh, you're awake, Mr. Lucent," said the sexy nurse.

Bruce worked his lips, but couldn't speak.

"Well, Mr. Lucent," the sexy voice went on. "You are probably wondering what you are doing here, honey chile." He realized the voice had the accent of a sexy Southern peach. "You were in an auto accident, Mr. Lucent, but don't worry. You'll be jess fine. This here is the finest hospital in Atlanta, and you are in the care of the finest doctor, Dr. Arthur Eastman."

Bruce tried to speak, but just moaned.

"Now, is there anything I can get you?" Nurse Eastman asked, moving around to the other sides of the bed, and fluffing the pillow.

Bruce wanted to feel those titties, that was what he wanted. Not that he could do much else, he realized. Everything hurt, right down to that thing, whatever it was, in his dick.

"Uh," he said.

Nurse Eastman's eyes lit up like Christmas tree light's. "Now you're talking! Oh," she gave a girlish giggle. "You are recovering jess fine! I have to go tell Dr. Eastman, right away."

"Wait . . ." he grated.

She paused, giggling again. A frightened giggle now. A childish giggle. As though a little girl on Halloween, going door to door, instead of seeing a paper Mackay witch or goblin suddenly was grabbed by the real thing.

"I don't remember . . ." Bruce croaked. "I don't remember!"

"No," she said, shaking her head vehemently. "You don't remember a thing. Now, you jess rest!"

She went to the door, her hips swaying like palm trees in a Hawaiian hurricane.

Bruce lied there in the bed, trying to recover his memory. All he could remember was the screeching of tires', like a steam engine gone crazy, and then there was just all that pain. Hell. Hell on wheels, that's what it was, yeses.

Hell.

On wheels.

* * *

While outside the door, Nurse Eastman leaned against the wall, her breasts rising and falling with passion as she tried to control her gasps. Oh no, she thought. How could it be? Out of all the hospitals in Georgia, they would bring him here.

She raised shaking fingers and outlined the shape of her lips, moaning softly as she remembered the one day she'd met Bruce Lucent. The single day, at the high school prom. She'd gone with her cousin to please their parents, since his date got sick and he had rented his tux and everything, even though she was in nursing college. Enchantment Under the Sea, it was called . . . she could remember it as if it was yesterday . . . their eye met across the room, locked, held, molding passionately. It was a gaze of molten heat, a supernova of total lust, even though he was only seventeen and she was twenty-three.

It was only a matter of time before she ditched her cousin and Bruce ditched his date, and they found themselves in the back of Bruce's Chevy . . .

She moaned, writhing in memory, until a voice splintered, shattered, pierced her memory. "Nurse Eastman!"

It was the Head Nurse! Her warty nose quivered, her eyes blazed with suspicion. The old bag! She wouldn't know what true love really was.

"I'm sorry," Margaret Eastman smiled. "I just had a cramp."

"If you are sick, you may be excused from your shift," the Head Nurse opined.

"I—I will be fine. But I promised Dr. Nance I would let him know when his patient woke up," Margaret gritted, and ran away before the Head Nurse could stop her, her high heels clattering on the floor like the death knells of doom.

Doctor Arthur Nance looked up when the nurse entered the room.

Arthur had always been the brightest star at school, from a very early age. He was always elected class president in grammar school, middle school, and high school. He was Class Valedictorian at his graduation, and when a lot of his friends went to mechanic school, or junior college to mess around with business, he went straight to the university medical school.

But their Arthur ran into something far worse than tough teachers or tough grades: prejudice. Yes, prejudice. Not race, but class. All the snobs from the wealthy families laughed at him for his accent, and when he tried to join the most popular fraternities on campus, they hazed him without letting him know until too late that he would never join.

Arthur got his medical degree, but he became embittered, against rich people, and politicians, and anyone in authority. Whereever he went, he was sure there was some conspiracy against him, by those in authority.

He was sure of it when he didn't get hired to any private hospitals, or to a lucrative practice among the rich, doing fat removal and face-lifts for twenty-five grand apiece. No, he could only get a job in this hellhole, where every night the ambulances brought in drunks and suicides and crazily homeless and the battered wrecks the EMTs scraped off the freeways.

Like this Lucent jerk.

Arthur was sitting there brooding about all these ills when Nurse Eastman came into the doctor room.

"Is my patient awake?" he asked.

"Yes," she said, and then she wiped her eyes and throatily whispered, "Doctor, I have to request that you excuse me from attending to this patient."

"Request denied," Dr. Nance said curtly. "I will not have one of those braided spies who work for the hospital trustees killing my patient! I'll go sees he now," he stormed, and stormed out of the room.

Margaret leaned against the wall and wept a sorrowing floodlike of tears.

She knew Bruce would emerge from the fog of the painkillers and he would recognize her. What if he told someone about that night at the prom?

All her life Margaret had worked hard, harder than anyone else. Her sisters, all of them far more beautiful than she, had coasted through life like a toboggan down the snow hill of life. But Margaret had a vision at an early age, and knew she was meant to be a nurse. Her mother had scorned her. Her father had laughed at her. So she put herself through nursing school by waiting tables at a low dive at night. Five long years she toiled, with never a day off, not even at Christmas, just so she could walk out with her head held high, and her degree in her hand.

Once, just once, she had strayed from the path of hard work. Just once she'd let herself relax. Do her cousin Ted a favor. Go as his date to the prom.

Well, she'd learned her lesson—she thought. She never thought she'd see Bruce Lucent again, but now, here, the cruelty of the fates laughed at her, just like her family. Bruce Lucent was here, helpless, in her hospital, and it was only a matter of time before he remembered who she was, and what would he do then?

She wept even harder.

Chapter 2

The Atlanta sun slanted low in the west, rain showers predicted for later that afternoon, then clearing. Bruce Lucent looked from the side window of his friend's shiny Maserati sports car as they wheeled their way westward against the afternoon traffic.

"I'm glad you could give me a ride," Bruce Lucent muttered, his pain-worn face reddened by the yellow sunlight. "What with my new car all smashed and all."

His old friend, Isadore, shook his massive head at him. "We know how it must be to have a lot of money but no working car," he said, the harsh Macon County drawl of his voice softened by his years in Atlanta high society. "It's my pleasure to bring you back to your fancy apartment, and we're all so happy that y'all is still alive. Y'all could have been killed in that dreadful wreck." Isadore paused to put on the turn signal before making a safe turn across rush-hour traffic into the parking lot of Bruce Lucent's luxury apartment building. "Y'all'll gets a new car on Monday."

"I don't know how I'll be able to drive it with my arm in a cast," Bruce Lucent shoots back. "It's lucky I wasn't killed outright like so many people are when they have horrid automobile wrecks."

"Fortunately, fast and efficient Emergency Medical Services, based on a program founded by Lyndon Baines Johnson the 36th President of the United States helped y'all survive an otherwise, deadly crash," Isadore chuckled. He nodded his head toward the towering apartment building, in the very shadow of Peachtree Avenue, where Bruce lived his luxurious life. So young, yet so wealthy, based on his skills as an expert software developer.

"I don't feel very fortunate," Bruce complained as his friend helped him from the low-slung red car, "I hurt all over and I don't remember a thing after I left that bar over on Martin Avenue. I wouldn't be surprised if the police didn't want to talk to me about what happened. Not that I could help them because I don't remember anything" he added as an afterthought.

Isadore pulled the collapsible wheelchair that he'd bought at Saint Irene's Hospital from the open trunk of his new Maserati and unfolded it on the curb beside where Bruce painfully stood, his recent ordeal only recently over. He helped his chum sit in the new wheelchair, and then pushed it rapidly toward the gleaming doors of the high-rise tower. The soft Southern breeze blew the sweet scent of magnolias over them as he said, "This is certainly something new for me."

"Never say that," he replied.

Isadore shook his head, his red ponytail flipping in the soft breeze, as he wheeled his best friend into the lobby, past the uniformed security guard named Amos who saluted them and then into the elevator to the fourteenth floor of the luxury high-rise apartment building, recently built in downtown Atlanta.

The longtime security guard saluted the pair as they passed. What lucky people, he thought, so young and rich, they can afford to live here. Not like me. I have to live across town and wear a uniform and salute the young rich kids who make more money in a minute than I can make in my whole life.

Bruce thought that the dark elevator walls were closing in on him and despite the chill in the air-conditioned air he could still smell the flower smells from outside. The upward elevator started slowly into motion as if it was reluctance to climb the hundreds of feet. "Hurry up," Bruce cried aloud.

Bruce pounded on the arm of his recently acquired wheelchair as his friend asked "Bruce, what's the matter? Is y'all so impatient to get home that the elevator is too slow for you? Imagine if y'all had to take the emergency stares in your condition" he chuckled.

Bruce glared at his friend who stood behind him and the wheelchair as the elevator hissed to a halt on the fourteenth floor, the dark paneled doors sliding open with the sound of well-oiled machinery, and then he was pushed by his friend out into the hall and then down to the door labeled 1414, his apartment door.

Bruce searched his pockets for the key that he knew he did not have. "Dammit," he said, and then, "They kept everything even my wallet at the hospital, how am I going to get it?"

Isadore knocked once at the door, and then it at once swung open. The stunning vision inside, an echo of pulchritude in a bright red dress, seemed to take their breath away, it was Penelope Urbain, Bruce Lucent's longtime and very beautiful girlfriends. Penelope, who had walked in the door of Lucent Software, asking for a job, and a good thing is being that she did, because he had one for her, a position, so to speak, that only a beautiful woman could fulfill, and she filled the role perfectly, as the beautiful girlfriend for those social occasions when he needed to appear on the front page of the newspaper with a beautiful woman on his arm. Everyone looked and thought he was lucky, but it wasn't just luck it was planning that he fell in love with this beautiful woman and her with him. He gave her his glance and she gave him hers.

Bruce looked at her and whistled, thanking whatever god was listening that the auto accident that he had apparently been in had spared his family jewels for he wasn't one to put to pasture his rampant desire for his stunning young woman, at least not yet. He snapped his fingers and snarled, "Take me inside, Isadore, or you're fired from my software company."

Something like anger stirred in Isadore's breast, yet Isadore laughed at Bruce's favorite joke as he pushed the millionaire software developer indoctrinated by New Agers into the stunning studio apartment that he rented in this exclusive high-rise tower. The walls were white as was the carpet. The walls met the ceiling at right angles, where glistening mirrors in gold frames studded the walls.

Penelope Urbain had been a poor girl she knew, though she pretended to have grown up rich and happy in the suburbs of Atlanta it was all a lie. Now she looked into one of the many mirrors on that studded the walls of her boyfriend Bruce's apartment and liked what she saw. Two hazel eyes with perky eyebrows, red like the hair of her head and other places, met her smoky gaze in the mirror. She smoothed the hair back from her elfin ears, making it tumble down her back, past her shoulders, broad but not too broad, broad enough to support the luxurious breasts that filled the front of her scarlet sun dress, glowing in the afternoon sun, the hot Georgia orb of fire, that came through the window, as she admired her trim shape and flat tummy, in the mirror. She looked, she thought, like the bad-girl heroine of a tawdry romance novel.

The expensive shoes she wore, high heels that matched her tight dress, and set off her red hair, were delicately shaped by the stiletto heels and sharp toes, the lift they gave curving her creamy calves and making her rounded bottom move like a semaphore of love as she walked past the framed mirror that she had been looking in. Her hazel eyes sparkled as she took in the sight of her newly-returned boyfriend in the wheeled chair that marked him some disabled person.

"Would you like a drinkie?" Penelope offered her recently returned beau as his friend pushed him in front of the wide-screen TV that dominated the west wall without making it seem overpowering.

"Dammit, yes," Bruce Lucent repeated, looking at this vision of feminine lust on two feet, "I've been in the lousy hospital and they don't let you have a little drink there," he opined. "Then I want to get to my new computer so I can check on my hot stock options and write more on my best-selling software development. I've wasted too much time locked in that smelly hospital. It's full of sick, people." Penelope and Isadore looked at each other, as only two redheads can look at one another as Bruce delivered himself of this comment.

"Then let me fix you something nice with expensive vodka and gin," Penelope giggled, as she went to the kitchen to make ice cubes. When she was young, she had been called Penny, but now she was worth a lot more she mused, as she busied herself at the full bar that filled the west wall beside the large television set that Bruce had bought with the first proceeds of his award-winning mutual software. He often went on the modern Internet, to make his money.

"And when Isadore's gone I can greet you properly," Penelope whispered as she handed the Old Fashioned to Bruce in his chrome wheelchair. She looked significantly at Bruce's tanned, lean frame as she handed him the crystal glass. "Yeah," Bruce responded "What's he still doing hear?" He turned to his old friend and pointed out, "Whys don't you go park the car? My old car is crashed. You know."

"Yes, Bruce," Isadore smirked, as he turned, knowing what kind of scene of wild debauchery was about to be enacted in that very room, because he had known it for himself first hand during the long week Bruce Lucent had been in the hospital. "I'll go park the car."

He went down the sleek elevator that he had so shortly before ascended, wondering if Bruce was going to be the man he had been, before losing consciousness in that horrible accident. Then the gleaming lobby doors were before him. He planned to take the Maserati out onto Peachtree Avenue in search of an empty parking place as upstairs a miracle of love was performed by Penelope and Bruce, young lovers at the very height of their beauty, wealth, power, desire.

"Going down," Isadore Trent chuckled as he pressed the down button, and laughing at his own joke. Had he but known what was to come he would have been laughing out of the other side of his mouth.

Chapter 3

"As you've probably heard Yvonne," began Penelope Urbain. Seriously brushing a gleaming scarlet tress out of her tearful eye "Bruce has come home from the hospital after his accident."

"Yes you must be very happy," said Yvonne sympathetically. "He was badly hurt in that auto accident."

"Yes he was badly hurt," responded Penelope honestly. "But he is home now and I am very happy about that."

"We need to have a very serious discussion about this," said Yvonne earnestly.

"Yes. We have some very serious things to discuss," agreed Penelope.

Yvonne Perrin raised her glass and began to gulp down the martini she had ordered and then she signaled the waiter to bring another one. Yvonne drank too much and did not eat right at all and Penelope was starting to get worried about her friend's habits in eating and drinking. Her cheeks were almost as red as her hair already, like red Delicious apples under green leaves which were her eyes and the dark pupils were like little curled up caterpillars in the middle.

"Do you think it is a good idea to have another 1 Yvonne?" interrogated Penelope.

"Yes one more will not hurt me and then I will quit," retorted Yvonne.

They did not notice that Steven Suffern was watching them secretly from his table across the dining room. They were at the Polo Club for lunch. The restaurant was a large room with a number of tables and some big windows looking out over the golf course and the lake. Both men and women and couples were eating lunch. Steven Suffern was the best masseuse the Club had ever had. After lunch Yvonne might get a massage. She thought he was a stud. Watching him across the room, with rippling muscles like a bull and well hung too. She could see his pulsing manhood stuffed into the tight silky blue gym shorts he always wore at work. She thought she should have made an appointment for a massage.

Steven Suffern thought Penelope was a real looker far too good for that stuffy software developer, Lucent who needed to work out once in a while and lose fifty pounds. He flexed his muscles and thought about the book he had just read, The Joy of Sex. It always surprised people that this athletic man was such a great reader and he liked that.

"Hello ladies," said Steven Suffern passing their table.

"Hello Steven." Purred Yvonne. She had a crush on the handsome masseuse at the Polo Club. Sometimes she saw him working out in the gym and she was turned on by the sweat smell of his sweet. She could not wait to think of a plan to try to get him into bed with her.

"Hello Steven." Penelope whispered softly.

"Do you have to work today? Maybe we could get a massage later," said Yvonne boldly.

"I only have room in my appointment book for one lady this afternoon," explained Steven.

"Oh that is all right. You go Yvonne," said Penelope kindly.

She knew her friend had a crush on Steven who was a real stud.

"I must get back to Bruce anyway. He needs me."

Steven would have liked to give her a massage but he was stuck with her friend. Yvonne was too old for him. He stood up and walked past their table and flexed a bicep for effect. "See you later then Yvonne," he said meaningfully.

Yvonne watched him go by his muscles pulsing and rippling like waves under a thin blanket of tanned skin like a freshly baked cinnamon cake. Penelope began to sip her mint julep. "I think he likes you Yvonne," said Penelope thoughtfully.

"Why do you think that Penelope?" asked Yvonne Urbain.

"He always comes over to talk to us when we are eating lunch at the Polo Club," explained Penelope. "He is cute, I think so too. But I have Bruce already."

"I think you are the main attraction here for him not I!" hissed Yvonne jealously.

"No, I am not," soothed Penelope. "Anyway you can get a massage and have him to yourself I will go home and take care of Bruce."

The waiter walked over to their table and brought another martini for Yvonne with a shot glass of extra vodka on the side.

"I did not order extra vodka!" Said Yvonne impatiently. She was mad from the conversation with her friend Penelope who all the men seemed to be attracted to. Her cheeks were flaming red fires like a volcano ready to explode through the cold emerald stones that were her eyes. She knew Penelope thought she drank too much.

The waiter said "I am sorry Miss but we are out of cocktail onions and the chef sent this instead with his complements."

Yvonne Perrin stood up and walked over to the waiter and took the shot glass full of vodka and poured it out in a planter that held a spindly rubber tree that never got enough light to grow properly even though it was near one of the windows that looked out onto the lake where some ducks were floating like they were waiting for someone to throw them some bread but there was nobody there at this time of day.

"Calm down. Yvonne people are staring at you," said Penelope worriedly. "Do you feel ok?" she asked questioningly.

"You never understand how I feel." moaned Yvonne. "I am just as good looking as you but I am older that is not fair. The men all go for you and you have Bruce already. I am afraid I will never find a man now that I am getting old."

Yvonne sipped her martini which tasted like liquid ice on her tongue. It helped her feel calmer. She asked the waiter "What brand of vodka is in this drink?"

"It is a French vodka imported specially for the Polo Club." Thinking that ought to impress her and picking up the empty glasses from their table. "Do you want to order something to eat now?"

"Yes. I will have steak," said Penelope decisively. "And I want it cooked rarely. I am a gourmet when it comes to beef so tell the cook not to overcook it."

"Yes Ma'am." The waiter said smoothly. "Anything else?" he added.

"French Fries and please bring the horseradish sauce."

"A Caesar salad for me with blue cheese dressing." Yvonne decided. "I am watching my weight."

"Leave room for the desert. It is our chef special today," suggested the waiter.

Yvonne could see the people at the next table eating chocolate cake. Everybody else had finished their lunch and gone now from the empty room. "Yes pleased," she said eagerly. She had gotten over her fit about the extra vodka.

The waiter walked away.

"Now back to talking about Bruce," said Penelope Urbain brushing a strand of red hair out of her eyes. "I hope he will recover soon from his accident."

"Do not worry about that," exclaimed Yvonne. "He is getting. The finest medical care money can buy. And if the accident leaves a scar he can go to a plastic surgeon and has it removed. I know a very good plastic surgeon in Atlanta. He did my nose for me last year," she argued.

Penelope wiped a teardrop from the corner of her lovely almond-shaped eyes. "I do not know what I would do without Bruce if something happened to him. You say Steven Suffern likes me but I do not think I could go for a masseuse if something happened and Bruce dies."

Yvonne Perrin got angry. "You are a snob, Penelope Urbain." She shouted angrily. The crowd of people eating in the restaurant at the Polo Club put down their knives and forks and stared at them.

"I am not," retorted Penelope in reply.

"You do not deserve the love of a man like Bruce Lucent. He is the absolute most eligible bachelors in Atlanta. And another one is Steven Suffern," Yvonne pointed out heatedly.

"We have been friends for a long time." Penelope said wistfully. "I do not want us to fight over men."

"You are right," sighed Yvonne. "Let us not talk about this again." Waving her hand to attract the waiter. "I will pay for lunch today."

The waiter stated "Yes misses what would you like?"

"I would like the bill," said Yvonne firmly.

"That will be one hundred and thirty-four dollars plus tax" responded the waiter.

"Put it on my tab I am a member of the Polo Club," said Yvonne grandly.

Penelope knew she could not afford a bill like that but she had her pride. She could not show her up before all the best society in Atlanta. She would never forgive her if she did. "I would be glad to pay half." She offered gently. But her friend waved the money away and stood up and began to walk to the door.

"I will make up for it when I get that massage from Steven Suffern." She exclaimed. "Steven is a real stud and I am looking forward to it!" She added eagerly.

Yvonne could not do anything more. She decided to go home and sees Bruce. But she was glad they had such a good discussion and cleared up things between them.

Chapter 4

Andrew Venice parked his car on the street in front of the house and double-checked the address he had written down on a slip of paper. Yeah, this was the place all right. It was an ordinary house, on an ordinary street. There was nothing special about it, just plain. Nothing here looked like it might be connected to murder or assault or anything like that. Richard Isaacs, the man he'd come to interview, were a stock manipulator, and you'd think he'd live in a fancier place, a nicer house, on a better street. But since he was also a police informant, maybe he wanted to keep a low profile, not do anything to stand out. Not exactly like the witnesses' protection program, but not all that different. Or maybe he just wasn't that good at manipulating stocks. Venice would try to find out, in addition to finding out what he really came here to ask about.

He put the note on the front seat, and his sunglasses in the glove compartment, checking his reflection in the rearview mirror and smoothing back his hair. Turning forty was hard. He didn't know what he'd been planning to do at forty, but he was damn sure this wasn't it. Oh well. It was his job, and he was the one to do it. He'd better get going, ask his questions, make his report. Then he'd have time to stop by the gym later, work out a bit, fight off the ravages of time. He was still in his prime, even if he had to work harder to maintain it.

Getting out of the car, he looked both ways, then shut the door and used the key fob to lock all the doors. It wasn't a bad neighborhood or anything like that, but he still didn't want to take any chances. He let a minivan go past, then an SUV, then he walked around the front of his car and up the long sidewalk to the porch. A bench sat on the porch, the kind you might sit on and drink some lemonade, but it didn't look used, like nobody had had any lemonade to drink there for a while, or maybe they just didn't like the porch or something. Isaacs probably had to keep a low profile anyway. He wasn't the kind of guy who spent a lot of time outside making friends with the neighbors.

Venice went to knock on the door and stopped. There was a flyer lying on the welcome mat. No, it was one of those bags of advertisements they paid neighborhood kids to deliver, one of those circulars. There was a cardboard box full of them just off to the side of the door. He picked up the new one and held it in his hand as he knocked on the door with his knuckles, loud enough so anyone inside could hear him but not pounding or anything like that. Watching his reflection in the storm door, smoothing the lapels on his suit jacket so he'd be sure to look nice, the door opened.

Richard Isaacs were the man who answered the door. He looked over Venice wondering who this guy was at his door, and what he was doing there. Venice got into his pocket and pulled out his wallet, flipped it open to a show hid badge.

"Hi, my name is Andrew Venice," he said cheerfully, like there was nothing unusual about him showing up there in the middle of the day. "I'm here to ask you a few questions. It's no big deal."

That was just what Venice wanted him to think, Isaacs thought. They always said it was no big deal when they were trying to nail you.

"I found this lying outside your door," Andrew said. "You want it?"

What was this guy trying to do, being friendly to him? "No, just toss it there into the circular file," Isaacs pointed.

"Toss it into where?"

"That box right there beside the door," he said, pointed to the box. He was getting mad.

"It's not a circle, it's more of a square," said Venice. "Or a rectangle maybe."

"It's a joke, all right?" Now Issacs was really really mad. "I put the circulars in the circular file."

But that crazy Venice guy just offered it again. "You sure you don't want it. They got good deals inside, could save you some money."

"Just throw it away. I wish the kids would stop delivering them."

"Hey, listen," said Venice, sticking his hands into his pockets. "I don't have all day here. I'm on an investigation. I came to ask you some important questions, and I want some answers."

"I don't have to answer anything you ask!" Richard Isaacs replied forcefully. He wanted to make a point. "Are you going to stay out there on the porch and scare off all the neighbors or you going to come inside?"

"I'll come inside and ask you my questions there. I want to ask you about Margaret Eastman."

Issacs knew he was going to be regretting this later. But he said, "Come on inside" anyway. Even though he didn't want the guy inside. But what were you going to do? That's what they expected from you once you got messed up with the police. But he didn't have to play their game.

Venice walked into the living room, not sure what to expect. Something about Isaacs didn't add up right. Either he was living in a plain house in this plain neighborhood because of frugality, because he was cheap, or there was some other reason. He couldn't figure Isaacs out, like there was something he was hiding. Even though Venice knew he was in his mid60s, he looked more like a tough guy than a stock market expert. He had broad shoulders, and a narrow waist, muscular. His cheeks were ruddy like he spent a lot of time outside in the sun and the wind. Damn genetics. Some people didn't have to work for anything and had it all anyway. He didn't look like a guy who had just turned 40 and needed Viagra to get it up anymore. But Venice wasn't here to feel sorry for himself. He had a job to do. And it was time to do it.

Isaacs sat down in the brown reclining chair with a plop, in front of the bigscreen TV, and he pointed to the couch. "Why don't you sit down," he suggested, like a man who meant it?

Venice wasn't going to let himself be pushed around that way by some informant. "I think I'll stand. This'll just take a few minutes."

"So get started already!" Isaacs would be glad when this interview was over so he could watch his football game. "You follow the Falcons at all?"

"I'm not really a football fan," said Venice, although he split a pair of season tickets with his brother-in-law, went to half the games. He looked at the TV for a second, trying to spot Bill in the crowd.

Bill was married to his little sister, Leslie, he adored Leslie. Bill was a great guy, just the kind of guy he'd rather be spending the afternoon with. Then he thought he sounded like some wuss for saying that, so he added, "I think the West Coast offense really ought to open things up for Vick though. They should make the playoffs next year."

"Yeah," said Isaacs, passionately. He loved football. He didn't mind all the damn questions now so much, not if this Venice character liked the Falcons. "So you wanted to ask me about somebody, some Mary, Maury . . . "

"Her name is Margaret Eastman," Venice said. His veins turned to ice at the mention of her name. Things like that shouldn't happen to a young woman like her.

"Who is she?" Issacs asked.

"Yeah! Who is she?" The door to the kitchen slammed open and in walked the most beautiful woman Venice had seen today, or maybe in a week. The more he looked at her, more he thought maybe in a lifetime, but he didn't have a whole lifetime of experience yet. But she was incredibly beautiful. Her eyes burst with curiosity. Or maybe it was jealousy. She was older, for a beautiful woman, maybe 40, maybe the exact same age as Venice. She was wearing a bra under her tight blouse and she was wearing lipstick too, and he couldn't help staring at her. Her hair was pretty too, like it was made out of silk, just that kind of shiny.

"Hey Monica, we need some privacy to discuss business," says Isaacs. "It's just man talk, nothing you'd be interested in."

"If it's another woman again, you bet I'm interested," she said, adjusting her breasts to make them stick out more. Venice was still staring at her, he couldn't take his eyes off her, and she was looking at his eyes, like she was touching herself for him, to be prettier for him. He couldn't believe it.

"I don't know who she is," Issacs said, and he was regretting inviting Venice into the house again.

"You sure you don't know anything about her?" Venice asked.

Monica stared at him with her lips making a little red pout. "If I knew anything about her, you can bet I'd let you know," she said, slapping Issacs on the top of his head.

"Ow!" he said, grabbing the top of his head.

He looked at Venice again and said "I said I don't know her or anything about her."

"She was the nurse at the hospital where Bruce Lucent recovered from his automobile accident," Venice said. "She's really beautiful, like you wouldn't believe. She has brown hair."

"I know you like women with brown hair, you two-timing jerks," Monica said, she was hitting Isaacs on the top of his head again, and he jumped up and yelled.

"Stop that, I said I don't know anything, and I don't know her!"

"I could show you pictures," Venice said. He had a lot of pictures of her, but he didn't want to share all of them, not with this scum. "It might help your memory some."

"Listen, buddies," Isaacs said. "You came here, so you take what you get and leave. I said I don't know anything, I don't know nothing, that's all there is to it."

"Why don't you take me?" Monica purred at him.

"Hey now, I don't like that," Isaacs said, and now he was mad at all of them for ruining his day. He was mad enough to hurt somebody. He'd killed a man before one time, with his bare hands, and he could do it again, if he put something in his bare hands like a knife or a gun or something that he could kill somebody with.

Venice sensed trouble ahead, but he wanted to see more of Monica. He had the sense though that they were just ships passing in the night, that she was just some temporary liaison of Richard Isaacs, probably just another cheap tramp or something like all the others. Maybe she could be different, but it wasn't going to be in this lifetime, not with him.

"Well, if you don't know anything, I guess I'll be going," he said.

Walking down the sidewalk, the car waited for him at the curb. He stopped before opening the door and looked back up at the house. He saw Isaacs standing in the window frame looking back at him. Somebody was hiding something here, but Venice knew he was a bulldog. He'd get to the bottom of it yet.

And it didn't matter who got hurt along the way, cause he was going to find out the answers.

Chapter 5

There she was, the pretty nurse Steven had seen while he was visiting Bruce Lucent in the hospital. It had just been luck, because he'd stepped out of Bruce's hospital room, thinking about Bruce's ass— a nice, tight ass—when he'd seen her. Her hospital Uniform, so lose on some of the nurses, was tight on her. It highlighted her ass, and her other assets, too. Even loose green scrubs couldn't hide those breasts, spraining at the fabric like they wanted to break free.

Steven licked his lips and rubbed his hands together. Women like his hands, they said. And men. He made more money than all the other masseuses at the Polo Club, tips from people who appreciated his hands.

"Hey," he hissed, and got her attention. She looked him up and down, taking in how his shirt strained over his sculptured abs, how the front of his tight jeans bulged, how his hair hung sexily over his eyes.

She smiled, those sexy eyes sparkled, those rosy lips pouted. "I saw you at the hospital," she said. "You came to see Mr. Lucent."

"Excellent memory," he congratulated. He knew his smile, lit up dark-brown his eyes, accented his tanned cheekbones. "Like the rest of you."

She blushed, and the warm rush of color colored her face and neck and on down into her cleavage. His eyes followed where it lead, and she saw him staring down her shirt. She seemed to like it. "Buy me a drink?"

Bars this close to the hospital had people drinking to forget what horrible sicknesses their loved ones had been sitting in them. They weren't very good places to start romances. So after one drink, Stephen queried, "Let's go somewhere else. This place is depressing!"

"It's raining outside," she moved closer to him, like he could keep her warm in the rain. "I'll keep you warm," he promised.

That's what she wants to hear! She leaned closer on the bar stool. He looked around at the sad people with their drinks. But no one met his eyes, so he leaned down and played with a piece of her sleek brown hair.

"I'm Steven," he explained. After a little while, when she didn't say anything.

"Do you ever try to forget things, Steven" the sexy nurse asked him?

"All the time. But I didn't forget you. You are not forgettable."

She turned her head around and smiled at him. That smile made her look younger, like she was a teenager. It was pretty, with straight white teeth. She didn't wear much lipstick, but he liked it that way. Probably for her job. "I'm Margaret. I didn't forget you, either. Even though, it was days ago, at the hospital. You are easy to remember."

He smiled lazily at her, glad that he worked out, because it must be his abs and his muscles that made him so easy to remember.

Their faces got closer together. He was looking at her in the dim light from the bar, ignoring the jangling music. It was noisy in here, and stank of beer and other things he didn't want to think about. So he thought about her. Looking down at her like this, her shirt gapped open more, and he could see the top of her bra. Those big, jiggle breasts, so close to him. They were making his jeans uncomfortable.

"Let's forget what you want to a fogey, then, "Steven encouraged. She smiled a little bit, and those rosy red lips parted. Her teeth shone like perfect pearls in the dim light. He wanted to taste those lips. She closed her eyes and tipped her head back some more. That was his cue, he could tell. So he pushed his lips against hers.

Her lips were warm and soft and tasted like breath mints. It was good. She sighed a little bit, and he thought she would pull away then, but she didn't. So he made the kiss better. He ran his tongue along those perfect teeth. The feeling made him more sure he wanted to get her out of this bar.

"This isn't a very good place to kiss," he stated.

"But it was a very good kiss." She exclaimed dreamily!

He paid the bill, then put his sweater around Margaret's shoulders. Wait her," he mentioned meaningfully. "I'll bring my car around."

His Miata, bright red like her lips, sparkled with raindrops like diamonds in the light from the streetlights. Margaret giggled whilst he held the sweater over her head and led her out to the car. "Climb in, fair princess," He chuckled, holding the door, open.

Soon that sexy nurse, was sitting close to him on his sculpted, dark-blue velvet sofa. The lava lamp glowed on her face. Blues made her look mysterious. Reds shouted "Sex!" Her eyes were deep pools of mystery.

He put in a DVD that his last girlfriend had said was sexy.
The music filled the room with drumbeats like heartbeats, and a rhythm like to people humping.

"Let me give you a massage" he said. "I give really good massages!"

"I'm waiting." She turned her back to him, and he laid his hands on that sexily slender neck. "I need to pull your shirt up." "Mmm hmm!"

He started to massage the tight muscles of her back. She was so tense, but he could fix that. A little oil. Patchouli. Down to her slender waist, then her voluptuous hips. Ease tension, and he could smell her reaction, even over the oil. Yes, she was ready. He turned her over, massaged those breasts, D cups at least, with his sc3ented fingers. Did he take off her bra? Did she? And who undid her skirt? All he knew was that her muscles softened and her tension went away under his skilled fingers, and then her muscles tightened again as she pulled frantically at the zipper of his jeans.

That was when he pushed his fingers, into her yielding brown hair and pulled her face to his. Their tongues met like wild beasts, their dance ageless and timeless. "You have a hell of a body," she exclaimed into his mouth. "So do you," he moaned. Even if she was older than I, she was still hot.

His raging manhood was bursting at the seams of his jeans, and so he undid the zipper she couldn't. She was moaning, lying on the soft velvet of the sofa, completely abandoned to his will. As they came together, he thought how much better this woman, who was experienced and sexy and had been padding on all the right places was to make love to than the teenagers who threw themselves at him for his body.

They writhed together, like wild beasts, on the velvet, somehow moving to the deep shag on the floor. His hands, still oily, massaged her ass as he moved inside her. She panted, against his chest, she breathes getting more and more agitate. Steven could tell she was really getting into this. He was turning her on. So he got faster and faster, and finally, she screamed "Henry!" and went limp underneath him.

Her waves of passion set off Stevens, and her passion pumped him dry. She lay with her head on his chest, looking up into his eyes. The light from the lava lamp was purples and golds now. Purple and gold—the colors of passion. It shown on her face, damp with sweat from their wild sex. The purple made her glazed brown hair look like some exotic African princess, naked and willing. After a few minutes, he started again.

* * *

Steven was tired the next day, because he and Margaret had made love more than one time. First in the living room, then in the bedroom, then in the bathroom in the shower. Then he took her home, and they had held hands like little kids and kissed outside her door. He couldn't remember any woman or boy as hot as she was. None of those teen-agers had ever been like this. He defiantly wanted to see her again.

He was giving a massage to one of the regulars at the Polo Club, and a guy named Isaac Stevens. Steven wasn't interested in Stevens, because the guy was too old. Besides that, he had Margaret on his mind. But he must have yawned one too many times. "Late night last night?" wondered Stevens. His voice was kind of muffled by the table he was laying face down on.

"Oh, yeah," Steven muttered dreamily. He wished it was Margaret's back he was massaging right now. Or maybe somebody else he could get a quickie in with. Thinking about Margaret was making Steven hard.

"She must have been something, "Stevens guffawed wickedly. "Or was it a he?"

"It was a girl, no a woman. Not just any woman. The best I ever met," enthused Steven.

Stevens wriggled on the massage table. He was probably getting hot, thinking about Stevens' night last night. "Does she have a name, or, are you keeping her, all to yourself?"

"You know those center folds of, naughty nurses? I think they're all true. That's what she is, a nurse. At the Atlanta General hospital, right across town."

Stevens mused, "Every time I ever went to the hospital the nurses, would hardly talk to me. Must be?"

"Probably." Stevens mind was not on the conversation. It was on Margaret. He could tell she did like his abs. And his ass, the way she had gripped it—

"Well, does, she have a name" Stevens said one more time?

"Oh, yes. Margaret Eastman. "He drew the name Margaret out like a kiss. "Maaar-gaaa-reeeet."

Chapter 6

Bruce rubbed the thick foam collar around his neck with his good hand. The stupid thing itched badly and he knew it looked darkies but the surgeon had insisted that he must ware it constantly for the next month or suffer the consequence. At least it kept his neck warm in the frigid air conditioning in this restraint. He followed Isaac Stevens who followed the waiter around past the side entrance and between tables and a booth at the back. Bruce stomped his cane down on a lady's foot at one of the tables and she swore at him: "Damn stupid gimp! Whence watch out were yes going' with that damnable misbegotten whoreson stupid cane you a dam adjt.!"

"Gaseous, you old bat!" he howled. "Watch your own feet and keep them out of the way so I don't trip over them! Don't you know who I am? Give me any more trouble and I'll have your ass arrested so far your false teeth will pop out of your head!"

Three waiters hurried over. "I'm so sorry Mr. lucent" they sniveled. One of them turned on the old lady and shouted "Backs off, you! That's Mr. Lucent and he owns half this town!" Another waiter spoke up and yelled "Why he owns more than half of this here Trotters Corners and that's a fact!" They gathered around her and knocked her out of her chair, then kicked her a few times to teach her a lesson.

Bruce limped on after Stevens, leaving the waiters to handle the woman. It was stupid people like that who had inspired him to climb to the top. He didn't ever want to be stuck with riffraff like that so he had used the computer skills he had learned from cracking play station games and writing viruses on the internet to build his company to a person was today. A giant among software development companies! Not bad for a guy just out of his teens.

He bumped another table with the cast on his leg but the people there cringed. "Sorry Mr. Lucent" one declaimed "I hope that didn't hurt you."

"No" he offered magnanimously, "I'm okay." He limped across to their booth and slid in across from Stevens. "So, what did you want to talk to me about?" he growled.

"Let's have a drink first and get something to eat" soothed Isaac. "That dumb old lady seems to have upset you so let's relax for a while and then we'll talk about business."

"Suits Me Fine" offered Bruce. He turned to the waiter. "I'll have a Shirley Temple Screwdriver with absolute vodka on the rocks." "Yes sir!" exclaimed the waiter. "And you, Mr. Stevens?"

"Spays burn, on the rocks, with a little Pepsi. A good single-malt needs a little sweetening."

"I prefer Mountain Dew with my single-malts" quibbled Bruce. "Or maybe prune juice. It's more natural somehow."

"My daughter, Irene, likes it with root beer, but she's a little weird." Chuckled Stevens. He rubbed his pepper and salt beard, then brushed backs his close-trimmed hair. "I heard about your accident at the Polo Club. Guesses you're lucky to be alive. Henry Archer went off the road on the same curve a few nights later in his Humvee but he didn't survive. The cops said someone had dumped a bunch of used oil on the shoulder near there. That might have been what got you and Henry."

"Could be? I was only doing 95 but I slid right off when I got there. Had to throw away the boxer shorts I was wearing. They were nice ones, too. Glow in the dark green with luscious red lips printed all over them. I miss those shorts" whined Bruce. He scratched at his crotch where the leg cast rubbed and itched.

The waiter returned with their drinks. He set them down and then set a big foaming mug of beer in front of each of them as well. "Compliments of the house, sirs. Mr. Gronomon said you two looked a little thirsty."

"Great! "Said Isaac. Nothing like a cold frosty mug of heavy dark beer to go with my single malt. Helps wash away the taste."

"What will you gentlemen have for lunch? "Quarried the waiter?

Isaac rubbed his pepper and salt beard, then brushed backs his close trimmed hair. "Lets starts with pate de foie gras and caviar and a basket of crackers to spread them on. Triscuits, wheat thins, stuff like that. And some stuffed mushrooms and truffles on the side. And a couple of triple thick chocolate mocha latte to drink." He might be 50 now but he could still pack it away. Nothing that a few good rounds of racquet ball and polo wouldn't burn back off. Too bad Bruce was all knocked up. Bruce had such a studly body, rock0-hard abs and massive shoulders from working out and weight lifting, but he was starting to get just a little pudgy since the accident. Isaac had seen him in the locker room at the gym. Kid was pretty well hung, too. Probably had chicks throwing themselves at him all the time. He'd better stay away from Isaac's daughter, Irene Stevens, though! Kid was making a lot of money with his software development company, too, and Isaac wanted a piece of that. If he could buy his way in now, he might be sitting really pretty in a few more years.

"I'd like some artichoke hearts and pickled eggs, too" mused Bruce lucent.

"And make sure there's plenty of whipped cream on my latte."

"Yes Sir!" exclaimed the waiter. He hurried off to do their bidding in the kitchen.

Bruce rubbed his rock-hard abs. I'm getting a little pudgy with all this inactivity since the accident he mused. I'll have to really work to get back in shape once I'm better. A good thing that shrapnel just nicked my thigh rather than cutting a little higher or I might be singing a little higher. Wouldn't want to? Disappoint the ladies.

The sunlight was very warm on his face and side from the window and he wondered if he was going to start sweating. Fire and ice he thought to himself. Too cold air-conditioning and too hot sun. I'm being frozen on one side and roasted on the other. I'll be shivering and sweating at the same time. Isaac will think I've got a fever. Fire and ice, ice cream and jalapeno, ice water and steam, cold and hot, freezing on one side and roasting on the other. He fled uncomfortable, like he had the flu and had a fever.

-43-

"It's kind of chilly in here " commiserated Isaac. "How come you look so hot?"

"It's this sunlight, groaned Bruce, "I'm boiling on one side and freezing on the other."

The waiter brought their appetizers and set them in front of them. "More beer," he queried? "It's on the house."

"Sure" quipped Bruce and Isaac together. The waiter refilled their mugs.

"Hot enough for you?" he quipped?

"Yes," shivered Bruce. I'm boiling on one side and freezing on the other."

"Like Fire and ice."

"Try the cold beer," offered the waiter. " That should help cool you down some."

Isaac rubbed his pepper and salt beard, then brushed backs his close trimmed hair. "Here's to further success with your company," he enjoined. Bruce returned the toast and they clanged their frosty mugs of dark beer together, than swilled large mouthfuls down."

"Ahhh . . . ," declaimed Bruce, "That was good. Cold."

They tucked into the appetizers. There was pate de foie gras and caviar and stuffed mushrooms and truffles and artichoke hearts and pickled eggs and crackers and they washed it all down with cold frosty dark beer in foamy mugs and sipped their latte.

"Aaaah . . . " exclaimed Bruce, "That was really good. How about some real food now?"

"Oh, yes, "agreed Isaac" some real food would really hit the spot now. Waiter, I'd like a half pound of rare T-bone steak smothered in mushrooms and onions and a baked potato with cheese and sour cream and bacon bits and steamed baby carrots and corn on the cob."

"Yes sir!" exclaimed the waiter. "And you Mr. Lucent?"

"I'll have a roasted chicken stuffed with truffle and cranberry dressing, a baked potato with butter and sour cream, and a side of some baby back ribs."

"Yes Sir!" he declaimed and hurried off to the kitchen.

Bruce scratched at his neck brace. "Who was that babe I saw you with at the party last week?" he simpered.

Isaac rubbed his pepper and salt beard, then brushed backs his close trimmed hair. "That was my daughter, Irene Stevens. She came to the party with me."

"Your daughter?" inquired Bruce? "Wow. She was really hot. I'd surely like to get to know her better."

"Well," countered Isaac, "That might be arranged, as long as things go all right, you understand."

"Cool," quipped Bruce, who was feeling hot on one side and cold on the other. "Fire and ice." Bruce wanted to get out of all these casts and things first, though. And to get all his stitches out. Or maybe not. She might feel more compassionate toward him if she saw him this way first and that could lead to more passionate fun later. What a hot babe! He could hardly wait to see her with her clothes off. They'd start slow, maybe a game of strip poker or something classy like that and then once they were ready they could go right for the brass ring. His slacks tightened and he winced as one of his stitches pulled out.

Bruce rubbed his throbbing crotch where the cast rubbed and the stitch had pulled out and his pants were too tight now. "So, " he inquired? "What did you want to talk about?"

Isaac rubbed his pepper and salt beard, then brushed backs his close trimmed hair. "Well, " he countered. "You've been very successful with your software company and I'd like to talk about that. I really admire a successful man who makes a lot of money and you're one. Especially as young as you are, to be so successful and making so much money, if you know what I mean. I admire that."

"Yes, " agreed Bruce. "I am doing rather well and I enjoy making money. Not the money so much as all the things it can buy. All the wonderful things I can do with it. I own half of this town, Trotter's Corner, now and someday I'd like to own half of Atlanta itself. First I'm going to name this town, though. I'm going to name it Lucentville! Do you hear that everyone? This town is now Lucentville! And someday Atlanta will be named Lucent City!"

Everybody cheered and the waiter brought their food. "More Beer," he carried? "It's on the house! ."

"Sure!" they quipped and dug into their food.

"Well," chewed Stevens around his steak and potatoes and onions and mushrooms and corn on the cob, "I'd like to invest in your company. I'd like to give you a lot of money so that I can have a part of your company and I'll introduce you to Irene, too."

Bruce scratched at his neck brace. "Well," he gobbled past his roast chicken and ribs, "That sounds quite decent of you. I think I'd like that. And I'm especially looking forward to getting to know Irene Stevens better, if you know what I mean." Wow, was she hot! Fire and ice! They devoured their food and drank more toasts from tall, foamy, mugs of ice cold beer. "To Lucentville!"

"To Lucent Software Development Corp.!"

"To Irene Stevens!"

"To Life!"

"Fire and ice!"

At last they finished their meals. Isaac rubbed his pepper and salt beard, then brushed backs his close trimmed hair. "How about some desert?" inquired Isaac.

Bruce rubbed his throbbing crotch where the cast rubbed against it and his stitch had pulled out and his pants were swollen with lust. "Dessert would be great!" declaimed Bruce. "I'm famished!."

Fire and ice.

Chapter 7

Margaret and Irene sat in silence for thirty-two minutes, each gathering their thoughts together, each afraid to say the first word, knowing that the first word could lead anywhere, including the truth.

Irene signaled for a latte with one hand and fingered her long blonde hair with the other twisting it again and again until it spiraled like a golden staircase leading to the top of her head. When the pain started, she wept, expostulating "I don't know what I'll do without Henry. He was the center of the world."

"Even the center of the world has to die sometime." Margaret sat sideways in her chair, her breasts a pair of protruding Alps.

"He didn't seem like the kind of man who died," Irene said. "Sometimes, when were in bed, making love, at the very edge of the surf where the waves washed over us again and again, I looked at his face and saw something there that not even all the forces of erosion could ever wash away. He was a determined man, and in his position he had to be: and I knew that, too, looking up at him wanting only for him to be there forever. He was old, you know: he was around in the seventies and everything. But there was an agelessness to him, a beautiful eternal foreverness that shone from him like the light from a lighthouse, or like the sunlight from the sun. He made me feel like a child again, and I wanted to stay in bed with him, feeling him warm my world, cooled by the waves that washed over us, until the stars went out. That what I expected anyway. That's what he promised. And now he's dead. His heart's stopped."

Margaret's eyes darted toward Irene in expressive regard. "Yes."

"What am I supposed to do without him?"

The unanswerable stolidity of the question echoed in the space between them, and there was nothing Margaret could say that could make the other woman feel any better. As a nurse who had been taking care of people about to die and who had died for longer than most people could guess, she had spoken to her share of people mourning the death of their loved ones. She had earned a nationwide reputation for her bedside management, as she always knew what to say to make people take the deaths of those they cared for most for just another part of life that needed to be endured and which would be one day feel better. Doctors always asked Margaret to help when their patients died. But some deaths were not like other deaths, some deaths were too much to be borne.

Some deaths hit those who were left behind like a bomb exploding in their houses, leaving just rubble behind. Margaret did not know what to say to this spectacularly beautiful woman before her, to make her feel better that the man she loved more than she loved life itself had been so cruelly taken from her.

A tear formed at the corner of her own eye (the left) as she shook her head and said, "I don't know. Sometimes we lose the whole reason we're alive.

Sometimes we have to go out somehow and find a new reason. A reason not dictated by law or morality or even sense. Some new person to love. Some new way to live. Some new purpose to make the night seems warmer. I think Henry was probably the kind of man who knew that if he ever died in a horrible car accident, leaving you behind, that you would find the courage to stand up and move on and climb out of this place where you are. He would not want you to be here, now. Or ever. He would want you at the beach where you were at your best, in the waves, in bed."

"Maybe." Irene swigged her steaming latte in one scalding gulp. "And maybe —"

"Maybe what?"

"I remember one night, the best night for us. He took me to Rome where we stood in the light of the Eiffel Tower and watched the people go by. There was one couple there who reminded us of us. There was another man Henries age and another woman my age and they were laughing together, just laughing, hard you know the way people laugh when they really feel the joy of life, the two of them, laughing! Laughing! Laughing, til the tears came down the sides of their faces in great cascades, and I was a little worried that they would not be able to breathe but Henry said, look at them, Irene, just look at them, look at her and look at him, look at them, the very themes of them, you know it's not a she and a him but a them, two of them together, in one unit, laughing and laughing here in the city of brotherly love, their laughs echoing and echoing and echoing up and up and up drowning out the traffic and the conversations of other tourists and the singing of the Christmas cajoler and even the motor noises, filling the world, it was a lot of laughing, and me remember Harry squeezing my hand's til the bones hurt and saying, you know, I laughed like that once, many years ago, when I was a boy, and I don't even remember the joke anymore but I always wanted to laugh that way again and sometimes when I take a good look at you I think I have a chance. And I never thought of it again but he also said that night, you know, honey, I'm much older than you and that means I'll be dead before you, and it will be worth dying even in a terrible car wreck if that means that between now and the moment of that car wreck we laugh at least once as hard as that couple walking by just now, though they were long past us by the time he got around to saying that. He said make me laugh like that again Irene. And I said surely, but you know, there was always the older-man, younger-woman thing and as much as I thought of him as some kind of God me never once got around to making him laughs." Twisting her hair into a braid using the same finger she had been using before she said, "And now I will have to live my entire life, however long that turns out to be, knowing that I never gave him what he wanted. I made him come but never made him guffaw."

The sun broke through the clouds then its brilliant golden disk burning a hole through the great puffs of water vapor to send a shaft of golden light zigzagging down through the layers of atmosphere and warm the earth in a way that no sunlight since the beginning of time had ever warmed the earth before. Somewhere a child was being born. Somewhere a dog was barking. Life was going on but in this one moment at this particular place in time and space. The two beautiful women, one twisting her hair into knots, the other sittings sideways, were not part of it. They were here only for each other and for the memory of a great man who had walked the earth like a rock in the sand. Life is like that sometimes, thought Margaret helplessly. Sometimes is just an interruption in the day and not a part of it. The trick is knowing when it's day and when it's night and the lightness or darkness has nothing to do with telling the difference between them. The death of a man like Henry Archer was definitely night even if it took place at noon. It was like an eclipse of the world. There must have been people even in distant primitive villages who had felt the moment he breathed his last. They must have looked up at the night sky or even the day sky and said, what was that, meaning him.

Irene lit a cigarette and blew out a huge cloud of smoke. "What am I going to do without him?" she wailed. "What?"

Margaret had no answer except for the ones she had already given.

Chapter 8

Richard studied the menu like a shark savoring a school of school of fish while the waiter impatiently tapped his fountain pen against his pad. Across the table, he felt Callie's eyes upon him, waiting for him to make up his minds. Yet his mind wasn't on lunch, but upon Callie; he could sense her own impatience with him, as if she was trying to decide whether she wanted to be dining with him at all, or whether she would be just as happy to be eating by herself.

"I'll take the filet mignons," he said. "Rare, please, and with the garlic mashed potatoes. And to start ... hmm, perhaps the New England clams chowder." He briefly consulted the wine list. "And perhaps a bottle of Riesling, please. 1999 vintage."

"Very good, sir." The young waiter, whose name tag said his name was Frederick, and who sported a pencil-thin mustache, studiously jotted it all down, then turned to Callie. "And for you, madam? May I recommend the calamari soufflé ... it's in a season."

"Yes, I think so," she said stiffly." And a chef's salad to start. But hold the dressing, please."

"As you wish, madam." Frederik clicked his pen, then moved off into the hustle and bustle of the restaurant. Le Bonhomie was busy today, busier than usual; Richard ate here often, usually with other Peachtree Street brokers who he was trying to get info from about deals they were making. It was one of the best, most fashionable bistros in Atlanta, which is why he liked it so much. The service was superb, and the food was pretty good, too.

"And so," Richard said, as he unfolded his napkin and laid it daintily across his lap, "how are you getting along, now that Henry is gone?"

Callie reached into her handbag, pulled out a compact. "As well as could be expected, I suppose," she said, opening it to study her reflection in its mirror. "Oh, I miss him so much, but ..." She sniffed, then closed it and tucked it back in her bag. "Well, life must go on, you know. Life must go on."

"Yes, it does." She wore a black silk dress to day, low-cut, better to expose the generous mounds of her bosom. Callie was a fine-looking woman, Richard had to admit, and the dress left little to his teeming imagination; her nipples, like the silver dollars he used to collect when he was a kid, pressed against the fabric, arousing him. "Yes it does indeed. Life must go on."

Callie observed his interest. She pouted, looking like the Mona Lisa having a bad day. "Is there a reason why you asked me to come here, Richard?" Then she lowered her voice to a husky contralto. "Or should I call you Dick?"

He caught her meaning, found his livid face turning red. "No," he said. "Richard would be just fine, Callie. I was just admiring your dress. From China, isn't it?"

"Yes," she said. "From Hong-Kong. Henry took me there many years ago, for one of his boring business trips. I loved the shops. I thin k I must have spent hours in them, bung things you can't buy here in America. And he was very generous, too. I think I must have maxed out an American Express Platinum Card just on clothes and jewelry. Oh, what a trip that was!"

"I can imagine," Richard said. He wondered if the police would be interested in her purchases when she was abroad. He had little doubt that many of them had not been declared with U.S. Customs. But a woman like her wouldn't have, have had much trouble dealing with lowly Customs inspectors, now would she? She would have just smiled her and winked and perhaps slipped a hundred-dollar bill across the counter, ands a horny young Customs inspector would have let the rich dame pass. Happens all the time. "And it fits you well, too," he added.

She glowered at him from across the table. "You're not here to ask me about my wardrobe," Callie said. "What do you really have on you're mind? Really?"

"Oh, you know." Richard Isaacs crossed his legs casually, like a king sitting upon his throne and examining a peasant who had come to him in supplication.

"Don't quote "Alice in Wonderland" to me," she quietly seethed. "You're up to something, and I want to know what it is!"

Oh, she was a tempestuous little wench, wasn't she? Henry Archer didn't deserve her … hadn't deserved, he reminded himself. 20 years younger than he was, and manipulative as Hell's own vixen, but she'd known how to spend his money, didn't she? But now Henry was gone, an ans. she had been left with his considerable fortune, along with his company, and Richard was interested in both. The company and the widow who controlled it that is.

"I'm wondering what you intend to do with Richard's company," he said, as the waiter returned with the first part of their meal. "Do you intend to keep it, or is it your intent to sell?"

She waited while the waiter, Frederic, placed her salad in front of her, then saved a generous portion of black pepper and Parmesan cheese on top of it. She glared at the plate. "There's anchovy on this," she huffed. "I cannot abide by anchovies. Remove it at once, please, and bring me another."

"Oui, madam. Anything to please." The waiter looked annoyed, but he disappeared with the plate, and came back a second later with a fresh salad, without anchovies. Satisfied, she speared a crouton with her silver fork and shoved it into her mouth. The waiter smirked with disdain, then carefully placed a bowl of New England Clam Chowder in front of Richard. It was hot and fragrant, just the way he liked it; he smiled and nodded. "Bon appetite," Frederick said, then he moved away to attend to his other customers.

"I haven't decided about the company yet," Callie drawled, chewing thoughtfully upon her food. "I suppose I could sell it, but . . . " She hesitated, daubing at the corners of her eyes with her napkin. "Oh, what would Henry say, if I sold the company he struggled so long and hard to build."

"I imagine he would want you to do what was best for you." Once again, Richard found himself examining her cleavage. So soft, so firm; like Florida cantaloupes, ripe for the picking. Although she was young enough to be his own child, he found himself wondering what it might be like to have her in bed, to run his hands through her silky black tresses, to knead and stroke and cajole her breasts into submission, to slip his hands between her thighs and explore the damp, warm secrets within. Henry Archer must have done this, time and time again, when they were married, and Henry had been only a few years younger. And now . . .

No! He couldn't! Once more, Richard found himself becoming aroused, and he fought to keep his mind on the immediate problem at hand. "You could do this," he said, idly stirring the bowl of chowder, "but the company stock, put on the open market now, could fetch quite a high price. Perhaps even ten times as much as it's presently worth on the New York exchange. You could be very rich."

"I'm already rich," Callie said, but there was a flash of avarice in her dark eyes as they rose to meet his. "Ten times as much, you say? Surely you jest!"

"I'm not joking. Have you seen today's "The Wall Street Journal?" The story about Henry's car crash has sent the prices through the ceiling. The NASDAQ itself is running wild. It's the talk of the town!" Richard stared back at her. "The time to sell is now, Callie, and I'd only too pleased to help. If only you'd let me."

Her breasts heaved against the taught fabric of her black dress, and again his eyes fell to them. Yes, she would be grateful. And once she'd properly expressed her gratitude, perhaps his friends in the police department would be grateful to him. Henry's tragic car accident had been too convenient, too swift. Callie Archer had more secrets than what she had hidden beneath her Victoria's Secret lingerie. And all he needed to do was to get at them, and he would be . . .

A dark shadow falls across the table, and a new voice interrupted them. "Pardon me," it said, "but is this seat taken?"

Richard jerked his head up, peered at the uninvited intruder. Bruce Lucent, the software developer. Young, handsome, well-known around Atlanta for the software he'd developed. What was he doing hear?

"I couldn't help but overhear," Bruce said, as if in answer to the unasked query. "Callie, I'm so sorry to hear about Henry's death. He meant so much to the rest of us."

"I didn't know you knew him well." Richard couldn't help but notice how Callie's eyes roved over him. Bruce was younger even than Callie, yet even despite the auto accident he'd suffered his body was lean and trim, with a youthful verve that Richard could barely remember. "Please, have a seat. We just ordered."

"Why, thank you. I think I will." Bruce moved to the empty chair at the table, then snapped his fingers for the waiter. "Garcon! A menu, please."

"Oui. At once, m'sieur!" And as the waiter hurried away to fetch a board for the unexpected interloper, Richard realized that the plot had thickened, indeed.

Chapter 9

Penelope Urbain let out the clutch as she sped around the curve. She felt a thrill — partly from the roaring engine, from the speed of the car (she was moving fast, too fast, on a suburban street, and she liked the speed too much). Partly, no, mostly — mostly it was the thrill of anticipation. She was going to meet Bruce Lucent, and she was eager to see him.

She could not have said why she wanted him so badly, but she did. Wanted to see him! That was all it was, she was curious, maybe more than curious. Eager, but — not too eager.

There. That was his home. That was where she meant to be.

She hit the brakes hard, skidded to a stop in front of his home.

He was in the doorway, waiting for her.

"Penny," he said. "I've been waiting for you."

There was a hint of suggestion in his smile, something that whispered to her dreams.

She embraced him, whispering his name. "Bruce," she whispered, and felt a chill at the turgid warmth of his body.

He kissed her, so lightly. He wanted her, she could feel it in his lips. She wanted him, too, but not so easily — not here, not now. (She thrilled at that thought. Here! Now! — No!) "Dinner," she said. "Where will we go?"

"I've got reservations for us at *Le Moulin de la Gallette,*" Bruce said.

Penelope Urbain knew the place — it was French, continental, lit by candles, elegant and intimate; she'd gone there once, alone, and eaten Saucisses de Francfort by a window in the back that looked over the moonlit garden . . .

"That'd be nice," she said. "I like the way you think, Bruce Lucent."

Bruce took a remote control from his pocket, pointed it at the garage. An engine roared to life as the door began to shudder open; in a moment a car emerged, its doors opening gently as a suggestion.

"It's ready when we are," said Bruce. He smiled. "I'm always ready. If you are . . ." He was already in, on the driver's side; no one had to ask Penelope twice.

# # #

There are moments when life, like a bad movie, gives us theme music. The good stuff is quiet — maybe Rachmaninoff, played softly in the background; Bach or Beethoven — in the classy films, it's one of those, or maybe Mozart. Bruce Lucent's life wasn't like that. More like, oh, more like "Popcorn" — the electronic pop version, quick, zippy, headed straight toward a climax. In the end, well, it's a little flat — too much air, too little substance; it just ain't Beethoven, you know what I mean? But it's something, and we can't all be Beethoven, there isn't talent enough in all the world for that.

Penelope nestled into the crook of Bruce's arm. It didn't matter to her that the music was "Popcorn"; for her it was Wagner and Valkyries, all the way.

"I love your lustrous hair," he whispered. "I love red hair, real red, it's so beautiful."

Only her hairdresser knew for sure, and it'd been years since he'd confided in Penelope. She didn't know what color she'd have without him, and shuddered at the thought.

"You're a sweet man," she said. "I love your passion."

Bruce grinned. "You make me rapturously happy," he said.

Penelope Urbain felt a chill that thrilled her. "Me too," she said. He raised an eyebrow. "I mean, you make me feel — so happy, too. *Rapturously happy.* Yeah, that's the word for it — rapturous."

She could feel his firm studly body under her left hand.

He was smiling at her. He looked hungry.

"I was in an auto accident, once," he said. "The doctors told me I'd never walk again. But they were wrong."

She smiled, nestling into the crook of his arm. "Of course they were," she said. "How did you recover?"

"I lived my dream," he said. "And didn't let their nay-saying dissuade me."

She pressed her voluptuous body against him. He was pulling into the restaurant's garage, turning, downshifting, jamming the brake — they were there, parked. The valet came to her door, helped her from her seat. Bruce gave the man his keys and a twenty; the man smiled knowingly.

Bruce took her arm and led her to the door, where they waited a long moment for the maitre d'.

"You're in software?" she said.

Bruce smiled. "I'm a software developer," he said. "Well-to-do — about 20. I have a studly body, don't you think?"

She looked him up and down. It was indeed the finest body that money could buy.

She smiled. "If I tell you you have a sexy body," she said, "would you hold it against me?"

He put an arm around her, pulled her close. "You know I would," he said.

She purred. "I like that," she said. "I like Atlanta. It's such a cosmopolitan city."

Bruce whispered in her ear. "It is."

"Atlanta is a great place for an enthusiastic would-be novelist to write about. The *Atlanta Journal-Constitution* is a first-rate paper, and CNN is headquartered right here in Atlanta!"

"Oh, Penelope!"

"Oh Brad!"

"I'm Bruce. My name is Bruce, beautiful."

"O Bruce!"

Dinner was amazing — Brad or Bruce or whatever the studmuffin's name was ordered the eponymous specialty of the house, les moulins de las gallettes, they call it the food that sings, and it sang for them before it was prepared. They drank before dinner — Bruce ordered, quietly speaking to the waiter. "Deux ouragans, si vous plait. Double fort."

With dinner there was a magnum of champagne, and after dinner there was coffee and brandy. Penelope felt her head swim as she rested it into the crook of Bruce's arm — it was an amazing meal, an experience she would always treasure. She wanted him so bad, and there, in the quiet that was the candle-lit restaurant, he touched her. She didn't resist. He wanted her, and she wanted him, too.

Chapter 10

The elegant Polo Club walls were adorned with a great plentitude of exquisite paintings, depicting a tremendous multitude of beautiful scenes, with still lives of flowers, horses, sailing boats, and landscapes. They are from all sorts of great painters and they had one every few feet. Their frames are gold gilt and filled with curlicues and fancy carving. The floors were polished white marble, with veins of luminous color running through them, and you can see your countenance in them because they polished every morning. A commodious, confident cloak room was standing discretely behind the double door, for coats, but was empty on this lovely, gorgeous, beautiful morning. There was an elegant, gracious, wide stairway to the second floor that had gilt on the black iron railing. It was orthogonal and it curved around it. The carpet was bright, vivid, glorious red. The French windows in the vestibule were open to the patio, and the sound of tennis games came in, and the scintillating, witty, sparkling chatter from the black wrought iron tables and chairs with all their twisting twining cingulated vines in their arms and legs there, where lunch was being served and the smell of the food came in, too. There was a guest book on a table in the center of the vestibule, open to hold the disguised names. There was a flower pot of Wedgewood china, blue and white, sat behind it, filled with a colorful, fragment, teeming profusion and arrangement of sweet-scented, multicolored flowers. Their vivid color contrasted with the stark, plain, severe starkness of the unadorned walls.

The Atlanta Polo Club was an old and respected and very venereal institution. It had been founded more than two centuries ago and was members from all the most respectable, notable and antique families in the area. When Sherman came marching through Georgia they had saved a few things from the old Polo Club, and the noble and distinguishable members were very proud of their traction. They gads been very poor after the war, but no presumptuous, odious, vial carpetbagger or scallywags had been permitted too scornfully, contemptuously darken the doors of the Polo Club. They had carefully rebuilt it of dark oak paneling and the lead-framed windows that were there now. They had spared no expense. They had played polo whit cavalry horse brought carefully back from the war, by young, handsome, honorable Calvary officers of immemorial memory from the war. They were very very proud of their disgusted memory and extended ancestry. They had antique cavalry swords crossed over every marble fireplace. Many people tried to join it and couldn't. It was very exclusive. Some of the aged members don't want anyone at all from the north to join, but there were other members who were retrogressive and onward-thinking and they managed to ease folks about those members, as long they stood docility and listed resentfully when the members talked prolixly about the novel war. Some of their new members were very good polo players and they had industriously managed too won many difficult games.

Irene Stevens starts to pertly walk into the Polo Club. She had long blonde hair and a voluptuous body. She was about 20. She was dressing in an expensive designer cerulean gown and not a bit of jewelry; her beauty needed no jewelry. She tried and signed the guest book.

She had come there from her hotel, where she had checked out that morning. She had driven here down the tortuous roads by all the Civil War monuments and past the pastures where they get the polo horses. They were all thoroughbreds and very beautiful. There had been flowers all along the way: roses and tulips and asters and crocuses and lilies and magnolias. She had managed to park her vehicle in the newest parking lot but she had been compiled to park it where the ferocious sunlight would infernally heat it up while she was leisurely enjoining the Polo Club. The soaring oak trees and maple trees had gloomily, dismally shaded the parking lot.

Elegantly, She walked up the stairs. The gown swished mysteriously about her legs. The sparkling mirror in the stairway considerately let her prudentially endeavor to carefully check her hair and jewelry. The artificial, incandescent light did not become her. It unflatteringly made her verdant dress and gold necklace look ghastly unbecoming. But nothing could, in its worst efforts, made her look less than marvelously stunning, could really detract from her gorgeous beauty and loveliness and she hurriedly took arctic comfort and consolation in that.

She urgently meandered down the marmoreal hallway to the opulent, exotic, expansive bar. It was very, very crowded and odorously noisy. All the men instantly stopped and ardently looked at her. She wearisomely sighs. She was getting very tired of the way all the men instantly stopped and ardently looked at her voluptuous body and long blonde hair and her vermilion dress and her gold watch with the diamonds. Especially when they were such tiresome stuffy old business men and none of them could adequately, competently, sufficiently play tennis let alone anything more private. And all the women cattily looked at her with sniffy expressions, when they were foolish wearing too much makeup and revolting, unsightly jewelry. She can be already heard the snide gossip began too perambulated its gossipy peregrinations about the ostentatiously crowded bar.

Swiftly, she sveltely walks up to the bar and smoothly orders a Bloody Mary. The bartender sagaciously nods. He competently takes a crystal glass. He swiftly gets the cold ice and put it in the empty glass. Consequently, he gets the imported, foreign vodka and put it in the glass with the red, opaque tomato juice. He sticks a fair wedge of easy lemon on the edge of it and promptly gives her it.

She comfortably sat back in her opulent, luxurious chair and leisurely sighed.

This was the right thing, after a long, wearisome, odious burdens and troubles of an appalling day like that.

She toyed with her pearls.

The comfortable chair was brown leather and very nice. She liked it.

And she was here in the bar.

Alone.

It was nice.

No one would talk here. She carefully tried and soothed out the skirt of her sallow dress.

She fortuitously remembered Henry Archer.

She managed too shivered in memory. No wonder no one was looking attentive anymore, next to him.

She sips her martini.

That was when Steven Suffern saw her.

Steven was a well-built and well-hung young masseuse at the Polo Club. He has an eye for the ladies, but bats for both teams.

His eyes narrowed when he saw her.

Irene Stevens.

Hear.

Alone.

There was no one around.

No one would come to the Polo Club on such a dreary, wet day, especially so entirely early in the morning.

Thunder cracked thunderously overhead. There was a loud, voluminous drumming and thumping of precipitous and abundant rain.

He walked toward her. Slowly. Took each step in leisure. Contemplating Irena with gimlet eyes. Taking in that voracious figure and the elongated blond hair. The carroty dress. The ruby band. He wanted to linger, to savor the moment, to pounce at once.

She leisurely drank from her gin and tonic again.

"Irena," he pontificates. "You are the daughter of Isaac Stevens. I will reveal your dark secret to your father unless you allow me to have my way with you."

"No," exclaimed she, horror stuck.

"Yes," grated he, harshly.

"You will not!" expostulated she.

"I will reveal your dark secret!" exclaimed he.

"I will not allow you to have you way with me!" she avowed.

"You will!" he averted.

"No, you won't reveal my dark secret," threatened she, numbly. "My father will never believe   you."

"I will, and he will," exerted her.

"You won't and he won't," claimed he.

"I will, and he will," remonstrated he.

"You won't," explained she, in an explanatory tone of voice. "My father will be very, very, very furious with you. He will certainly blame you."

"I will and he won't," demonstrated he, contemptuously.

"You won't and he will," proclaimed her, definitely.

"I will and he won't," declared he, defiantly.

"You won't," denounced her, angrily. "I already told him last Tuesday."

It was as if a copious galleon of wintry water had been surreptitiously poured over his hansom head. He sat stonily and goggled explicitly and gaped impassively as if he were a fish precipitously extracted from its appropriately aqueous environment. He boisterously, wordlessly, softly sputtered like a boiling tea kettle. He stolidly sat like an ancient, moss-overgrown statue from the radiantly fragrant gardens that the noble city was plenteously, bountifully endowed with.

She contentiously got up and stylishly walked away, her amethystine dress swirling about her ankles, fondly remembering his exquisite, superb physique and form of his well-proportionate, muscled body. She dazedly walked down the polished wood of the stairway and out of the Polo Club and up the hill and under the oaks and over to her vehicle.

Chapter 11

The nightclub was the Blue Velvet. It was noisy and hot and Callie was thinking how the sweat made her look hot. The heat of the Atlanta last night made it even hotter inside. Bruce didn't like the Blue Velvet because it was full of old people who thought it was still a cool place only it wasn't any more. He did think Callie looked hot.

"Hey, do you want to dance?" he said.
"Sure."

Bruce wasn't hot and thought if he tired Callie out he might get a better deal on the merging companies. Callie thinks Bruce is studly looking, and she liked to dance anyway, so she said yes.

They danced for a long time. Until she says she was tired and could they sit down at a table.

Now she felt really tired but was sure the sweat made her look really hot to Bruce. She smoothed her glossy black tresses.

"You didn't put any drugs in this drink, did you?" she said. She thought Bruce might try to take advantage of her to get a better deal on the merger.

"Speaking of the merger," Bruce asked, "what did you want to do about that?" He has to shout over the noise of the band. The band was a retro 80's punk rock band. They were a local group and looked like high school boys. Callie thought one of them looked pretty hunky, but not as hunky as Bruce.

"I think it's a good idea." She whispered, "what couples a million?"

Bruce decided he should think about it and said, "I'm going to have to think about it."

"Did you want more?"

"Well, sure, of course I want more. Why would I want less?" He really thought he could get a lot more. He wasn't thinking just about that one kind of merger, either.

"It's pretty warm in here, maybe later we could go somewhere quieter and talk about the details."

"Like what kind of details?"

"Like who will run the merged company for one thing."

"I sort of thought I would and you'd be my second in command."

"I think we'll have to talk about that. But I think we should dance some more right now."

They danced for a long time.

While they were dancing Bruce asked Callie about her husband.

"Did you wear him out dancing like this?"

"You mean like dance so much until he had a heart attack or something?"

"Yeah."

"No."

Bruce laughed. "I almost died once."

"I heard about that. I did a lot of research on you before I agreed our companies should merge."

"It was a car crash."

"You seem pretty well recovered."

"I have some pretty nasty scars though. I was 16 and I run the car into a pole."

"I'll have to see them sometime."

"Maybe later, if we go somewhere quieter to talk about the merger."

She spills her drink all over him. "Oh, I'm so sorry! I guess we'll have to go now."

"No, it's ok. I can dry it off with these napkins." He wiped at his shirt. He was starting to get hot and it kind of made he feels cooler in a way. Besides he wasn't ready to talk about details of the merger yet. He wanted to make sure Callie was more tireder first. "See that all dry?" he said. "By the way, I think it's pretty cool what your company does. Transatlantic shipping is pretty interesting."

"Yes it will be good to be merged with your software company. I know you make a lot of money with your Internet multi-level-marketing software. With the money you make from all those people sending you money and from my shipping, we'll be able to take trips all over the world all the time." Besides, she thought he was pretty studly and if it didn't work out after a while they could un merge their companies too.

"You're older than a lot of the women I talk to," he said, and he meant it.

"My husband said the opposite thing when he was alive. He said I was younger than the people his age. But I learned a lot from him about running business. Nobody thought I could run it after he died, but I showed them." Bruce thinks she has a pretty good body for someone her age. She was probably the same age as his mother only his mother wasn't very good looking like Callie. She had a voluptuous body even if she wasn't twice as old as I.

"Well it's getting late isn't it? Do you think we should stop dancing now and talk about business?"

She really wanted to get the big deal finished tonight and not have to involve all the lawyers.

"I don't know." Bruce wasn't sure if she was tired enough. Since she was older, she was probably wiser. Even though he was well-to-do himself from his software company, she was twice his age and had probably learned a lot more about business than he did so he has to be careful of any tricks she might pull. "Are you pretty tired? We could go back to my place."

"It's pretty hot in here." She said.

"Then let's have another drink. Since you spilled that one before you didn't get to finish it."

"Okay but just one more."

"Could we get another drink?" Bruce asked the bartender. She was pretty hot too and more Bruce's type since she was younger. Bruce liked her red hair. Callie's hair was black which was okay with Bruce but he liked red better. The bartender was maybe exactly 22. He knew she had to be more than 21 to serve. He thought he should order more drinks just to have her come over to where they were sitting at the bar.

"Here you are."

"Thanks."

"You're welcome."

"Thanks," Callie said too.

"And you're welcome too."

Bruce liked the way the bartender said "you're welcome." But he was here with Callie and thought he should pay attention to her instead. They were here to talk about the merger was another reason.

"We could merge our offices together too."

"That might be nice."

Callie didn't like her office all that well. It was on the top floor of the NationsBank building in downtown. That's being the tallest building in Atlanta. The view was good but she didn't like how long it took to get up in the elevator every time. "I don't really like my office," she said.

"Well then we can all use my office." His office was back in California and had a lot of plants in it. Bruce thought it was cool that they hired someone to come in with a tank of water to water the plants since they were real and not fake. It didn't look out over the city or anything but he didn't know what kind of view Callie's office had anyway so it didn't matter.

"When we go to your place to talk about the merger, you can show me your scars. I bet you have impressive scars."

"From the car crash. Yes, they are impressive." He sipped his beer. "I could show you here but I'd have to take off my shirt and I think they don't allow that here." He smiled.

Callie smiled too. She wanted to make sure she didn't get too drunk so she finished this one which was a scotch and ordered a beer. You don't get as drunk from a beer. She held her drinks pretty good anyway because she learned to drink scotches from her husband who had been a heavy drinker. It was too. Bad Bruce was playing hard to get about the merger. He was wondering if she had enough to drink yet so he could get a good deal. She was thinking they were having one of those awkward silent times in a conversation and she should say something.

"If we did merge what will that do to the depreciation do you think?"

Bruce didn't know anything about depreciation and was now getting worried. "You're not thinking of backing out being you?"

"No, I don't think so."

"The depreciation thing is worrying you I think."

"It's always a worry, isn't it?"

"Well it's different on shipping than on software I'm pretty sure."

"We'll make a lot of money if we merge though. We both know that."

Bruce stretched. She thought she could see the outline of his scars under his tight black shirt that was the same color as her hair. He was afraid he might be getting tired and it was probably time to move things along. Merging their companies was going to be a good idea no matter what the objections and he told her, "I think merging will be a good idea no matter what, don't you?" He was a little worried about driving because he'd had his car crash at night like this and it was when he was maybe a little drunk so he was hoping he could drive okay.

They would really make a lot of money if they merged. He had done a lot of mergers and this was going good. His accountant would be really happy with this merger.

"Do you want to have another glass of wine or do you think we should go somewhere quieter? I can hardly hear you in here."

She could hardly hear him either.

So they went back to his place and hammered out the details of the merger and signed the papers. "Then that's it. We're all merged!"

She toasted him with the champagne glasses.

That wasn't all that got merged that night. They had wild sex.

Chapter 12

Bruce Lucent limped out onto the patio in the hot light of the late afternoon sun, carrying a tray where a mound of freshly chopped up hamburger gleamed red and wet like a pile of bloody spaghetti, and put the tray down on the gleaming glass patio table with its matching set of six wrought-up iron chairs, where Penelope Urbain sat with her long legs as graceful as the fronds of a willow tree crossed in a provocative pose that made him think about last night and the passion they'd shared hour after hour till the turgid light of dawn folded down over Atlanta like the petals of a bloody rose and they were both too exhausted to move another muscle. Maybe, he'd thought as they sank into sleep like two swimmers who'd just won a race across the English Channel, just maybe things were going to work out after all. Maybe they could get it together at last. Seeing her now, as beautiful and fresh as a sunny morning in May, even though it was August, his heart skipped a bat.

"Hey, babe," Bruce offered. "Wanna grill some hamburgers?"

The happy expression fell off of Penelope Urbain's finely featured visage. She pressed her slender hand to her moist red lips and shook her lustrous red hair back over her shoulders, bouncing like the vibrant mane of a thoroughbred horse.

"Is that . . . meat?" she gasped, her eyes, the color of a warm blue sky in springtime, falling onto the tray. "Red . . . meat?"

"Yeah, babes," Bruce affirmed proudly. "Bona fide 100% sirloin."

Penelope fluttered, her corn flower blue eyes still stuck to the tray. "It's really grizzly."

"Honey, don't you like hamburgers?" Bruce wanted to know, crestfallen. "That beef is chalked full of protein!" Bruce grinned contagiously. "And we could both use some protein, after last night! If you know what I mean!"

"But . . . don't you remember, Bruce?" Penelope reproached, her sapphire orbs now grasping his. "I'm a vegetarian!"

Bruce's lungs ricocheted with shock, causing him to let out a gasp, and remorse swept over him in a stunning tide. *Darn,* he exclaimed to himself. *How could I forget that?*

"Wow, babe," Bruce stumbled, "I'm . . . I'm really sorry. I...I guesses should have picked up a carrot or something while I was at the store."

"It's . . . it's OK, honey," Penelope tried to smile forgivingly, but he could see the betrayal in her limpid azure eyes exactly like she'd said it out loud. "I'm . . . I'm not really all that hungry. I'll just watch while you and Isadore eat. He . . . he is coming, isn't he?"

"He's Enright right now."

"Good. I...I was hoping he would," she commented softly.

Bruce Lucent put the tray down on the table. He began to shape the hamburger patties, shaping the meat into round, circular shapes with his strong hands. Usually he caressed the hamburger like a lover, loving the way the soft red meat squished yieldingly between his hands and the sensuous sucking sounds it made when he pulled his hands away once he got the round shapes just the way he wanted them, not too thick and not too thin, not too wide and not too small, but just right, like the Three Bears, except it was hamburger and not porridge. He was an artist with hamburger, everyone said so.

But today it wasn't good like usual. The way Penelope's exquisite features had fallen when her eyes swooped down onto the meat had taken roots inside his brain like the tentacles of a poisonous black spider.

I let her down again, he berated himself savagely. *I betrayed her. Again.*

Why didn't I remember that she's a vegetarian? he ruminated to himself worriedly. *This must be the fourth time I've forgotten. Or is it the fifth? But I'm forgetting a lot of things,* his thoughts veered off on a tangent. *So many things I can't remember since my accident. Like . . . like making hamburgers with my mother.*

He remembered a lot about his mother. Too much, in fact. The alcohol binges. The beatings. The way she'd sit in front of the TV smoking crack and watching infomercial. The time the cops had to come to the house because she'd set the dog on fire. He'd loved that dog—Fluffy, his name had been, and there were times when he'd been sure that he was his only friend. The time she went into his closet and cut up all his clothes. The time she stole the money he'd saved up from his crappy evening job at the roller rink and spent it all on nail extensions. The way her fat legs bulged inside her spandex stirrup pants, so different from Penelope's slender frond like limbs. The way she'd cut him down all the time, laughing at him, telling him he'd never amount to anything, never get anywhere in the world. *Well, ma, you aren't laughing now,* he asserted to himself. *I'm not a pimply wimp anymore. I'm a stud, a rich businessman, with a fabulous house and a voluminous redheaded girlfriend and lots of friends. How does ya like them hamburgers?* He'd always wanted to shout those words into her fat face, her ugly fat hateful face with its garish caked on makeup and glittery paste on eyelashes. But she died before any of the good stuff happened and he'd never gotten to yell it into her fat face like he wanted. She'd choked to death on a cocktail frank while watching infomercial. He'd found her there the next morning, stiff as beef jerky.

I remember all that, his thoughts continued, squashing the red meat between his fingers like he was squashing his mother's throat. *I remember it like it was yesterday. But not the hamburgers. I...don't . . . remember . . . the hamburgers? Why? Why?*

"Sweetie, are you . . . , IS your OK?" came Penelope Urbain's soft voice, sliding into his tortured thoughts like a cool shaft of evening rain into the fiery heart of hell. "You look like you're trying to crush it or something!" she exclaimed worriedly.

Bruce Lucent gusted a sigh that siphoned up from the bottom of his heart and hoisted his thoughts up out of the black stinking mineshaft of memory. Mom was dead. She'd never laugh at him again. That part of his life was over. He didn't have to think about her now. Who cared if he couldn't remember the hamburgers? He'd learned how to make them himself. *Yeah, ma!* He affirmed. A contemptuous smile squirming across his well shaped lips. *I learned it all myself!*

"Howdy folks!" resounded a cheery voice from inside the house. "We grilling yet?"

Isadore Trent came striding out onto the patio, his washboard abs tight as a drum underneath his skintight white tee shirt. His red hair in its ponytail hung down his strong muscular back like the vibrant mane of a thoroughbred hose.

"Isadore!" cried Penelope, her soft tones vibrating joyfully.

"Is . . . ,, is it you?"

"One in the same!" Isadore cried.

"It's . . . it's so good to see you!"

"Great to see you too, Pen!" Isadore exclaimed, turning to Bruce. "Say, Bruce, great patties!"

Bruce Lucent's head gave a stiff nod. He didn't like the way Penelope had said hello to Isadore. Why was she so glad to see him? She hardly knew him. Or at least . . . he thought she hardly knew him.

"Guess I'll get these on the grill," he informed. The two of them didn't seem to notice. He picked up the tray and walked over to the grill. Opening the grill, he put the tray down on the table beside it and put the patties on the grill. They hissed and spattered from the grill while behind his back Isadore and Penelope were talking about vegetables.

"What's your favorite, Pen?" Isadore wanted to know.

"Oh, I . . . I don't know," Penelope responded breathily. "I...I think maybe lettuce. Or a broccoli. I...I like them to be green."

Bruce flipped the spluttering patties on the grill with an expert flick of his strong wrist. Inside his chest, his hart seemed to splutter too. *Why were they talking about vegetables?* he wondered darkly. *Well, Penelope was a vegetarian . . . but he'd never known that Isadore cared about things like that.*

"I'm an artichoke man myself," Isadore declared. "Give me a good artichoke anytime. You know . . . " his confident voice kicked down a notch. "It's the way you have to peel them. One leaf . . . after another . . . and by the time you get down to the heart, the soft warm luscious gleaming heart, you're . . . ready. Really . . . ready."

"Isadore!" Penelope fluttered with her soft voice. "I...I didn't know you were so poetic."

"There's lots of things you don't know about me, Pen," Isadore asserted confidently. "*Lots* of things."

This is wrong, but Bruce's thoughts told him. It was all going wrong. And he didn't know why.

Bruce Lucent piled the now-over-cooked patties back onto the tray and carried them over to the patio table where Isadore and Penelope were now laughing hardily at something Isadore had said. He banged the tray down on the table, the glass making a ringing sound that echoed the ringing that was sounding in his ears. A ringing of fury. A ringing of despair. He was losing her, but he knew it. Last night had been an illusion. Some briefs spurt of happiness that was all. It hadn't meant anything— not to her. It was all going wrong.

"There," he growled, his tone of voice betraying his deep seeded anger. "The burgers are cooked."

Penelope drew back from his rough behavior, her lovely face shaping itself into puzzled lines. "Honey," she ventured, "you . . . you sound so angry."

"I'm not angry!" Bruce denied. Pulling out his wrought iron patio chair with a clatter, he hurled himself down onto it, his actions contra punting his words. He shoved the tray toward them. "Go on. Eat them."

Isadore surged to his feet, his rock-hard muscles rippling and his red tail bouncing. "I don't think Pen wants to," he barked.

"Oh no?" Bruce shot back. "And how would you know?"

"Because," Isadore tilted forward, his eyes clutching Bruce's like pincers, his tone low and menacing. "*I* know she's a vegetarian. Which you, my friends, seem to have forgotten."

Penelope let out a soft gasp. Bruce sat like a statue turned to stone feeling despair engulf him like a black blanket of horror dragging itself over all his senses. *Isadore is right,* he acknowledged to himself in heart rendering misery. *I did forget. It's all my fault.*

"Ready to go, Pen?" Isadore demanded masterfully.

"I...I guess so," she hesitated.

Isadore gave Penelope his arm, his rock-hard biceps bulging under the sleeve of his white tee shirt like potatoes in a flour sack. Hesitatingly she took it. Together they strode out of the patio and vanished into the night, leaving Bruce sitting forlornly at the table staring at the hamburger patties on their tray, smoking like the charred ashes of his dreams, while inside his head he was listening to his mother's laughter.

Chapter 12

The reception was a disaster for Callie from the moment she stepped into the hall. Clearly famished from weeks of living on Xenadrin and Diet Pepsi, she made a beeline for the appetizers. The Swedish meatballs were obviously the most fatty thing on the table. To her dilated pupils those little red tinged morsels of mad cow must have looked like manna in the making. But as soon as she picked up a tasseled toothpick, the damn meatball launched itself off the stick and made its sticky, greasy, ambling way down the corset of her Vera Wang bridal gown, over all that hand crocheted tulle, and splattered its death throes on the open toe of her Jimmy Choo shoes.

The bride backed away from the table, letting out a strangled gurgle and waving her French manicured fingers in the air. She began hyperventilating. A cadre of caterers descended upon her, seltzer, bleached linen napkins, and industrial strength cleansers at the ready. Those wedding pictures were going to have to be photoshopped for days to make that dress ever look ivory again.

I backed up, trying to hide the fact that I was laughing so hard I was afraid I was going to spray shrimp cocktail all over my Manolo Blahniks. Of course, I backed right into Richard Isaacs. We hadn't said three words to each other at the church, but I'd immediately spotted him there. His Armani suit was so sharply pressed I imagined you could cut cheese with the creases. Being a stock manipulator, and a police stoolie, he'd probably stolen more cheeses than he'd cut. Still, it was hard to ignore his ruddy, good looks. I knew he had a yacht anchored on the Outerbanks, and his aftershave helped his allure by retaining a hint of sea air. The blue in his Ralph Lauren tie made his eyes seem more piercing, and the gray encroaching around his temples had yet to establish a firm beachhead on the rest of his scalp.

"Yvonne," he said, in a gravelly voice that hinted of a two-pack a day habit only recently dropped. "I was hoping I would bump into you."

Rub up against me was more like it. He hadn't moved more than a millimeter since my well-toned derriere had grazed his hip. We both watched in silent amusement as Callie's groom, Bruce, forced his way through the sea of starched aprons to comfort his fainting flower of a bride.

"Now Bruce," I heard the frail flower snap. "You just go away and let these professionals do their work. Go get mah Aunt Eustace some champagne."

Dutifully, Bruce left Callie to her staff and went to get some liquor for Aunt Eustace.

Echoing what I was thinking, Richard whispered, "Do you think she sent him to the oldest, ugliest broad here because she's already afraid of comparisons to younger, prettier company?" Here he patted me on my back as if to let me know who the young, pretty, company was.

Now Callie's only got maybe five years on me. And I know for a fact that she's still got all her natural software and she keeps it in good shape at the gym. Being a lady I would never mention some of her other habits. Besides, what's a little Botox between us girls? Still, I was flattered that Richard would include me with the younger set. Considering Callie was totally robbing the cradle marrying dear, little Bruce (for Gawd's sake, she's old enough to be his Mother!) I was enjoying Richard's attention. Of course, he's old enough to be my father. But let's just say I like them with a little steel in their girders. Plus he still has shoulders you could hang a lion off of.

I decided to go for the gusto. "So, Richard," I said. Think you can help me with a little problem I'm having?

Richard backed up a few inches. *What did he think I was going to ask him for? Help with insurance? Stocks tips? What to do about some incorrigible STD?*

"I lost my navel ring. Somewhere over by the gift table. I was hoping you could help me look for it."

His eyes lit up with a predatory gleam. I hoped it wasn't just the idea of finding gold. I planned to have him panning for more than a little circle. I was looking for the big O myself.

Over at the gift table I did a full bend over to scan the floor. From his position I was sure he couldn't miss a good gander at my leopard thong. It didn't really go with the fuchsia bridesmaid's confection I was stuck in, but I felt it added a little *je ne sais quoi* to a rather dowdy outfit. Besides, it set off my auburn tresses better than fuchsia.

Fuchsia, for Gawd's sake. Callie wasn't being shy about trying to make all us other girls look bad!

Ah, but back to my prey. "It's just a little old, navel ring with an emerald on it. I heard it go clink when I dropped Callie's gift off. I felt I needed some fortification before hunting under the table for it." Here, I raised my glass of Veuve Clicquot, and he gallantly clinked his Baccarat crystal against mine. "Care to help me look? " I asked, straightening up and giving him the benefit of my fully bleached smile.

He gave me a frank, appraising stare. At least I hope the stare was for me. He could have been tallying up how much silver and how many checks there were lying on that big, round, table, but I suspected the thought of my thong was more enticing.

"Coming?" I asked, holding up a corner of the tablecloth. Taking a quick glance around the room, I saw that only a bemused waiter, who was holding his champagne bottle at the ready, was watching us. All the other guests were too involved with the dress drama to give our portion of the room a gander

Without looking to see if he would follow, I crawled under the table. Fortunately, the cream carpeting was very thick. Now I'd see what he was made of. If he was as stuffed as his shirt, he would probably beat a quick retreat from such a silly situation.

I held my breath for a few moments. Just as I was starting to feel really foolish, I heard him enter our little domain from the rear. He was awkwardly clutching a nearly full bottle of champagne.

"I brought reinforcements," he said, as he poured more bubbly into my glass. "In case we get stuck here for a while and need to fortify ourselves for the search."

Ah, a man after my own heart. All ready to liquor up for love.

We clinked glasses again.

"Now what exactly are we looking for?" he asked with a grin.

"Oh, just a little golden O," I say. "It's got a bit of green emerald, just like my eyes." I batted my eyelashes at him, in case he had somehow failed to notice my startlingly beautiful color.

Encouraged by his attention, I continued. "First we pat the rug," I say. Kicking off my slingbacks, I run my feet seductively over the carpet and all around his pant leg.

To his credit, Richard immediately took off his shoes, and socks, and began running his toes through the lush carpeting. "So what do we do when this doesn't work?" he asked.

"Well we can start crawling around looking for it on hands and knees," I say. Taking care not to bump my head on the bottom of the table, I yet again favored him with a view of my pert derriere. Leaving his shoes behind, he clambered onto his own hands and knees and followed me around.

"Ooh," I say. "Feel here." I move his hand just over my knee. "Is that something we should be looking into further?" I ask.

"I don't know," he responds, fondling my knee in earnest. "Let me see if I can find the gold." In a move I would think was practiced, if not for the awkward angles we are at which keep our head from bopping on the table, he climbs swiftly over me, and shoves his knees up between my legs. "Let me see what I can feel," he whispers. Moving his hands up from my knees to run over my hips, then my tummy, they come to rest on the points of my push-up bra. He rubs his fingers in concentric circles around my breasts. I haven't had such a thorough feel since my last gyno exam. And Richard's hands are mercifully warm. His tongue reaches up to caress my ear. I can feel him nibble around the diamonds in my lobe. Unable to resist I say, "But what about my navel ring? One hand leaves my breast and tries to find a way to enter my skintight dress. When he can't find an easy entry, he reaches up under the skirt and pinches my belly button.

"Your navel feels perfect without ornamentation," he whispers breathily in my ear. "But for engineering this rather unique experience, I promise to take you to Tiffany's where you can pick out the emerald of your choice. Unless," and here he pushes my bum into the rug, leaning his full weight against me, so I can feel how ready he is for an adventure. "Unless," he says again, "You want to roll around some more and see what we can find."

I struggle slightly, wondering when I lost the upper hand in this seduction. My foot hits the champagne bottle and cold bubbly spills over, adding a tingly sensation to my toes. As his hand has now slipped from my navel to my love shack, I'm in no position to do more than wiggle. I have to muffle my moans by biting down hard on his tie, because all around us I hear guests returning to the room. His hand moves inside of me with the skill of many years of experience. *This is why I like my men with a little steel in their girders*, I think. *None of these pretty boys of Callie's will ever know how to do this so quickly or so well.*

The band finally stops playing that insipid "Butterfly Kisses". Trust Callie to choose something so banal, and it moves on to the Stones. Richard seemed more than ready to "Pump me up". He moved his hand from my boob and we were so close I could feel the tension of the teeth as his zipper slowly uncoiled. When I felt his muscle move against me I realized he had been going commando. I got wet just thinking about it. Proving how strong he was he snapped the reinforced lace waistband on my thong one-handed. As I felt his missile seeking my silo with all the power of American know-how behind it, I readied for the first strike.

All of a sudden, I saw the unmistakably cheap shoes of the champagne toting waiter appear inches from my nose. There was a soft knock on the table over my head. "Cheesit, the jig is up," I heard the waiter say. "Your champagne has soaked into the tablecloth and they're bringing over a new one, before all the gifts get wet."

I moaned with frustration and rolled my hips, trying to get a taste of Nirvana before the world could stop my fun. But Richard was already rolling over and zipping up. "Another time, Ma Cherie," he said. Without even a final kiss, he was gone.

Ooh, he'll pay for that, I thought. And gathering up my thong, along with the scattered threads of my dignity, I prepared to dance my ass off for the rest of the night.

Chapter 13

The Atlanta rain came down hard and glitzy-blue and transparent in a gorgeous murky haze over the bustling city, as the popular and highly exclusive café reposed in its cozy yet diffidently a corner nest along the posh avenue lined with trees and littered with pedestrians and people walking and their various and sun-dried pets.

They sat at a table near the window, watching the traffic and the gentle yet soothing pitter patter of the little feet that sounded in their earlobes but that was the purity of the rain. Rain soothed and made gently the soul's musings.

Isadore Trent lazily perused the menu of this trendy place, filled with extravagantly outrageous and overpriced items such as *foie de grass* and *pate*. The wine list alone made his pocketbook shudder with delicacy, but of course he pretended he could afford it all and more and then he merely put down the menu with a sniffling disdain and addressed the companions across the table from him.

"What a great lunch, eh, Isaac? What will you be having?"

"Not sure yet," replied Isaac Stevens, the older man, hair close-trimmed and distinctive and beard pepper-and-salt imposing, and gave a satisfied smirk and a wink. "I think I'd like to watch the scenery first. I know how you and Bruce Lucent love this kind of thing too. Young rutting fellows that you are." And he motioned with a brave and subtle rotation of his steady eyes, not toward the rainy window, but at the passing buxom and slender waitresses and well-dressed young women being seated a little away from them, two tables down. His eyes were visibly popping with sensual overloads.

"Yes, keep looking, old man," said Henry Archer in the empty seat next to them.

Only Isadore could hear that voice, ringing like a bell of the Notre Dame Cathedral in his mind, and resounding in the dinnerware, and rebounding in the cutlery and the window glass, for Henry Archer was dead and buried, his post-accident twisted body rotting in his resplendent grave, for he could definitely afford it, and his wife Callie who'd inherited his millions, was just decent enough to respect his last wishes regarding his own corpse of his very self. Callie, the frigid socialite arrogant woman.

"How is business, or should I even ask?" said Isadore, with his red hair pulled back in a casual yet stylish ponytail, hard-bodied, and gushing sex appeal as only a 20-year-old young man could, in his very prime of existence and radical experience of life. He had no need to stare at the women passing by, because they continuously stared at him, watched his redheaded careless macho yet a sensitive ponytail, his rippling muscles concealed under neat casual wear. He drew them like a magnet drew hungry flies.

"That's what you think you are," said Henry Archer, the eternal voices in his very mind. "But you are not, you know. You are not. Not ever."

The rain continued to beat down, first patter then come down in drizzles, and for a moment Isadore was distracted enough by the eternal rhythmic sound to gaze outside the window, and just look at the sublime incandescent beauty of the city nature flourishing before him. Weeping, crying, haze and silvery shadows stood leaning in the air before the window. A young passerby woman paused, leaning to pick up a bag that fell into a puddle, and for a moment she reminded him of Irene with her long blond hair and voluptuous straining body, oh so a ripe acacia-fragrant mouth.

"Yes, she was a hot number, that one," mused Henry Archer, ghostly and virile just below his ear, and across the table in that empty and ominous seat. "Hush, bastard, you devil!" Isadore wanted to say, but couldn't, because Irene's father, Isaac Stevens would think he mad, or worse, he would begin to suspect. Irene was there in his mind, and so was Henry Archer who grinned in his suave manner, once again reminding by his confident glossy white teeth why her had been his willing mistress and lover.

"There is the matter of Richard Isaacs, of course," said Isaac suddenly and quietly through the sedate thicket of his distinctive beard, putting down the menu on top of the plate and inadvertently making the water glass clank gently and ricochet merrily against the salad fork.

"Yes, I know."

The rain pitter-pattered and there was silence in the noisy café, or maybe in their minds.

Silence.

Noisy café noise.

Moments later, their young strawberry-auburn-headed waitress attended them with a pleasing winsome grin full of healthy teeth and gums. Her generous bosom swept forward in her tightfitting blouse, unbuttoned precariously and yet full of devious intent to reveal the tender rosy heaving flesh under the starched straining cotton.

"What may I get you, gentlemen?" she said in a honey pert voice, and a flash of white pearly teeth in a face of unusual refinement for such a creature. What was she doing hear in this seething and empties a trendy morass of human dross and raging worldly clamor?

"Ah," mused, Isadore to himself, "She is another unfortunate, probably alone in the world and needing to pay her way in the world of men. She may be writing a novel in secret, and I know her kind." And he had an immediate need to comfort and console her, and felt a pang of desire in his southern regions of the hard young body.

"Give us another minute, honey, will you?" said Isaac, grinning at the waitress and winking gently like an older man who is respectable, no doubt, yet has spent a wild youth sowing his wild oats and a bit of wheat and barley too.

"Would you like some more water, sir?" said the nubile waitress, addressing Isaac, but Isadore felt her posture straining toward him like Jack toward the beanstalk of his dreams. He could almost read her eagerness to serve him, not the other. The world narrowed and spun, then receded like the glory of the outer rain and inner worldliness.

Silence and moments of pitter-patter.

"You are the one with a sex-death wish," hissed Henry Archer in his ghostly presence permeating the room. "Just look at her, you know she wants you. They all want you. Except Irene! You could never have her, because she will always be mine. She cannot ever forget my youthful bodybuilder physique, the firmness and the rock-hardness of me, the only things that would satisfy. Her father does not know that his sweet innocent Irene was a wildcat in my bed. I could always make her mew. And to my musical key, none other. She purred for me like a bobcat kitten before it became fully grown, gained poundage and muscle bulk, and discovered other wildlife of its kind and ilk. Vibrant, innocent but sensual, purring. Ever purring for me, she was"

"Actually, I think I am ready to order now," said Isadore, firmly ignoring it all, flipping back his red forelocks out of his face and beyond the back to where the bulk of the abundant and suggestive ponytail rested against his wide strongly utterly virile back – a back that could do the beast with two backs so well, when one of the two backs came into question and under scrutiny (but the other back of course depended on the woman writhing with him, under him and on top of him ah, the beasts they would make!).

He ignored the voice of Henry Archer and the ghostly vacant and evacuated presence among them, and concentrated on thoughts of lunch and thoughts of Richard Isaacs, while retracting and folding away all distracting thoughts such as Irene's blond fairness to the back of his subconscious mentality.

"We really should talk to Richard about his behavior," said Isaac's low baritone while the waitress deftly and smoothly poured water over his shoulder into Isadore's glass and then Isaac's glass.

Her bosom was almost spilling outside and the depth of her cleavage was undeniable, like the depths of the liquid in the clear cool jug and the profundity of the dripping rain outside.

Isadore visibly forced himself to unglue his eyes from the panorama of mummeries and femininity, and said, "I will have the lightly-braised spring lamb *au jus*, and a vinaigrette *au coq*."

"Would you like soup or salad?" said the waitress in a breathless soprano. Her impressive mammary watch was inches away from Isaac's distinctive bearded face.

"Salad, please, and what kind of dressing do you have?" said Isadore, lifting his sensual narrowed eyes from his table setting and allowing them free reign and bounce over her lovely face.
"We have French, Italian, Sun-ripened tomato and Avocado, Thousand Islands, honey mustard, low-cal French, low-cal Italian, low-cal Thousand Island, Oriental Thai Oregano, and a house dressing with secret ingredients, which I highly recommend —"

"Go ahead, order the French," mocked Henry Archer. "You know Irene's French kisses were sublime and yes I tasted them repeatedly and dolefully."

"Low-cal Italian," said Isadore, never blinking, yet narrowing his eyes and then widening them in involuntary but firm pupil dilation and watching the wavelength and frequency of her eyes, so that the waitress was the first one to blink away, but first she heaved her chest in an automotive reflex that was not to be denied.

"As I was saying, Richard has gone too far at this point," interjected Isaac Stevens, pulling down the white linen napkin – sterile like Cassie Archer yet pure like Irene Stevens – on his lap. "I saw him the other day at the Racquet Club, and he looked pale and just sick with exhaustion. Wonder what's the matter this time."

The waitress jotted down Isadore's order, then looked at Isaac with the patience of a saint who has to work tables in order to support a family and possibly just a writing habits, not to mention, pay bills and federal taxes.

Isadore picked up his water glass ruefully, considering what was within, a cousin of the rain pattering on the window, and drew the parallel between the microcosm in the glass and the macro cosmos outside.

"No, one is pure, not even the rain," said Henry Archer's hateful ghostly voice.

Isadore's fingers shook so that in that moment he spilled some of the cool and refreshing once tap but now double-filtered contents of the glass — just droplets of mountain-spring purity — onto his shirt. "Ah!" Isadore exclaimed, and grabbed a napkin to dab at his shirt in some confusion, while Isaac and the waitress, and the whole restaurant, and possibly the whole world stared at him, and the moment extended itself into eternity and then redoubled upon itself like the emulsifying and moisturizing nature of the rain.

In the empty seat across the table, Henry Archer cackled like an evil genie without a bottle to return to, nor needing one, since he was fully dead, and Isadore could make himself believe it at long last.

His spirit and conscience hung boldly in the air while the rain outside continued to come down in the greatest flood.

And Isadore suddenly felt himself refreshed and free of shame and guilt and able to speak at last.

He opened his mouth, cleared his throat, swallowed the past, digested the moment, and started to honestly speak to Isaac Stevens about Richard Isaacs.

In the deepest closet back of his mind, however, there will always be the rain and Irene with her raining liquid blond hair, the complex daughter of his lunch companion and confidante.

The rain came down.

Oh, joyous yet serene emancipated rain.

Chapter 14

Penelope sat, sipping a Peach Martini (her third) while the staff hustled all around her table. She hadn't been back to Atlanta's Food 101 restaurant since graduating college, but it had the merits of terrific food, no loud music, and excellent bartender, and, above all else, there was absolutely no connection to her time with Bruce. She had no few fond memories of the place, and the memories were justified. Just since she'd arrived, no fewer than 3 guys (2 Pro hockey players and a Minor League pitcher) had hit on her. Once, she would have enjoyed their attentions. Now, she was impatiently awaiting Andrea's arrival.

Andrea who never came on time unless she happened to be laying on someone's watch during sex. Andrea who was gorgeous in ways even Penelope could appreciate, since Bruce had never given Andrea a second glance. Yet, she was engaged to Bruce's college roommate, Jeff, and still had managed to retain her friendship with Penelope despite Jeff's requests not to.

Penelope was just signaling her buff, young waiter Greg to bring another Martini when Andrea appeared, striding swift toward her table. Her lean, 5-6 frame and dancers leg with calves pulling tautly as she approached, had heads turning up-and-down the aisle. When she bent over and kissed Penelope on the cheek, 2 guys nearly fell off their chairs, and another received a vicious, teeth-rattling smack from his female companion.

Andrea was breathless, causing her chest to heave enough to sea sicken even the mightiest of sailors. "I'm so sorry I'm late. We were in a planning meeting this morning when the main server failed, and it's been nonstop phone time with our clients all day." So spoke Ms. Temporary Secretary.

Penelope waved over Greg. "It's OK. Let's just get you a drink." Within moments there were delivered 2 Peach Martini, and a Sex on The Beach for Andrea. The women sipped and made small talk over a plate of appetizers, though Penelope was itching to get to her main concern.

Penelope's simple Caesar Salad and Andrea's North Georgia Trout had finally arrived when she finally broached the main issue. "Are you going to tell me? Or are we both going to pretend it never happened?"

Andrea said with a sigh, "How about let's do that, Penny? It's done. Terminado. Do we have to go through all the details? The Pre-Nup is singed, the rings are exchanged, and the gift checks cashed. Let it go. Let *him* go."

Penelope shook her head, her ponytail waving behind her as if to swat a platoon of troublesome flies. "I need to hear it, Andrea. I need to hear it for myself before I can relegate him to the arms of that woman, and move on. Once you tell me about the wedding, I can put Bruce behind me for good." A small, childlike part of her petulantly crossed the dainty fingers of her left hand where it lay out of sight in her lap.

Andrea took a deep breath that nearly shattered the already precarious equilibrium of her blouse's buttons. "All right. If you really need to torture yourself, I will. The ceremony and reception were held at the Archer place."

Penelope snorted. "It was probably as much an exorcism of her husband's spirit as it was a wedding."

Andrea raised her hand with all the authority of a 20-year veteran school crossing guard on a rainy Spring afternoon. "If you're going to be like that, I'm not going to continue. Jeff isn't thrilled that you and I are still friends, but out of respect for me, let's just get this over with."

Penelope nodded. "Sorry. Go on."

Andrea nibbled as she spoke, covering the initially distasteful taste of the tale with the smoky richness of restaurants' special recipe BBQ sauce. "There were only about 50 guests, mostly on Bruce's side. Callie doesn't have much family, and I guess most of her guests were business associates from Archer's business."

Andrea paused for a sip of Sex before plunging on with all the subtlety of the neckline of her favorite blouse. "Before you ruin this already awkward story, yes, Callie wore white. And her bouquet was Calla Lillies. Cute touch, no? That Personal Assistant of hers . . . Maude? ... Milicent? ... whoever . . . was the Maid of Honor. Bruce and Jeff wore gray tuxes, with white sneakers. It was a very simple ceremony, and Bruce's mother cried the whole time. To be honest, I half-expected you to jump out of the shrubbery, or from a helicopter, or something screaming 'Stop this mockery of a marriage!' when the minister asked if anyone knew any reason why these two should not be married."

Penelope glowered a bit, but Andrea rushed ahead having warmed greatly to her tale. "Jeff gave a marvelous toast. He told that story about the night Bruce and those basketball players stole all the bread that had been delivered to the college cafeteria, and there was no bread for meals the next day, and how he woke Jeff at 3 a.m., and clobbered him with a loaf of French bread, and there was bread all over the floor of their room, and Jeff ended up cleaning it up, but how they've stayed friends ever since. That story still cracks me up, though I guess it's more touching now that I see what a bonding moment it was for them."

Penelope waited while Andrea finished off the last of her ribs. Much as she generally liked Andrea, the girl had a certain flighty — no, make that "airheaded" — quality to her personality that was scratching at Penelope's nerves like a cat with 7 paws in a sofa factory. Why couldn't she see that Bruce's marriage was not a subject to be taken humorously.

Andrea let out a burp, not so manly a belch as to attract undue attention to them, but not so ladylike that one or two heads did not turn their way again. Wiping her mouth delicately and fiddling about with the few tiny fish bones on her plate, she went blithely on. "And their vows were so lovely, Penny. They wrote them themselves, and I never knew a computer geek like Bruce could be so eloquent. Callie went first, and she said the loveliest things about Bruce and them and their relationship. How he had pulled her up from the deepest depths of her mourning, and given her reason to rise from her bed in the morning light, and yet still more and greater reason to return to it at nightfall. She swore to love him all the days of his life."

Penelope's mind decided this was a fine moment to play heckler to this divine comedy. *"Wonderful. She means to outlive this husband, too!"*

Andrea was oblivious to this bleak internal exchange. "And Bruce's vows. Oh, Penny! You would have been so proud to hear him say such things. He went on about how Callie was the Tech Support Agent who had taken him off a Musales Hold and brought him through the ultimate upgrade of the Operating System of his heart, and made his thus-far sad and lonely existence 100% compatible with life, the universe and everything. I was so moved I made Jeff quote every tech specification he could remember while we made love that night. You have no idea how hot that stuff can make a girl! We should try to get you a computer nerd of your own."

Penelope barely registered the last of Andrea's tale, as the harsh reality of the situation struck her with all the destructive force of reality. Bruce had no feelings for her. That demanding woman had rebooted his memory, erasing all the good, warm, tender history they'd shared. She was nothing but a part of that "sad and lonely existence" from which he was fleeing. He felt nothing for the time they'd shared. Nothing for all the amazingly raunchy and kinky things she'd allowed him to do to her (or had she do to him) when his Internet explorations had introduced him to one of the many particularly exotic forms of foreplay that had kept them abed on many a night, and many a feigned sick day from work.

Penelope's vision slowly closed in on her, leaving her finally aware of only two things: Andrea licking her lips while describing the decadently delicious German Black Forest wedding cake. The thought *"Why did Henry Archer have to die? Why couldn't it have been Bruce?"* With that, she lapsed into unconsciousness, earning a bruise on her forehead from her fork, and a crouton up her nose before buff Greg carried her to the manager's office, and called 911.

Chapter 15

Less than sixty seconds after she'd come through the front door at Bruce Lucent and Callie Archer's wedding reception, Yvonne Perrin knew she was in trouble.

"Hey there! How's my very favoritest bridesmaid?"

Yvonne looked around just in time to dodge a beefy-faced and obviously drunk man who was trying to kiss her.

"I'm *not-*"

"You remember me-I'm Uncle Roger!" he said. "I was at the rehearsal dinner." He tottered slightly, then pulled a mashed-looking disposable camera out of his pocket. "Let's get one of these nice people to take our picture together, huh?"

She knew how *that* would work: he'd get his arm around her for a good long grope and a couple of wet kisses, while some other hapless guest took forever to figure out the camera's dead-simple controls. She privately vowed that if she couldn't get out of it, she was going to do the whole thing with a lovely smile on her face and one of her spike heels planted squarely in the middle of Uncle Roger's foot.

Mercifully, the little cellphone in her handbag chose that moment to start ringing. She transferred the bag to her Uncle-Roger-side hand, made an apologetic "just a sec" face, and flipped open the phone. *"Maria Lisa?"* said an unfamiliar voice.

Yvonne beamed. "Hi, honey! I've been looking for you, too."

"Maria?   Estas?" The guy on the phone sounded urgent. That was probably why he'd dialed the wrong number.

"Estoy en mi casa. Necesito ir a mi trabajo."

"They *are*? Right now?" Yvonne turned and made a quick "this is going to take a teeny bit longer" gesture to Uncle Roger, then went back to the call. "Tell them to wait and I'll be right there."

"Por favor, Maria—estoy muy tarde para mi trabajo."

"Sweetie, where are you? I'm right by the front door."

Yvonne stood on tiptoe and scanned the room, looking for a good escape route. The big arched doorway over to her right looked promising. "Just tell me which way to go, and I'll be there quick as a bunny," she told the guy.

He let out a furious burst of idiomatic Spanish and hung up, hard.

"Thanks, honey, I'll be right there!" she caroled, and snapped the phone shut. "Gotta run," she told Uncle Roger, and took off through the crowd.

* * *

She should have known, Yvonne reflected bitterly. God knows Callie had e-mailed her enough pictures while the wedding was in its planning stages. Trouble was, she'd never been able to get the attachments to open. They were bin-hexed, or something like that. Probably a virus.

But even without seeing the pictures, it should have occurred to her that if anyone in the world were capable of picking out non-sucky bridesmaids' dresses, it was Callie. And so she'd discovered, when she'd arrived at the church and gotten a glimpse of them. They weren't sucky at all. Not the problem.

"Oh lord," she'd said out loud. "It's practically the same dress — and hat!"

She'd had just enough time to dash back to her car to grab a lightweight shawl she'd providentially left lying on the back seat two weeks earlier, then come back and find an out-of-the-way seat at the rear of the church. During the ceremony, who'd be looking at her anyway?

But that wasn't going to work during the reception. At close range the shawl just looked tatty, and when she was standing up it did nothing to camouflage the rest of her gown-so distinctive, with its subtly off-shade organza overdress that looked like absolutely nothing else being worn at the party Š except by the bridesmaids, of course.

Sometimes, life is just not fair.

* * *

A few minutes later, Yvonne found what she needed: An out-of-the-way dressing area with a good mirror, in the pool house way over on the other side of the grounds. It wasn't exactly private, but it was around three corners from the poolhouse entrance, and the pool house itself was reassuringly dark inside. Besides, with all the guests still up at the main house doing their initial meet-greet-and-congratulate, she had the place to herself.

She switched on the overhead lights directly above the mirror and took a long hard look at her dress. Would the organza come off without leaving the underdress in rags? It seemed a shame to remove it—she'd loved this dress—but consoled herself with the thought that if six other women in their social circle had the exact same thing hanging in their closets, she'd never have been able to wear it anyway.

Yvonne unzipped the dress to her waist, and took down her bodice so she could look at its construction. She was in luck! There, underneath the facing, was a neat little row of hand-set stitches fastening the overdress to the underlying material. It must have been designed to be removable all along. She rummaged in her purse for the ornate little silver pocketknife she'd inherited from her grandmother, then went to work ripping stitches.

The front came away easily, and the back was nearly as quick. That left the waist. She looked around, sighed, shrugged, and peeled her dress off entirely.

When she was done, she bundled up the remains and put her dress back on to see what she had. "Less dress; that's for sure," she said aloud to the mirror. It was still pretty, but now it showed far more skin; and with the organza draping gone, she'd had to forego her bra and its attached slip. She shimmied her shoulders experimentally and watched the effect. She didn't *quite* fall out.

The matching organza sunhat would have to go as well. Before, it had matched the dress perfectly. Now all it matched was the oddly forlorn-looking roll of fabric she'd tucked safely away on a high shelf. Yvonne started carefully removing the hatpins that had secured the hat to her elaborate hairdo.

The minute the hat was off, her glossy red hair came tumbling down around her back and shoulders. Yvonne sighed in exasperation. In this humidity, she could see it was already starting to curl. She twisted the unruly red hank into a loose knot at the nape of her neck, tying it off with the hatband and cluster of silk flowers from her castoff hat.

"Very nice," a male voice said lazily from somewhere behind her. "It says a lot for a dress that I don't mind seeing you put it back on."

Yvonne gasped and whirled around, looking for the source of the voice while she groped behind her for her long hatpins. "Who-"

"Sorry," said the voice. There was the ratcheting click of a Zippo lighter, and in the brief flare of its light she saw an older man in formal wear sitting in an ornate high-backed wicker armchair. Then the lighter clicked shut, and all she could see in the shadows was the red glow at the end of his cigarillo.

"How long have you—-" she began, then stopped. "I'd have heard you come in."

"I'm afraid so," he said. "I'll have to beg your pardon. I had just finished making a phone call when you walked in."

"In the *dark*?" she said.

"Not too dark to make a phone call. You're blinded by those overheads."

Inside her head, an inane little voice was busily calculating *I had the slip on when I took the dress off, I put the dress back on over the slip, I pulled the slip off over my head while I still had the dress on, he didn't see much* — Another voice was saying *formal wear, he's either a guest or he's an employee who has something to lose, still not safe but maybe I'll be okay, keep him talking, where's my knife where's my phone* — And something that wasn't exactly a voice was thinking something like *Mmmmmm?*

"I expect you're right." She walked over to the switch plate and turned on the rest of the room lights. The mysterious man in the chair now looked less mysterious, but perhaps more intriguing: wide shoulders, narrow waist, a ruddy complexion; not young, but neither afraid of nor defeated by his age. He looked, she suddenly thought, like a man who was lightly sparring with his age, and enjoying the fight. His suit was perfectly tailored. *He never rented that suit*, she thought; *not with his build.* She approved of both.

The man returned her attention, studying her as she did him. He looked pleased.

Yvonne felt herself blushing, and the vexations and frantic pace of the day evaporating as though they'd never happened. She was in her thirties, her girlhood long behind her, and she'd never lacked for male companionship; but she suddenly felt that little pleasurable dizziness of the dance beginning again, as always feeling like it was the first time in the history of the world.

The nice thing about being in your thirties, she reflected, *is that you can appreciate that feeling for what it's worth, and not worry about what it isn't.*

Then memory kicked in. "Richard Isaacs," she said. "I've met you. One of Bruce Lucent's parties."

His smile widened. "Yvonne," he said. "I didn't catch the rest of your name. It was noisy. You were wearing green silk, the exact shade of the philodendron hanging behind you."

She laughed then, feeling absurdly flattered, and walked across the room to offer him her hand. "How do you do?" she said. "I'm pleased to finally make your acquaintance."

He took her hand and held it lightly in his own for a few seconds. "I'm afraid I really am going to have to ask for your forgiveness," he said. "I should have said something when you came in, but I didn't, and after that I was fascinated. I had no idea that women were capable of transformation on such short notice."

"You mean my dress? I had to. I was ambushed."

"What kind of ambush makes you take your dress apart?"

As Yvonne walked back to the narrow shelf in front of the mirror to collect her bits of belongings and stow them back her purse, she said, "I cleverly deduce that you weren't at the wedding ceremony."

"You are correct. What did I miss?"

"Bridesmaids. Six of them. Every one of them wearing that same dress and hat."

His jaw dropped. "My god. Isn't there some kind of law against that? Bridesmaids aren't supposed to dress like human beings."

"You'd think, wouldn't you?" Yvonne said. "But Callie picked them out."

He shook his head; and then a thought struck him, and he began to laugh.

Yvonne watched, feeling a little wary. "Share?" she asked.

"I was just thinking that you're being terribly brave. My first wife once wore the same dress worn by just *one* other woman at a party, and she sulked about it for a week and a half. If she'd arrived to find *six* other women wearing her dress-"

"Spontaneous human combustion," Yvonne said solemnly. "I'd always wondered what caused it."

Then a brief silence fell between them, and she found herself wondering self-consciously whether she was keeping him from the party. Just as she was wondering whether she should say something about it, he said, "This is lovely, and so are you—but should I ask whether I'm keeping you from the party?"

"Oh!" she said, at once relieved and afraid she looked too relieved. "I was about to ask you the same. I have no obligations, besides attending; and if I know Bruce and Callie, this party will run through tomorrow morning. How about you?"

"I'm here for the party. I do have one other item on my agenda, which is to try to have a conversation with a former business associate of one of my former business associates. "He grimaced. "A man named Roger. I don't know his last name. I'm supposed to recognize him from an old snapshot they found in the files."

"If it's the Uncle Roger I met as soon as I came in the door, you're too late."

"He's left already?"

"He's three sheets to the wind. That was the other reason I came back here and started hacking my dress apart."

Richard studied her bare shoulders. "And this is supposed to discourage him?"

"It's supposed to put a crimp in any further rounds of 'Hey, sweetheart, didn't I meet you at the rehearsal dinner."

"Ah," he said. "Now I understand. You took off your uniform and buried it."

"Exactly. I'm a noncombatant. Now, shall I take a look at this snapshot of yours? I think I'd recognize him if I saw him."

Richard shook his head. "I left it behind." He picked up a cane she hadn't noticed he was carrying, and got up out of his chair. He was moving a little stiffly. "I don't remember that from the party," Yvonne said. "When were you hurt?" "An auto accident. Nothing worth mentioning. I'll get over it; I just haven't yet." He limped over to what Yvonne had taken for a section of wall. "Could you turn out the lights? There now. Good. This is a louvered window. You can see most of the yard from here. Tell me if you spot Uncle Roger."

Richard started turning the crank that would open the louvers, and Yvonne came and stood beside him. She abruptly realized she was close enough to smell him—a good smell, hard work and clean skin and a hint of Old Spice—and to feel the slight radiant warmth of his body, there in the darkness. There was a single sharp knock in her chest, as though her sternum had been kicked from the inside, and for a moment she closed her eyes and fought to keep her balance. Her heart was hammering so hard that she thought he must surely be able to hear it.

"There," he said, and she blinked; and shook her head a little, trying to clear it. Outside the louvered window, the late afternoon was turning into early evening. The lamps strung up around the yard made little pools of light in the dusk, and partygoers clustered underneath them.

Richard was right. You could see everything from here. She looked carefully, mentally dividing up the area and thoroughly scanning one section before moving on to the next. And — "There!"

"You can see him?"

"Yes." She glanced up at Richard. He was staring out the window, his eyes fixed on some object. She turned back to the scene. "Medium-blue suit, going bald?—over there, next to the woman in the red caftan and all the gold beads—see? That man who keeps bouncing up on his toes when he talks?" "Him, yes. I'd already thought so from seeing that picture. If he told you his name's Roger, I'd say that just about settles it." He watched a little longer. "Definitely too drunk to talk to."

Then he turned to face her, and once more she could feel her heart hammering. She paused a moment, listening. There was a second sound mixed in with it. "I can hear your heart beating," she whispered, and impulsively laid her hand on his chest. He put his arms around her, and pulled her close; and then they kissed, and for a while the rest of the universe went away. When they broke off the kiss, the way he looked down at her was like someone reading, and he looked at her for a long time. "As a matter of fact, no," he said con-versationally. "I don't do this sort of thing often." He kissed her again. "And neither do you," he added."Thank you," Yvonne said. "I was about to say something stupider than that. What do you want to do?"

"A lot of things. Take my hand. You really can't see in the dark, can you? There's a door over in the corner. It has a lock on it."

"And on the other side of it?"

"A big, lumpy old sofa and a dead TV set. And something even better."

"What's that?" she said, feeling for the wall. She heard the door open somewhere in front of her.

"A fuse box switch that'll turn off the power to the whole poorhouse. Nobody will come bothering us if they have to make their way through a couple of unlit rooms to do it."

"Oh, you *are* clever," she said. "Are you sure you haven't done this before?"

"I'm sure. It's the sheer inspiration that's making me ingenious."

* * *

A long time later, he shifted position, kissed her neck and ear, and murmured "I lied."

"Past pluperfect subjunctive," she said sleepily.

"What did you lie about?"

"The 'not doing this very often' part."

"Already having some doubts about that."

"Shucks, ma'am, that weren't nothin'." He ran his finger slowly up the inside of her thigh, starting from her knee, and smiled in satisfaction to feel her spine arch backward, and hear her long soft gasp as she inhaled. "What I meant to say," he continued, "is that I'm not really committed to that interactive model."

"Is that so?" She squirmed slightly to get better leverage, then wrapped one leg around his waist and tucked her heel into the small of his back. "I think I can live with that."

Chapter 16

Yvonne felt a thrill as she was finally able to leave the expanse that was I-85 and enter the four-lane road that is 316, the Atlanta Highway. She unconsciously began singing the B-52s "Love Shack" to herself. She reflected joyously that she had passed the CNN Center, Fulton County Stadium, and the other relics of the days when Ted Turner seemed to run a country, instead of trying to give all his money away to places such as the United Nations. It isn't, she thought, that everything in Atlanta is named Peachtree Something—only bad novelists believe that—so much as the city has moved beyond Peach trees. That thought shifted the soundtrack of her mind to Aerosmith.

I'm not a Rag Doll myself, she reaffirmed to herself. Her thoughts moving to Rory Edwards. Richard Isaacs had been a pleasant fling—it had, after all, lasted one night more than she had expected. She had ultimately (that second night) decided that even his skill at selecting clothes that made him look five years younger was not enough. It would not compensate for the fact that his life was spent playing games, and that he would play her for as long as he wanted. Her friend Sue Young had once told her, "Every once in a while, you just have to bend over and take it." Sue had casually continued, being explicit about where, and Yvonne had been appropriately offended. She also realized her friend would never understand that sex was about power, not love. Putting yourself into such a position would forever reduce your role in the relationship, until you both started hating you for doing it.

(Yvonne had seen articles that noted that some *hot tramps* who might be seen as her competition proclaimed their enjoyment of that particular proclivity. She shuddered at the thought, wondering idly if that meant that the next generation would be romanticizing the Ordinary Housewife of yesterlore. She couldn't romanticize women who had thrived in the South by feeding their husbands high cholesterol foods and encouraging them to go hunting and fishing in all types of weather. The "premature" deaths may have produced pensions, life insurance, and financial security, but "steel magnolias" could only enjoy the second half of their life, and then only when the affairs of the first half went unacknowledged.)

She drove toward the exurban area that allowed Atlanta to describe itself as a metropolis. Even the names—Alpharetta, Marietta—indicated places where the Man of the House kept the "little woman." It was as if the transition to soccer mom from Ordinary Housewife had never occurred. Metropolitan Atlanta was more an extended backwoods area than an accelerated city. Now that Turner had taken the cash, and the suits in New York had destroyed much of the rest of the empire, Yvonne wondered how the next generation would fare.

Not that she cared about the twenty-somethings with tongue piercings. They were a large reason she found her greatest successes with the Levitra generation. She preferred men who no longer found drug-enhanced pleasures of the flesh more important than a woman who could keep them interested for the half-hour or so before the drug was effective. Her men were those whose definition of foreplay largely consisted of being able to look fondly, share a glass of expensive wine, and listen nostalgically to Doo-Wop or other "classic rock." Pleasant conversation and lubricated condoms did the rest.

Today, thinking of Rory, Yvonne pondered what to wear. She approached the well-monikered Commerce, with its delightful selection of stores. She even enjoyed watching those *daddy's little cuties* spend far too much at Petite Sophisticate and J. Crew on clothes that did far too little for them. N*ot*, she reflected uncharitably, *that they* need *their clothes to do as much for them as I do.*

She imagined how she would approach Rory. She would shyly reach out, the very model of an ingénue, which both of them would believe for the moment she was. She would seductively remove his glasses from his face. Should she speak? What is the male equivalent of "You're beautiful without your glasses"? No, just to act silently would be better.

She would move simply. Gently touch him her fingers, hinting of nail. Caress that solid torso. Add a heartfelt coo about how strong he must be. To tilt her head slightly, hinting at supplication. He should see worship in her eyes. To slowly move her other hand to his Grecian-formula temples, running the fingers (more nail this time) through it. To exalt how impressive it is that his hair is still intact, while widening her grin to highlight her White Stripes teeth. (Should she show a hint of tongue?)

Finally, there would be a slow, apparently natural, motion of the hand from hair to removing the glasses. Is he nearsighted? His age hinted not. He would still be able to see her. She decided to proceed directly to moving the glasses slowly down to her side, and rub them with her blouse as if cleaning them thoroughly, forcing his eyes to travel down her body? Another tap of his fabulous torso, lingering this time with a comment about his not needing the Vaseline and oils of a Stallone. She would note his lack of love handles while tilting her own torso to highlight her glorious 38Ds. They were impressive, she knew, even now when they were no longer supported by nature. *Thank God for Howard Hughes,* she mused. *If he'd gone for those boy-girls, instead of Jane Russell, women's rights would have been set back twenty years.*

Yvonne pulled into the Tangers Outlet Mall, reassuring herself that Rory would not track fashions intensely, the way Richard does. (She remembered the pivotal scene in some clothing movie, where the blonde woman catches the man knowing fashion and realizes he is gay. She could not, for the hundredth time, consider Richard in those terms. Rejecting the possibility again, for the hundredth time, she tried to concentrate on Rory Edwards.

She was distracted by the list of things she needed to buy, clear from her scenario. There would be a tasteful-shade-of-red nail polish, lip gloss, hand cream, moisturizer, tooth polish, and a flavored mouthwash. For the latter, she contemplated mint, but had a breakthrough with the idea of cinnamon, something to surprise him.

She considered a touch of dye, *not that I need it*, but gloried once again in her glowing auburn tresses. Her mother claimed she had inherited them from her grandmother. She decided a green hair clip, which would also highlight her eyes, would be sufficient.

But the most important part was the outfit. If she was going to be rail meat on his yacht, she would have to look the part, and nothing in her wardrobe was *quite* perfect yet. There was a purple silk blouse from she had bought at Neimann Marcus, but she had worn it to a party of Callie's three years ago. She was afraid Rory had been there and would remember it. She couldn't remember him from that party, but had been during her enchantment by Calvin. *And men claim only women are bewitching.*

She skirted past the Georgia Tech and UGA girls grabbing last year's halter-tops and tube dresses for the coming summer. While she fancied that her body could still support a tube dress, she needed something more traditional for Rory. There was no point in emphasizing the difference in their ages, trivial though she thought of it. She knew this quest well, given her natural proclivity toward men who could legitimately be considered "late middle aged," old enough to know better, but careful enough about their bodies to keep them in peak shape. This expedition required an outfit that would have been daring in his day, but would appear restrained among what currently passed for "fashion." Which meant a bright green dress (the hair clip would have to be purple), fishnet stockings, and, most importantly, a good-fitting push-up bra.

So, it was to the bra shopping first. She wanted a nice lace, wondering if black would be too daring and rejecting red out of hand. Perhaps white would be safer, especially since the dress was likely to be a bit translucent.

Selecting a bra, she thought, *is one of those tasks that makes women wish for a penis, a flat chest, or both.* The hours she had wasted in just the past few years, not to mention all those she expected to waste over the next several decades were frightening. Not even two bras of supposedly the same size and make would fit well—or, often, even similarly. And two different labels were a sure sign that a 38D would be a 40E would be a 36C. Heaven help her when she realized that Calvin had been correct in saying that her left breast was smaller than her right. Bra shopping was like trying two pairs of shoes to make one pair.

Still, whether it was Life with Rory or there was some Mr. Right who followed him in her pantheon, this roundelay would not end. Even while her plan was still hatching and the glories of an anticipated seduction could still be savored, Yvonne suspected this would not be her last relationship.

Exhausted before she began, she eschewed the L'eggs Hanes Bali Playtex store for Claire's. Yvonne searched first for a NuBra. She knew that Playtex might be the result of her search for something to signal a longer term, traditional woman. The temptation of going strapless and backless in the world of A-cups, WonderBra, and plastic surgery for 54-year-olds was tempting, though.

The result she finally found was worth the effort. Black lace top, solid white cups, support, comfortable sweat-absorbing interior, and a silk exterior for that first maneuver of his hand. Even that it had been made in China, where all of the women who worked on it probably did not measure to her own endowment, did not stop Yvonne from wondering at the marvels of modern American culture.

The bra found, she moved on to Elisabeth for dresses, glorying again that her flowing locks meant that she really had but two basic choices in color, green or purple. And the climate of Atlanta allowed either color to appear appropriate at least ten months out of the year, setting herself off against the verdant landscape and the glories of the sunsets as if it were natural, instead of planned down to the hour. She thought ruefully of the fashion disaster that would have come from living in Chicago, where Calvin now cohabited with his not-even-a-handful trust-fund bimbo.

She considered the timing of her impending liaison and decided she should take a Lavender Sunset approach to the evening. A 7:30 meeting could be leveraged to its fullest. His view as she approached their outdoor table, fashionably late, would be of herself set off by the glowing yellow-red backdrop and highlighted by the verdancy of the surrounding deciduous trees.

She decided this meant that her hair would have to be down and around her shoulders. Maybe a flower—lilac? daisy?—instead of a hair clip. It would appear positively antebellum, with a hint of knowing couture.

A lavender Donna Karan, with a neckline that did not plunge so much as gracefully hint (well, it may have been intended to gracefully hint, but her pulchritude always more favored grace than hinting), tapered at the waist to highlight the firms of her hips and derriere, ending slightly below the knee to show her calves off in good stead while hiding the scars from the skiing accident that had caused her to meet Calvin at that lodge in Vail, selected, Yvonne left the store, wet with both the success of the expedition and the anticipation of the night to come.

Chapter 17

Andrew Venice parked his car on the street in front of the house and double-checked the address he had written down on a slip of paper. Yeah, this was the place all right. It was an ordinary house, on an ordinary street. There was nothing special about it, just plain. Nothing here looked like it might be connected to murder or assault or anything like that. Richard Isaac, the man he'd come to interview, was a stock manipulator, and you'd think he'd live in a fancier place, a nicer house, on a better street. But since he was also a police informant, maybe he wanted to keep a low profile, not do anything to stand out. Not exactly like the witnesses' protection program, but not all that different. Or maybe he just wasn't that good at manipulating stocks. Venice would try to find out, in addition to finding out what he really came here to ask about.

He put the note on the front seat, and his sunglasses in the glove compartment, checking his reflection in the rearview mirror and smoothing back his hair. Turning forty was hard. He didn't know what he'd been planning to do at forty, but he was damn sure this wasn't it. Oh well. It was his job, and he was the one to do it. He'd better get going, ask his questions, make his report. Then he'd have time to stop by the gym later, work out a bit, fight off the ravages of time. He was still in his prime, even if he had to work harder to maintain it.

Getting out of the car, he looked both ways, then shut the door and used the keyfob to lock all the doors. It wasn't a bad neighborhood or anything like that, but he still didn't want to take any chances. He let a minivan go past, then an SUV, then he walked around the front of his car and up the long sidewalk to the porch. A bench sat on the porch, the kind you might sit on and drink some lemonade, but it didn't look used, like nobody had had any lemonade to drink there for a while, or maybe they just didn't like the porch or something. Isaacs probably had to keep a low profile anyway. He wasn't the kind of guy who spent a lot of time outside making friends with the neighbors.

Venice went to knock on the door and stopped. There was a flyer lying on the welcome mat. No, it was one of those bags of advertisements they paid neighborhood kids to deliver, one of those circulars. There was a cardboard box full of them just off to the side of the door. He picked up the new one and held it in his hand as he knocked on the door with his knuckles, loud enough so anyone inside could hear him but not pounding or anything like that. Watching his reflection in the storm door, smoothing the lapels on his suit jacket so he'd be sure to look nice, the door opened.

Richard Isaacs was the man who answered the door. He looked over Venice wondering who this guy was at his door, and what he was doing there. Venice got into his pocket and pulled out his wallet, flipped it open to a show hid badge.

"Hi, my name is Andrew Venice," he said cheerfully, like there was nothing unusual about him showing up there in the middle of the day. "I'm here to ask you a few questions. It's no big deal."

That was just what Venice wanted him to think, Isaacs thought. They always said it was no big deal when they were trying to nail you.

"I found this lying outside your door," Andrew said. "You want it?"

What was this guy trying to do, being friendly to him. "No, just toss it there into the circular file," Isaacs pointed.

"Toss it into where?"

"That box right there beside the door," he said, pointed to the box. He was getting mad.

"It's not a circle, it's more of a square," said Venice. "Or a rectangle maybe."

"It's a joke, all right?" Now Issacs was really really mad. "I put the circulars in the circular file."

But that crazy Venice guy just offered it again. "You sure you don't want it. They got good deals inside, could save you some money."

"Just throw it away. I wish the kids would stop delivering them."

"Hey, listen," said Venice, sticking his hands into his pockets. "I don't have all day here. I'm on an investigation. I came to ask you some important questions, and I want some answers."

"I don't have to answer anything you ask!" Richard Isaacs replied forcefully. He wanted to make a point. "Are you going to stay out there on the porch and scare off all the neighbors or you going to come inside?"

"I'll come inside and ask you my questions there. I want to ask you about Margaret Eastman."

Issacs knew he was going to be regretting this later. But he said, "Come on inside" anyway. Even

-127-

though he didn't want the guy inside. But what were you going to do? That's what they expected from you once you got messed up with the police. But he didn't have to play their game.

Venice walked into the living room, not sure what to expect. Something about Isaacs didn't add up right. Either he was living in a plain house in this plain neighborhood because of frugality, because he was cheap, or there was some other reason. He couldn't figure Isaacs out, like there was something he was hiding. Even though Venice knew he was in his mid60s, he looked more like a tough guy than a stock market expert. He had broad shoulders, and a narrow waist, muscular. His cheeks were ruddy like he spent a lot of time outside in the sun and the wind. Damn genetics. Some people didn't have to work for anything and had it all anyway. He didn't look like a guy who had just turned 40 and needed Viagra to get it up anymore. But Venice wasn't here to feel sorry for himself. He had a job to do. And it was time to do it.

Isaacs sat down in the brown reclining chair with a plop, in front of the big screen TV, and he pointed to the couch. "Why don't you sit down," he suggested, like a man who meant it?

Venice wasn't going to let himself be pushed around that way by some informant. "I think I'll stand. This'll just take a few minutes."

"So get started already!" Isaacs would be glad when this interview was over so he could watch his football game. "You follow the Falcons at all?"

"I'm not really a football fan," said Venice, although he split a pair of season tickets with his brother-in-law, went to half the games. He looked at the TV for a second, trying to spot Bill in the crowd.

Bill was married to his little sister, Leslie, he adored Leslie. Bill was a great guy, just the kind of guy he'd rather be spending the afternoon with. Then he thought he sounded like some wuss for saying that, so he added, "I think the West Coast offense really ought to open things up for Vick though. They should make the playoffs next year."

"Yeah," said Isaacs, passionately. He loved football. He didn't mind all the damn questions now so much, not if this Venice character liked the Falcons. "So you wanted to ask me about somebody, some Mary, Maury."

"Her name is Margaret Eastman," Venice said. His veins turned to ice at the mention of her name. Things like that shouldn't happen to a young woman like her.

"Who is she?" Issacs asked.

"Yeah! Who is she?" The door to the kitchen slammed open and in walked the most beautiful woman Venice had seen today, or maybe in a week. The more he looked at her, more he thought maybe in a lifetime, but he didn't have a whole lifetime of experience yet. But she was incredibly beautiful. Her eyes burst with curiosity. Or maybe it was jealousy. She was older, for a beautiful woman, maybe 40, maybe the exact same age as Venice. She was wearing a bra under her tight blouse and she was wearing lipstick too, and he couldn't help staring at her. Her hair was pretty too, like it was made out of silk, just that kind of shiny.

"Hey Monica, we need some privacy to discuss business," says Isaacs. "It's just man talk, nothing you'd be interested in."

"If it's another woman again, you bet I'm interested," she said, adjusting her breasts to make them stick out more. Venice was still staring at her, he couldn't take his eyes off her, and she was looking at his eyes, like she was touching herself for him, to be prettier for him. He couldn't believe it.

"I don't know who she is," Issacs said, and he was regretting inviting Venice into the house again.

"You sure you don't know anything about her?" Venice asked.

Monica stared at him with her lips making a little red pout. "If I knew anything about her, you can bet I'd let you know," she said, slapping Issacs on the top of his head.

"Ow!" he said, grabbing the top of his head.

He looked at Venice again and said "I said I don't know her or anything about her."

"She was the nurse at the hospital where Bruce Lucent recovered from his automobile accident," Venice said. "She's really beautiful, like you wouldn't believe. She has brown hair."

"I know you like women with brown hair, you two-timing jerks," Monica said, she was hitting Isaacs on the top of his head again, and he jumped up and yelled.

"Stop that, I said I don't know anything, and I don't know her!"

"I could show you pictures," Venice said. He had a lot of pictures of her, but he didn't want to share all of them, not with this scum. "It might help your memory some."

"Listen, buddies," Isaacs said. "You came here, so you take what you get and leave. I said I don't know nothing, I don't know nothing, that's all there is to it."

"Why don't you take me?" Monica purred at him.

"Hey now, I don't like that," Isaacs said, and now he was mad at all of them for ruining his day. He was mad enough to hurt somebody. He'd killed a man before one time, with his bare hands, and he could do it again, if he put something in his bare hands like a knife or a gun or something that he could kill somebody with.

Venice sensed trouble ahead, but he wanted to see more of Monica. He had the sense though that they were just ships passing in the night, that she was just some temporary liaison of Richard Isaacs, probably just another cheap tramp or something like all the others. Maybe she could be different, but it wasn't going to be in this lifetime, not with him.

"Well, if you don't know anything, I guess I'll be going," he said.

Walking down the sidewalk, the car waited for him at the curb. He stopped before opening the door and looked back up at the house. He saw Isaacs standing in the window frame looking back at him. Somebody was hiding something here, but Venice knew he was a bulldog. He'd get to the bottom of it yet.

And it didn't matter who got hurt along the way, cause he was going to find out the answers.

Chapter 18

Richard Isaacs stood gazing out the window from the 32nd floor executive office, Atlanta at his feet. The streets were empty below but for a few pedestrians dashing for cover beneath umbrellas. Timing was everything in this business. You couldn't make a killing when people are dying. Especially if you hadn't planned for their death. Business thrived on stability and growth. And for that stability, sometimes you had to play cut throats.

He heard the soft click as the door to the boardroom opened behind him.

The man's broad shoulders and slim builds made his silhouette against the window belie how close he was to retirement. As if you would retire in the middle of the biggest hand of your life, not when you're playing cut throats.

He turned. The sunlight slanting in through the window shimmered from the obsidian tresses of Callie Archer. She glided into the room, perfect, as always. She may have been wearing widows' black, but the swell of her breast, the shift of her hip against silk, assured him she wouldn't be alone for long, not if he had anything to do with it. Stability. All of them needed to be in Richard Isaacs' pocket if he was going to keep this ship on course.

Archer Industries must thrive. He'd invested too much in what he knew about this company, the way it operated and the under-the-table trick's Henry Archer had used to build it. All good products did not make a company great. Most of it was knowing how to manipulate money and power and the markets, to find the loopholes in the laws, trade just a little closer to the inside than many might feel comfortable doing. And when the players get nervous, when they start worrying that their house of cards might fall, it was Richard who knew just where to leak the word to investigators to break up the game. And when the dust settled, Isaacs always walked away unscathed with obscene amounts of cash in his pocket and ever more power. It was Henry Archer who had taught Richard the game at which Richard excelled.

Archer Industries had been poised to make the next great leap. Richard and Henry planned to bring in Isaac Stevens, a heavy if there ever was one in the corporate battleground. But he'd crossed Richard one too many times, the last when he'd forced his daughter Irene to end her relationship with Richard, right there, loudly, on the grounds of the Polo Club before hundreds of Atlanta's most well-heeled citizens. Stevens would give Isaacs the distance he needed when they started taking over their rivals, company by company, and piecing them out, converting the stock options, doing the deals, raking in the dough. And if someone must fall, all along the plan had been to take Isaac down, while Archer Industries subsidiaries concealed the deals. Richard and Henry were too good at this game to fail. They'd only miscalculate once in their 30-year partnership: they hadn't expected Archer to drive off a cliff.

Callie gave Isaacs a bare nod, a hint of a smile as she turned her back to him and walked along the bookcases that lined one wall. She ran her fingers along the spines, letting them linger on the masters, books that had never been cracked. Of course, Henry Archer was too important to be troubled with reading fiction, poetry, plays. But a wealthy man who had built his company from nothing needed a library, and he needed to surround himself with art and the accouterments that demonstrated he was a thinking man. But Henry's passions were the machinery of business, economics and industry. Those were the well-thumbed books closest to the desk. And his passions had been serious as well. Invention, transportation, and keeping his wife content. The last mattered most to Callie, of course. She would be well cared for; her prenuptial agreement assured her of that. But prestige that was something a little harder to come by in this city. And with a background like hers, prestige came from marrying well.

At last, she settled in the seat behind that massive imposing desk from which Henry Archer ran his world.

"You wanted to see me?" Callie asked him pointedly. One brow arched up, almost lost in a lock of hair that had drifted lower on her brow, like the question mark punctuating her sentence.

"I know this is a difficult time for you Mrs. Archer, but you must understand, the business of the company must move forward," Richard said brusquely. He bent over the desk toward her, his ruddy cheeks so close to hers she could see his pores. She leaned back a little, then followed his gazes that had so briefly touched on her breast before it moved to linger at her throat, in her hair, and at was pulled deep into her eyes.

"Henry and I spoke at length about the direction the company needs to take to be competitive," Richard crooned as he gazed into her eyes. "This company was a passion of his, you know, and I was about to help him double, triple its value. You need someone in place to make those decisions now that Henry can't."

"Why, Mr. Isaacs, I'm so pleased to hear your confidence in me," she said demurely, though he could see a devil lurking behind those eyes of hers; it kindled the flames smoldering in her gaze. "Of course, I haven't had much experience running a company like Archer Industries. But, sure Henry would be pleased that it stayed in the family."

Richard leaned back. Was she playing him as he was trying to play her? What had fired up that spark in her eye? Was she planning to take over the company? Did she have the gall to do something like that? With effort he pulled his gaze from hers and strode to the window.

"What's your game, Mrs. Archer?" He asked, staring over Atlanta, his voice barely raising a little with a unconcealed anger. "You know you don't have the experience to run a company like this. Henry and I worked side by side for thirty years." He pounded one fist into his open other palm, in rhythm to his words. "We built this company together. I know what his plans were for growing the business," he said angrily.

"So you think you should be running it?" Callie asked with that disarmingly innocent gaze of hers, the one that seemed to flash like the lightning playing across the rooftops of Atlanta, moving swiftly from chimney to gable, until it reached its target with a burst of heat and smoke. That was Callie Archer's gaze.

"I wouldn't presume to, Mrs. Archer," he enunciated somewhat crisply, turning from the window to lay a gentle hand on her shoulder. "You are entitled as owner of the company to sit at its head. But Henry had planned for some time to bring in Isaac Stevens to coordinate some buyouts and sell-offs, all of it tricky and confusing and more than a grieving wife should have to bear," he said in a tone Callie thought might be paternal, or condescending, or even genuinely caring. Did Richard Isaacs even know how to grieve for Henry Archer? She wasn't sure even she could grieve a man who treated his wife like any of the other baubles he'd collected to build his image.

Richard read the hesitation in her eyes and leaned in close, over her shoulder. "Let me guide you, Mrs. Archer. First, we bring on Stevens, as planned. Once he's installed, he'll begin buying up Archer Industries' competitors and dividing them up into existing divisions, then sell them off, bit by bit, exercising options, and building this company into the large cap company it ought to be." He turned her in the chair so that she faced him, the sunlight blinding on her dark waves of hair, the fire lit again in those eyes of hers as her breasts rose in breaths that seemed to quicken beneath his gaze.

"Think of it Mrs. Archer, Callie, think of it!" he exclaimed. "You can carry on your life as you always have, leaving the tedious business dealings to me. But the power will be yours. You will be Archer Industries. It'll be your books that line the walls, your charity events in the news, your parties the town will be talking about. Who knows, you may even find love again. I imagine a woman of your uncommon beauty and means would never need to be alone."

Alone. As if Callie didn't already know alone. Hadn't she survived ten years as the bauble of Henry Archer? Callie Archer rose from her chair, faced Richard squarely, then turned on her heel. She again glided through the room, touching a sculpture here, a painting there, at last coming to the broad mahogany doors out of her office. Her office. She turned. Isaacs was again a black silhouette against a blazing sunset, fiery red, as if he were some demon standing at the open gates to Hell. The entire board room had taken on the devilish glow.

She swept open the door.

"I imagine I'll be meeting Mr. Stevens before I have the opportunity to hire him?" she inquired.

He swept toward her, his silhouette resolving into a well-built man only slightly older than Henry's 60 years, his face quickly fading from the silhouette of a dark demon to a ruddy cheeked imp who looked like he'd be at home on a soccer field.

"If that's your wish," he offered deferentially.

"It is," she said, catching her breath. Something about him made her heart pound, as if she had agreed to work in a league with the devil himself.

It's time for it to be about me, isn't it? She thought to herself.

"Then you will meet him," he said forcefully. "We have an agreement, then, you'll accept my counsel?" He thrust out his hand.

She took it in both of hers and leaned toward him, tilting her head to look him in the eye, her breasts jostling within the black satin dress she wore. "I look forward to . . . working with you."

Again, she gave him that glinting glance, an almost wicked smile playing across her lips. What was her game?!

Chapter 19

Arthur Nance looked around the country club parking lot, crowded with cars, minivans, and SUVs old and new, battered and gleaming, cheap and priceless. Squinting into the late afternoon sun, the cars reflected the red-tinged light off windshields and bumpers and mirrors and doorknobs like a pack of bicyclists caught in a searchlight late at night on a deserted road. "Well, Jason," he said impatiently, "do you recognize any of them?"

"No, Doctor Nance," answered his nerdy young assistant with the pocket protector and horn-rimmed glasses that he seemed to wear as a badge of honor. "But I'm not a big car guy, you know that, and I haven't got all their cars in here yet anyway." He waved the sleek brushed-chrome Compaq iPac in Arthur Nance's face, as if Arthur could see that it was so light that he really couldn't have any cars in there yet.

"Well, you'll have to work on that, because I really hate it when I have to leave a place I wouldn't have gone into if I'd known whose car was parked out front. Okay? Start on it tomorrow; has it done by the Miller's pool party on Saturday?"

"Okay, Doctor Nance, will do. Want me to go inside   now?

"Yeah, you do that, Jason."

He wished he could smoke a cigarette while he waited for Jason to return, but the gravel-topped parking lot was just too public a place for one of Atlanta's top doctors to light up and hurt his image, which was of a trim, muscular, athletic medical genius who played a mean game of a racket ball with a golf disability of two. He'd just have to wait until he got home, assuming he went home alone, which he rather doubted because so many women wanted him, what with his near-perfect body, huge mansion, and astronomical salary, that he almost never went home alone unless he felt like it.

Behind his back, stiletto heels clicked, but not sharply and intensely like they would on wood or marble, rather with a little sogginess to them, a sort of muffled slurping caused by their impacting asphalt that had gone soft and resilient in the hot Atlanta sun. He liked stiletto heels a lot, so he turned to see who was coming.

It was Callie Archer, old Henry's widow. God, she was a looker, with those glossy black tresses and fine, fines hooters. She smiled and came toward him. Even though she was about forty, she still had an ass to die for, although he was more of a leg and foot man himself, which is why he preferred stiletto heels to pumps or running shoes. "Hello, Arthur," she said saucily, laying a perfectly manicured hand on his arm in a way that promised interesting things to come, "is Jason inside making sure it's safe for you to go in?"

"Yes," he exclaimed, studying the smooth white fingers tipped with crimson and filed to glossy perfection. "Yes, he is," he laughed, because it was a joke between them, even though when you came right down to it, it didn't much amuse him when he wasn't with Callie.

Arthur Nance had a very poor memory for faces, especially women's faces, because he almost never looked at their faces, especially if they were wearing open-toed shoes with stiletto heels and had bright red polish on their toenails, like Callie was. He had a fantastic memory for bare boobs and naked apses, of course, but those weren't likely to be on display in the country club's party room, at least not so early in the evening. In fact, the only reason he recognized Callie was she'd been his patient for going on twenty years, now, and after twenty years, it's hard not to recognize somebody, unless the light's bad or they've got a new haircut or something.

So wherever he went, he took his assistant Jason with him, because Jason not only had a photographic memory, he liked to look at women's faces, and besides, he had all their pictures in his Palm Pilot anyway, just in case.

Callie squeezed his forearm and leaned so close to him that her big breasts brushed his bicep. "How many are you up too now, Artie?" she demanded.

"Fourteen, I think, maybe fifteen. And don't call me Artie in public, okay? It diminishes the authority a doctor needs to do his job right."

"But I can call you Artie when we're alone together and I'm kneeling at your feet and your pants are down around your ankles, can't I?" her eyes flashed dangerously. "Because if I can't, then maybe I'll have to wash my hair on Friday night instead of on Saturday morning, if you know what I mean."

"Aw, shucks, Callie, sure you can call me – that – when we're somewhere nobody can hear us, it's just, you know, when we're somewhere with lots of people." His voice trailed off as he waved his free hand at the empty parking lot.

"That's good, Artie." She patted his hand. "Shall we go in together?"

"As soon as Jason oh, here he is."

The nerdy young assistant stood before them, his eyes fixed on Callie's beautiful cheekbones. "Okay, Doctor Nance, it's safe. There's not some singles woman in there with a restraining order against you."

"You're sure?" he inquired. "Last Thursday, at the Gaieties"

"Yeah, I feel bad about that," he said sadly, "but who would have expected Melissa Kriegel to be in a bedroom with somebody so early in the party?"

"Melissa?" asked Callie indulgently. "Was she with Walter?"

"No," he said sardonically, "Dorothy."

"Ah," she said and put more meaning into that one single unbroken syllable than an entire stack of a psychology textbook. "Well, then, if the coast is clear, let's go in. Are you coming, Jason?"

He blushed at the question, and shook his head form side to side. "No, Doctor Nance likes me to wait out front so that if anybody on the list shows up, I can warn him before they get within fifty feet of him."

Arthur nodded. Those fifty feet were important. He'd spent a whole night in a county lockup once because he'd thought fifty, forty, what's the difference? Ten feet, the cops had told him belligerently, as they'd taken his belt and shoelaces and neckties and fingerprints. He tucked Callie's right hand under his left arm and led her inside.

It was noisy, the kinds of noisy that only happening when you stuff a hundred people into a room built for seventy-five, give them all a couple of high-powered drinks, and let the band crank its amps to max. The air-conditioners were probably raising a ruckus, too, but who could hear them over the roar of the crowd?

From the far side of the room, Isaac Stevens raised a hand to Arthur and picked his way through the press of humanity to him, pulling a beautiful young woman along with him by the hand. "Arthur," he said softly, "just the man I've been looking for." He crossed the last ten feet and thrust out his hand. "Hello, Callie."

"Hello, Isaac," she responded sedately, but her grip tightened on Arthur's forearm.

"Arthur," he said, taking a pull on his drink, and his speech was a little slurred, so it was as clear the vodka in his glass that this wasn't his first drink of the night, or even his fifth, for that matter, "you know my daughter Irene, don't you?"

"Yes, of course," he said at once, inwardly glad that Isaac had told her who she was because he really hadn't recognized her, not in this setting or that skin-tight emerald cocktail gown cut so low that it made a man want to punch his fist at the sky and shout "Wee-hah!" After all, the last time he'd seen she was in a dimly-lit restaurant on Peach Street, sitting in a booth at the back with Henry Archer so close that it was hard to tell where one began and the other left off, her right hand under the table but apparently in Henry's lap, from the contented yet anticipatory gleam in old Henry's good eye.

"And Callie," said Isaac, his expression simmering, "I do believe I haven't seen you since the funeral. You're looking lovely tonight, my dear, as you always do, whatever the circumstances. May I present my daughter Irene? Irene, this is Mrs. Archer, whose husband Henry died recently."

Callie extended her hand to the blonde young thing and murmured, "It's a pleasure to make your acquaintance."

Irene took a deep breath, some breaths that made her large breasts look as though an anti-gravity beam had just rippled through them, and then took Callie's hand. "It's very nice to meet you, Mrs. Archer. I'm sorry to hear about your husband."

"Why, that's very kind of you," she riposted.

Watching all this, Arthur Nance quirked an eyebrow, but so inconspicuously that no one but he could see. Very interesting, he thought to himself. Old Henry's widow and old Henry's bereaved mistress, pretending not to know each other, when to Arthur's certain knowledge, the two had, on more than one occasion, shared the same bed in order to pleasure the old man and make sure he never developed eyes for anyone else. Yes, very interesting, he thought to himself. I wonder what's raising? Besides that, I mean, as he subtly adjusted his trousers.

Chapter 20

As Yvonne Perrin climbed the stairs to Rory
Edward's penthouse, she could not shake the
ominous feeling of dreadful fear that dampened her
day. It was a beautiful day in Atlanta, Georgia, fair
too partly cloudy, with temperatures in the low 80s,
dropping to 60 around midnight, it was the type of
day Yvonne usually found to make her feel like a
child again. But it was not to be that way today, as
cruel fate would have it.

Rory's penthouse was on Peachtree Street in
Atlanta, Georgia. Rory often wondered how he
would afford it, secretly afraid that his job might be
not as secure as he was led to believe. Just the other
day, Mr. Ricketts, his boss, had called him on the
carpet and read him the riot act over the problem
with the Zimmerman telegram. This made him feel
bad. But Rory never told anyone this, so Yvonne
had not known of his fears. But he appreciated her
visits, and today Yvonne was bringing him a box of
doughnuts wrapped in bright red plastic wraps that
reminded her of the day she boiled the eggs, even
though she knew Rory wouldn't be there to
appreciate it.

Rory's door was open when Yvonne Perrin got
to the top of the stairs that were unusual. It was a
large wooden door, usually painted white, that Rory
bought at an estate sale in Milledgeville, Georgia,

the capital of the state before the Civil War and General William Tecumseh Sherman's famous march through Georgia during the Civil War burned the city to the ground, both cities, actually, It (the door) had three hinges and a doorknob, as well as a doorknocker in the shape of a horseshoe that didn't work. It was a real find and Rory often regretted the fact he had never gotten it properly appraised by a licensed appraiser. It was one of Rory's biggest regrets, eating at him like a monster devouring his soul and spitting out the remnants of his shoes in little bits of leather and oil.

Yvonne went inside Rory Edward's penthouse. It was decorated with yellow walls, with an 8-x 10 color glossy photos of Rory's pet dog Barky on one of the walls. The dog was a champion show dog, winners of many gold medals, but had to be put down after. Rory had never gotten over it, sobbing uncontrollably whenever he ate at Burgher King. The picture window faced East, overlooking the river, a thin blue ribbon in the distance. Yvonne and Rory love to hold their hands and watch the sun setting, especially in winter, when the average high temperature was only 53 degrees. There was a smell in the air that Yvonne couldn't identify.

Callie Archer suddenly entered. She was wearing only a bathrobe! Naked underneath! Yvonne was shocked and startled! What was Callie doing there?!

Callie was wondering the same thing!

"What are you doing here?" she demanded. Callie didn't know what was going on. "I had not expected you today, Yvonne," she commented cattily.

"Never mind that!" Yvonne exclaimed. "Where is your husband, Bruce?"

"Well, you know," Callie cried hesitantly, her long glossy black hair hanging in front of her face. She hated when that happened and slid it aside.

Yvonne was confused. This was impossible! "Would you like some donuts?" she offered, holding the bag.

"Do you have any chocolate?" Callie asked.

"I think they were out," stated Yvonne bitterly, opening the box. There were a dozen — three jelly, four glazed, two strawberries frosted, three peanut butter, and Yvonne's favorite, a coconut glazed. "Would you like a cream filled?"

Callie pounded the table. "Damn!" she cursed. "Why does everything happen to *me*!" she exclaimed. She dropped her robe on the floor. "I never get a break!" she hissed.

Yvonne felt really badly! She had known Callie for years, since the summer of '91 when a cloud the shape of a ball of dust opened the sky to the heavens and turned their life into one big fun time. It was late in the evening and Callie was wearing a bright green skirt and matching red top with pink lace at the neck and sleeves. It had a slight paisley pattern that caught the sun. It was before Bruce's accident. Though he would never say so, Rory Edwards thought she was the most beautiful woman he'd seen. He often wished that Callie wasn't married, or that Bruce was dead or something!

The night was magical, and the band played disco into the night.

"Are you doing something with Rory?" she asked, deciding to take the bull by the horns and get to the root of the situation and let the chips fall as they may.

"I refuse to answer that," Callie said pigheadedly. "I don't have to answer that!"

This was a fine how-de-do! "After all we've done together, you-all won't tell me what you're doing!" she cried loudly.

"O, for crying out loud, Yvonne!" Callie shouted back like a bellowing mule, "What do you think? What does it look like?"

"Is Rory here?" Yvonne sobbed.

"He left." Callie informed her. She went to the refrigerator and opened a can of Diet Pepsi. "He . . . he couldn't perform."

"Yes," agreed Yvonne. "He often has that problem."

"What! You, too!" Callie blurted. This was a big surprise! What in the world was Callie thinking?!

Rory was always afraid this could happen. Despite his macho exterior, he was a bundle of fears inside, an writhing masses of phobias that made him tremble in nervousness. If he knew what the two girls were saying about him right now, his ears would probably burn red hot! Or hotter!

Callie sat on the red leather couch that Rory had picked up on sale in Sears at the Peachtree Mall. She suddenly felt like a fool! How could she not have guessed? The signs were all there, the skim milk instead of 2%, the sudden change in Rory's manor, the time he spent "working" at the office.

"Pepsi?" offered Yvonne, sensing her pain and offering her can. She had had her share of bad love affairs, like that handsome doctor with the office on Peachtree Street who dumped her when she had hinted that she wanted more from the relationship than donuts. Suddenly, the box of doughnuts depressed her. She wanted to drown in their rich, creamy taste, become for gotten in their sweet crunch that reminded her of the death of Arky. It was even worse with the weightlifter.

Callie took the peace offering gratefully. "I'm not a bad person," she pointed out, drawing her robe around her. "I'm just cursed."

Suddenly, there was someone at the door! Callie could tell by the sound of the corduroys that it was her husband, Bruce! What a predicament! If Bruce found out about this, it's being all over!

"What should we do?" fretted Callie, her eyes beseeching her longtime friend. It was a scary situation! Callie didn't want Bruce to know, but after the accident, he had become different. "Yvonne, but I need your help!" she begged.

Yvonne felt sorry for her friend Callie, who had such beautiful glossy black hair.

"Rory," called Bruce, lisping slightly. "Have you seen my hard drive? I'm a software developer, you know."

"We need to do something!" Callie whispered. "Bruce doesn't know about Rory!"

It was scary! If Bruce found out, there was no telling what he might do! He was insanely jealous, given to furious rages at the drop of a hat!

"What should we do?" Callie asked? "We need to do something!"

Yvonne thought about it. The needed to do something! But what could they do? Bruce hadn't been the same since the accident. It was all so hopeless! Yvonne should have known better than to bring the donuts; Bruce was sure to blame her!

Suddenly, she had an idea!

"Go into the bedroom!" she urged Callie. "I have an idea!"

"An idea?" asked Callie. She had ideas of her own, dreams of beautiful winter knights in Tallahassee, Georgia, watching the ships come in from the sea. With a handsome man by her side, his strong many arms mannishly comforting her with his male strength. She dreamed that idea many nights, but when she woke up, the arms were gone and she was in a stone cold bed with no joy except for her tropical fish. Dead all these many years.

"I should go into the bedroom," Callie opined. She picked the robe up off the floor and did so.

"This had better work," Yvonne muttered as she opened the door that could mean a matter of life or death!

Chapter 22

Atlanta was a hot city that day, and the air conditioner was dribbling and leaving a pool on the floor. Too bad it wasn't helping to keep the station house cool. I hate summer in Atlanta, Andrew Venice thought. He'd give anything to be hanging around up north some where—anywhere so long as it wasn't 90 degrees in the shade and full of concrete.

He had half way convinced himself to go down to the cantina and get a cold tall one when someone shouted at him.

"Hey Andy, you got a visitor!"

Andrew raised his bleary eyes from the mass of papers on his desk. It had been a long day, and in spite of all his efforts to dig up everything he could on this case, he was still no closer to figuring out who has killed Henry Archer than he had been when they found Archer dead. The scattering of evidence wasn't producing any clues that he could use. Suffice to say, he was not a happy camper just now and it was playing "Old Harry" with his temper. The last thing he wanted was a visitor. Probably some wino coming in to report seeing pink elephants in the alleyways of Atlanta. The city was full of crazy drunks, and most of them ended up at the police station at one time or another.

Of course, being a detective, Andrew didn't usually have to put up with them. The desk officer at the door was usually the one who was inundated with drunks and floosies and every other whacko in the street.

I'm just the murder guy...

"Who is it, Sergeant?" Andrew growled. He hated interruptions, especially when he had not had enough sleep. He'd been up all night staring at the photos of Archer's body. It had been too hot to go to sleep last night. Even sleeping in his underwear had not been comfortable. He would have stripped naked, but old lady Carson in the flat across the way was already on her last pace maker. No use in giving the old girl a kick-off before her time, though she would have gone with a smile on her prune face.

The Sergeant merely stepped aside, pulling his police hat off his head and holding it in both hands. His cheeks had a sort of apple glow. He turned his eyes to look just down the hall, and he smiled.

"Well?" Andrew barked.

A woman with a head full of hair as red as a roaring fire stepped through the doorway. She had green eyes like the rich emeralds in a princess' crown and they settled on Andrew the way a fox looks at a chicken that's strayed from the hen house. Hungry but hesitant, and wary in case there was a dog nearby. He puffed his chest and stood up, enjoying the way her eyes rode up and down his well-built frame. Clearly, she appreciated how well set-up he was. In turn, he stared unabashed at her voluptuous figure clad in a short tight black leather skirt and pink frilly blouse open nearly to the navel. He put her about thirty-five, though she might have been able to pass for younger.

"Hi there," she said in her thick Southern drawl. "Are you Andrew Venice?" she asked.

"I might be," Andrew said. "Who's asking?"

She sauntered into the room, walked over to the chair before his desk and seated herself demurely without even being asked. The angle gave Andrew a better look at her cleavage. He was starting to feel warm.

"My name is Yvonne Perrin, and I'm a friend of Callie Archer," she said.

Callie Archer? "Henry Archer's wife?" Andrew dropped into his chair and started pushing papers aside in search of the report of Callie Archer.

"Widow, actually." Yvonne smiled, and Andrew knew then that she was too hot of a woman to be handling in the summer. Those green eyes were starting to mesmerize him. He cleared his throat roughly.

"So...what can I do for you?" Venice said, trying to keep his mind on his work.

"Well, you see, I heard on the TV that the police were asking that if anyone knew anything about the Archer case to please come forward." She pushed a hand through her thick red tresses, brushing them out of her green eyes. "So I thought I should come forward and tell you what I know."

"And just what do you know?" Andrew asked.

For a moment, Yvonne glanced over her shoulder. Then she looked back at him and leaned so she was braced on the far side of his desk.

"I'm not the sort of girl who rats on her friends, mind you. Callie and I go back a few years. She's always been like a big sister to me, if you know what I mean."

"Yeah, I know," Archer said.

"And you'll probably think I'm terrible for telling you this." She looked at her hands.

"I make that decision after you tell me," Archer said.

Yvonne pursed her luscious lips. "Well, as I said, Callie and I go back a ways...to when she was Callie Lucent. Before she married Henry. She tells me everything...well, almost everything. Anyway, I knew her older brother Bruce too. He's over at the hospital right now recovering from an automobile accident. I though I would drop in and visit him...just to make him feel better. Callie said he was sorta blue. But he was asleep when I got there, and I didn't want to wake him up, but I didn't know what to do.

"I was going to leave when I decided to use that little bathroom in his room, and while I was in there, I heard people coming into the room. I was going to call out and let them know I was in there, but I heard Callie...and I heard Dr. Nance."

"Dr. Nance?" Andrew asked.

"Arthur Nance." Yvonne waived her hand around in the air as though shoeing flies. "He's some big time doctor over there. Anyway, I heard Callie say, Is he still asleep, and Dr. Nance said, "Oh, yeah, he's going to be out for a while..."

She paused.

"And?" Andrew insisted.

"It got quiet, and I opened the door...and Callie was kissing Dr. Nance like he was an old flame."

Andrew frowned. "So what did you do?"

"Well, I didn't want them to know I was in there, and that I heard them and saw them, so I sorta slipped out of the room and left." She cocked her head like a little girl afraid of being scolded. "Was that wrong of me? I just didn't want to embarrass them..."

"Just like that?" Andrew asked. "They didn't see you leave?"

Yvonne shook her head so the cascades of red hair shimmered like flames in a fireplace. God, he wished it was winter...

"I was real quiet," she said. "Anyway, that's what I know. It's what I saw."

"And just why are you telling me this now?"

"Because...it was back before Henry died...and it made me wonder if he knew Callie might actually be having an affair with the doctor who was looking after her older brother."

Andrew sighed. "Well, I want to thank you for coming in and telling me this," he said as he stood up.

Yvonne pulled herself out of the chair and nodded.

"Thanks for letting me tell you," she said. "It's a load off my mind, and can sure tell you."

"If you think of anything else," Andrew said. "Give me a call."

"I will," she said and smiled. "Bye, now."

She sauntered back out of the office just as Sergeant was returning. Sergeant pulled off his hat again and nodded to her as she passed. Then he took his hat and started to fan himself while smiling at Andrew.

"Now that's what I call one hot little lady," the Sergeant said. "I wish I was a few years younger, I do. Are you gonna ask her out?"

"Don't be ridiculous," Andrew snarled and motioned the Sergeant to leave. Still grinning like a hyena, the Sergeant wandered away. Then Andrew sat down and started staring at his papers.

"So Arthur Nance and Callie Archer have a past," Andrew muttered.

That was something to ponder.

Chapter 23

Irene Stevens nibbled at her sautéed crab cake (it was nestled in a mild golden curry sauce and garnished with micro basil), and gazed at Bruce Lucent, who was sitting at the head of the 42-seat table with his wife, that positively ancient Callie Archer with her glossy raven hair (that had to be Miss Clairol or Irene wasn't the reigning Georgia Peach Princess for 2003!) and her gravity-defying 38DD boobs. Bruce (who had the studliest body ever, but a face like a turnip, round and a little purple around the bottom where his skin was still recovering from the laser peel to get rid of those nasty acne scars) was in a midst of a long, boring presentation about his newest software package, LuceLips, an interactive speech-recognition program that could do everything from read you're morning newspaper to you to book you're lunch reservation.

At this point in the long presentation (too too long, as far as Irene was concerned), chef Joel himself clapped his hand to his mouth in amazement. "You mean a *computer* reserved my special Cellar Room for this function?" the handsome and dashing chef gasped, smiling broadly, and everyone set down their salad forks and applauded with appropriate little oohs and ahhs and titters of appreciation. It was enough to make a girl gag.

"How's the crab cake?" Rory Edwards asked.

Rory Edwards, sixty (but he didn't look a day over forty, not with that absolute hard body!), was Irene's best—and at the moment only—friend in the whole sunny state of Georgia. She just didn't understand why other girls didn't like her. All the men she met did.

In answer, Irene popped a bite of the crab cake into her mouth and gave a little shivering moan of ecstasy. That little shiver made her ample bosom quiver on an even larger scale, causing the computer geek across from her to nearly poke himself in the cheek with his fork. Now there was a man who could stand some buzzing with a laser! That unibrow simply had to go, and that tattoo, *UNIX Rulz!* was just too icky for words. Especially on his neck. Imagine having to look at that every single day of you're life!

"It's delish," Irene simpered. "Thanks *so* much for bringing me, Roar."

Rory Edwards's tanned cheeks turned pink in response to her use of her pet name for him, "Roar," and he took off his spectacles and polished them feverishly, something he always did, Irene noticed archly, whenever she paid him a compliment. He looked pretty darn good for sixty, thought Irene. She'd always thought golf was an even bigger bore than computers, but Rory Edwards was living proof positive the sport had something going for it. Either that or Rory was sinking his considerable fortune into liposuction and face-lifts.

Bruce Lucent aimed the laser pointer he was holding at the giant screen and said, "Next slide, please," in his slightly boyish (but not in a bad kind of way) voice, but instead of the silver and black Lucent banner, an error screen popped up.

At the same moment, a woman's sultry voice issued from the speakers, "Oh, Bruce, darling, I'm afraid something's gone *terribly* wrong."

The raven-haired beauty sitting beside Bruce made a wide-eyed moue of astonishment and shook her magnificent mane of raven hair. "Why, Bruce, darling . . . !" she cried, smiling widely, her teeth like snowy Chickens and her lips like glossy red satin pillows, and pointed to the computer to make sure even the dumbest of the dumb got the joke. "That's *my* voice!"

Irene stifled the urge to roll her eyes and stick her finger down her throat and pantomime a person throwing up. Oh, as *if* . . . ! She thought. Could any of this *be* any more fake?

Bruce cleared his throat and frowned in mock displeasure. He tipped his head on one side, stroking his rugged chin with his long fingers, fingers that looked as if they really knew how to pleasure a woman, Irene thought dreamily. She squirmed a little in her chair, entertaining racy fantasies about what she'd like to do with a studly body like Bruce Lucent's. Bruce opened his voice to give a command, but before Bruce could speak the computer voice that was exactly the same as Callie Lucent's voice asked in a husky drawl that sounded like she'd been positively gargling straight tequila, "What can I do to make it up to you?" It sounded, Irene thought with uncharacteristic lack of charity, as if Callie Lucent's computer voice was asking if Bruce wanted a blow job.

Stabbing ferociously at her crab cake, Irene pretended for a moment that the golden-sauced crustacean cake was Callie's face. Her oh-so-perfect Baptist face, clear of wrinkles, clear of unsightly hairs, clear of pimples. The arrogant woman. Irene's hand crept to her chin to surreptitiously fondle the hard red zit that was swelling under her creamy skin. It was the kind of zit that hovered under the surface for days, not really showing but *feeling*, if you touched it, which Irene did about a zillion times a day, to see whether it was forming a head or not. Sometimes Irene hated being a mere twenty-two, even if it did mean she could go braless without worrying she'd look like she was carrying two droopy water balloons under her trendy Donna Karan tank top. She had firm, upright breasts, the left just a teensy-tiny big bigger than the first, something her doctor told her not to worry about. It just made them more kissable, he'd assured her as he pleasured her atop the examining table, her feet in the stirrups, his hand over her mouth to stop her unstoppable little cries of ecstasy.

Irene's nostrils flared with delicate disdain as she glared at Callie Archer's ample bosom. There was more silicon floating in that woman's chest than there was in the laptop computer Bruce Lucent was showing off this very minute to the two men at the table. Irene wondered momentarily who they were, and if they were as well-to-do as Bruce. One of them (Irene could tell she was a computer geek from the fact he was wearing a Star Trek T-shirt under his sports jacket, a jacket so old and tatty it had shiny elbows, and blue jeans from Gap. There was even a plastic strip running down the leg that said "38-38-38-38" all the way down to his calf) was engrossed in whatever was on the screen. The other, a young redheaded man with ginger freckles and a studly body but a really ugly face and the worst teeth Irene had ever seen on a man, was ogling the five or six acres of cleavage Callie Lucent was displaying. Irene sniffed. That any woman over forty would dare wear a Betsey Johnson, especially in a high-end upper-class place like Joel's, positively reeking of good taste, was just unthinkable. All she needed to complete the ensemble, Irene thought with uncharacteristic sarcasm, was a pair of castanets and a guitar player shouting "Ole!"

That made her smile, and she dabbed her glossy lips delicately with her napkin (good thing she'd remembered to use her new Clinique "Stay the Day" lipstick!) before once more putting her attention back on her crab cake. Swirling a forkful in the mild golden curry sauce, she took a bite. It really was scrumptious, but if she ate the whole thing, and the *pôt de chocolat* served with *crème fraiche* sorbet and a rolled sugar wafer cookie she'd been eyeing on the menu (or maybe the delicious-sounding *crème caramel* with honey-vanilla ice cream and a sweet almond wafer cookie—they both sounded *so* good!), and a couple more glasses of this positively yummy 1999 Marsannay *rosé* from Domaine B. Clair in Burgundy, France, she'd either have to skip dinner tonight or march right into the washroom and throw it up.

Suddenly, just like he was right there across the table from her, his laugh lines deep as the Grand Canyon and his merry eyes twinkling like stars, Irene could hear her dearly-departed and oh-so deeply missed dead lover Henry Archer's gruff down-home rumble: *If'n ya'll are gonna just upchuck it the second y'all finish eatin' it, Reeny-bean, what's the gol-dang point of spendin' this kind of cash on lunch?*

Her china-blue eyes welled with tears. *Oh, Daddy Hank . . . !* she thought. (He wasn't really like her real daddy, but since he'd been so much older than she was and took care of her better than her real daddy ever did, never hitting her—except when they played "Spanky Pants"—and never forcing her to do anything she didn't honestly truly want to—except when they played "Rape Me Till I Squeal!" or maybe sometimes when they played "Good Till the Last Drop," which really wasn't her favorite game, to tell the honest truth—and never, ever calling her horrible cruel names like "Daddy's Little Blow-Up Dolly.") *How could you leave me like that, my sweet Daddy Hank, without even saying goodbye to you're darling Reeny-Bean?* It had been six months, but not a day went by that she didn't miss her darling "daddy." It was, in fact, why she was sitting here in swanky Joel's restaurant: today was their first anniversary.

Well, it would have been their first anniversary, that is, if Henry Archer hadn't been so tragically killed in that tragic car accident out on the Parkway. Could it really be six months since he'd been killed so tragically? It seemed like only yesterday they were snuggling on his big round king-size bed or kissing in his kidney-shaped pool or just holding hands like a pair of giddy freshmen away at college.

That was Daddy Hank had still been married to that positively vulpine Callie Archer then— "vulpine" was Irene's "New Word of the Day," one of the many self-improvement things Irene was

-162-

doing to improve herself so she could rise up above the red-dirt-poor country-style life she'd grown up in—but she obviously wasn't satisfying him, not like a *real* woman could. *Not like I could*, thought Irene, tossing her glorious mane of flaxen hair in vexation. There was no one in the world she hated more than Callie Archer, who used to be married to Daddy Hank before he met Irene and found out what *true love* really was. Daddy Hank had promised to leave his wife for Irene—he'd even started the divorce proceedings—but then he'd died so tragically in that tragic car accident, before he could change his will, before he could divorce Callie, before he could marry his beloved Reeny-Bean and make an honest woman out of her.

And then, to add insults to injury, to make matters worse—as if they could ever get any worse!—the straw that broke the camel's back was when Callie turned around and married Bruce Lucent just a week—a week!—after poor Daddy Hank died. Callie inherited everything, and Irene was left practically penniless. Callie even cancelled the lease on that cute little Lexus coupe Daddy Hank had given Irene, the merciless, heartless, cruel witch. It was enough to make Daddy Hank turn over in his grave—if he had a grave, that was, but he didn't, being cremated, after all, since Callie was too cheap to buy a plot and casket and cement liner. She'd had him stuffed into the cheapest cardboard box the funeral home had, and then mailed the box to Irene. Postage due. The arrogant woman.

If only there was a way I could make her pay, Irene thought, fiercely fighting back the tears that welled to her lovely china-blue eyes. If only there was something, I could take away from her . . . !

Bruce Lucent was finished his part of the presentation, nodding and smiling at the applause. As his technical assistant took over explaining the technical parts of the software, Bruce put his hand on Callie's shoulder and murmured, "Back in a sec, hon." Then he headed out of the 42-seat private Chef's Room, which was just off the kitchen. It had beautiful art, high ceilings, and state-of-the-art technology available to rent, which is probably why Bruce Lucent chose it for his software presentation.

And suddenly—like she'd been struck by lightning—a light bulb went off over Irene's pretty head. Once more patting her glossy lips (and tucking her Clinique "Stay the Day!" lipstick in the pocket of the chic little Versace number she'd carefully picked out that morning, knowing it accentuated her voluptuous perfect size-6 body), Irene slid out of her chair and leaned close to Rory to confide, "Just going to powder my nose, Roar. Order me the *pôt de chocolat* served with *crème fraiche* sorbet and a rolled sugar wafer cookie, will you?"

She had a feeling she'd be hungry when she got back.

* * *

Steven Suffern eyed the voluptuous young blonde as she left the room, her round ass looking like a juicy Georgia peach in that sexy little number she was wearing. Steven, a masseuse at Atlanta's Polo Club, had an eye for the ladies, but he liked to bat for both teams. In fact, he had his eye on the studly older guy she'd been sitting with—Steven had asked around and found out quite a bit about Rory

Edwards, who was sixty but didn't look a day over forty. One was that the hard body was just as good without the clothes—no corset for Mr. Edwards!—and the other was that Rory Edwards was loaded, rich, rolling in the dough. And unattached.

The "unattached" part was the one Steven was hoping to personally change, and hopefully by this afternoon, suppertime maybe, or this evening at the latest. He'd scored a ticket to the $200-a-plate luncheon presentation by giving an extra-special massage to fat old Mrs. Decatur. He'd never be able to watch the movie *Deliverance* again without thinking fondly on the moment. He'd known there would be dozens of fat, rich pigeons at a do like this; no reason he couldn't pluck one. And Mr. Rory Edwards was the perfect pigeon. Steven had seen the way his eyes, a lovely chocolate-brown behind his spectacles, had kept roving his way. He might have a chubby for the luscious blonde, but put a bat in his hands, and he'd nail one out of the park.

Steven rose, unconsciously checking his handsome visage in the mirror for errant flecks of micro basil (he'd had the crab cakes) and made his way over to Rory Edwards. "Mind if I sit down and chat for a moment?" he asked, his pleasant baritone warm and inviting. He put out his hand and offered a manly squeeze, which Rory Edwards returned with equal fervor.

"Uh, er, my companion will return shortly . . . " Edwards stammered.

Steven slid his hand under the table, expertly flicking the snowy linen tablecloth over Edwards's lap to cover the fact that his nimble fingers were even now sliding down the zipper of Edwards's expensive Ralph Lauren stain-repellant slacks.

"Don't sweat it, handsome," he murmured with a throaty growl that made perspiration beads pop out on Edwards's surprised face. "This won't take long . . . "

* * *

Irene smoothed the skirt of her natty little Versace number over her curvy hips, smiling a secret smile to herself as she re-entered the 42-seat private dining room. She was a little out of breath, and if truths are told, her "Stay the Day!" lipstick hadn't quite held up to it's advertised promise of lasting through everything, but otherwise, no one would guess that she'd just moments before been riding Bruce Lucent like a champion bucking-bronc rider at a Texas rodeo, his face buried between her firm, high breasts that bounce unfettered and free.

There was a young man sitting in Irene's seat, but he jumped to his feet the moment he saw Irene, giving her a smile that showed off his perfect white teeth. He had the most startlingly green eyes, like a cat's, an emerald color that showed off his golden tan and sculpted features. Irene's own China-blue eyes strayed down to his crotch, noting with expert quickness that he dressed left and was hung like a stallion. She licked her lips, smiling as she lifted her hungry eyes off his crotch. Surely she'd worked off enough calories with Bruce that she could have her two desserts, after all.

"You'd never guess what I've been doing, Roar," Irene confided, sure the young man couldn't hear her (not realizing that he could indeed, and was hanging on every word). "I've just given Bruce Lucent the ride of his life!"

Irene laughed merrily, her laugh like a dozen little tinkling bells, and tossed her magnificent mane of flaxen hair. "I followed him into the men's room," she said in a purring voice. "Caught he with his pants down, so to speak!"

Rory Edwards just blinked at her, his mouth open a little. Irene laughed again, gaily, enjoying the effect she was having. This would certainly get him in the mood for what she had planned later this afternoon!

"I pretended I didn't know I was in the men's and got all flustered and excited," Irene said. "So excited, my breasts just *popped* out of the top of my Versace! These darn criss-cross tops just don't hold *anything* in! And as soon as he saw my bobbies—that's what Daddy Hank liked to call them—well, Roar, he just about popped, too!"

Irene's pretty face was flushed as she excitedly recounted the tale of what had happened in the men's room: "I said to him, 'Ooo, Mr. President, I've always wanted to try one of those big cigars . . . ! Can I have just a teensy little taste?' Roar, I thought his eyes were going to fall right out of his head he was staring so hard, and he couldn't say a word, just kept making these funny little noises like a puppy on his mama's teat, so I just went to my knees and went to work."

Rory Edwards groped in his pocket for his handkerchief and mopped his sweating face. It was a rather violent red, Irene noticed, but she was having too much fun telling her story to bother asking if he was feeling all right.

"He pulled me to my feet," Irene said, her China-blue eyes sparkling at the memory of how manly Bruce had been, "and he picked me up and set me on the imported Italian marble counter top, and pulled my panties down with his teeth! And oh,

Roar, he pleasured me with his probing tongue and nimble fingers . . . ! Just when I thought I had reached the utmost peak of bliss, he thrust his throbbing member deep inside my hot little juicy love-box, and pounded me like a snorting stallion on a broody mare—well, except that a stallion would have had her doggy-style, or horsey-style, I guess you'd have to say, taking her roughly and manfully from behind, but Bruce mounted me from the front—until I shrieked so loudly and with such unsurpassed abandon that he had to put his hand over my mouth to stifle my cries of ecstasy as he filled me with his steaming love-juices! Oh, Roar . . . ! I've never felt such bliss, such ecstasy, such rapture, such elation, such"

Irene stopped, suddenly aware that Rory Edwards' eyes had stopped blinking. His hand clutching his handkerchief had fallen to his lap, pushing aside the tablecloth that had, until that fateful moment, been covering the fact that his fly was down and his rather large and still a tumescent member was fully exposed and his Ralph Laurens' stain-free slacks hadn't lived up to their reputation.

Rory Edwards, in fact, had stopped together. His heart, at least. Strained to it's very limit's from Steven Suffern's expert ministrations, it had been pushed beyond the very limit's of human endurance by listening to Irene's spirited and passionate exposition of her washroom conquest of software developer Bruce Lucent.

Irene's lovely China-blue eyes filled with horror and flew to Steven Suffern, who was standing stock-still and frozen with utter shock behind them. Then she began to scream, loud and long, even louder than she'd shrieked while being pleasured by

Bruce Lucent. But this time, no one moved to put his hand over her glossy lips and stop her anguished cries. Like an ululating siren, klaxoning on and on and on and on and on, she kept it up for a full twenty-three piercing minutes until the police arrived and a craggy officer finally slapped her to shut her the hell up.

Chapter 24

The doorbell rang and Irene looked up from the magazine article she had been reading over and over again for the last half-an-hour. She would not have been able to tell anyone, not even her best friend Abbey O'Neil, what the article was about. Oh, she could have guessed of course, and said the article was about women's fashion, the latest rage in New York, jodhpurs or henna hand tattoos, but she would have just been guessing. The article was just chicken scratch that her usually well-tuned mind could not comprehend. Her thoughts were of nothing at all, nothing but the death of her lover Henry Archer.

Never again would their bodies glide together in union. Never again would she be able to run her fingers along his ample muscles. Never again would he kiss her voluptuous breasts or caress her beautiful blonde hair. Death was the cruelest break-up of all.

The doorbell rang again and Irene came back from her thoughts of Henry. It was all she had left of Henry. That and the apartment. The mink was also hers. He had been giving to her, and she to him where she could. Very giving. But then Henry had been so handsome. Her best friend, green-eyed, slender Abbey had laughed at the idea of twenty-year-old, blue-eyed, blonde-haired Irene dating a sixty-year-old, until she had seen his ripped pecs and bulging biceps on the trip to the Cayman Island Henry had arrange for the three of them and Henry's friend Rory Edwards. Henry spent an hour in the gym every day. His pecs, abs, and biceps were to die for.

But no longer. Henry was in the ground, dead from the car crash that took his life and that of his Mercedes. Both were blackened hulks now, one buried in the ground of exclusive Peach Barrow Cemetery, the other in a police impound lot. She would miss that Mercedes.

The doorbell rang a third time and Irene stood. She placed the magazine on the end table in its place next to the previous month's issue. All things in their place in Irene's living room. All things in their place.

Her heels clicked on the marble of the foyer. She paused in front of the gold-edged mirror. Her level, blue-eyed stare answered her look. Her shoulder-length blonde hair was pulled back into a tight bun, the same style she had worn to Henry's funeral. A thigh-length black skirt covered her voluptuous chest and buttocks. Below the perfect hem of the dress, her legs reached exactly to the floor. The three inch heels accentuated the bulge of her calf. The mirror had no doubt she was a beautiful, strong woman. Nor would any man have doubted it, nor many women, at least those women so inclined to appreciate a perfect female body. Irene knew many who did. Abbey for one.

Checking her eyes one last time for any redness, she pulled open the door, and said in her contralto voice, "Yes, may I help you?"

Andrew Venice had heard many contralto voices before, but none attached to a woman as beautiful as the one standing before him right then. Blue-eyed, blonde-haired, and round in all the right places, Irene Stevens, the mistress of the burnt and blackened millionaire industrialist and ex-body-builder Henry Archer, was a sight that sent a shiver down his rock-solid, forty-year-old body. What that now blackened old geezer had seen in this twenty-year-old beauty was clear. What she had seen in him was his money.

Andrew Venice knew her type well. He saw them on Peach Bottom Avenue, the ladies of the night who came out to offer their nylon- and fishnet-covered wares. Irene Stevens was the same, but her price was higher when she could get it. Looking at the well-filled skirt she wore, Andrew Venice expected that she would fetch that price for a long time to come. Until the Botox stopped working and the force of gravity could no longer be fought.

"Hello, I'm Andrew Venice, police detective," he said in his deep voice. "We met briefly at your... friend Henry Archer's funeral."

Irene knew what Andrew Venice was thinking, that she was a high-priced whore, a woman of the night. She was, but it was a velvet night with champagne stars.

"I know who you are, and I know what you're thinking," Irene said. "But you're wrong where it counts most."

"I bet I am. May I come in, Miss Stevens."

"Do I have a choice?" she asked, stepping aside.

"We all have choices, Miss Stevens."

Irene led the buff police detective into the living room.

"What do you want with me during my time of grief?"

"Answers, Miss Stevens. Answers to some questions."

"Ask your questions, Police Detective." She sat on the sofa and crossed her legs slowly. The slide of nylon on nylon was the rasp of a thousand tiny saws.

"I'll come straight to the point. We know Henry Archer was murdered."

Irene stood, her hand over her left breast. "Murdered? How do you know?"

The act was good, Andrew thought. Very good indeed. Andrew could almost believe the shock was real.

"Forensics, Miss Stevens. Forensics."

"Oh, forensics." The police detective was watching her closely. He'd meant to startle her, to scare her. Perhaps he suspected her. The thought scared her and excited her at the same time. Her, Irene Stevens, a suspect in the murder of Henry Archer.

"The brakes on his car had been tampered with, Miss Stevens."

The thought of Henry stamping uselessly on the German-made break pedal of his Mercedes over and over again to no avail sent a shiver down Irene's spine. Her stomach clenched at the thought of Henry's last frantic moments. She hoped that his last desperate thoughts were of her. Surely he had not been thinking of his wife Callie.

"How horrid!"

"Indeed. But I face the horrid every day, Miss Stevens."

"How do you do it?"

"With a strong stomach and a thousand push-ups every morning."

Irene could see the cut of Andrew Venice's body even through the dark suit he were. For a police detective, the suit's quality seemed out of place, Italian, if she guessed right. The bulge at his side was not just from the gun in its holster.

Andrew continued, "Someone with access to the car, someone close to him, someone who knew German cars, someone who perhaps spent a year in school in Munich and took auto shop there, tampered with the breaks on his car causing it to carom out of control on Peach Valley Road on that fateful night."

"I went to school in Germany! I took auto shop!"

"I know."

"But— but—"

"I know quite a bit about you, Miss Stevens. I know you are — I mean, were, — Henry Archer's mistress. I know you were one of the last people to see him alive."

"But when my father was stationed in Germany, we studied the C230 in auto class. Henry drove an E-series."

"Not hard for a dedicated murderer to figure out, Miss Stevens."

"I did not murder Henry!"

"Then who did, Miss Stevens? Tell me and I'll go easy on you."

"I know nothing about it."

"A day after Henry's death, you were seen coming out of Rory Edward's house." It was a lie. Andrew Venice didn't like saying it, but Irene Stevens was a nut that he had to crack one way or another, and he didn't mind using all his bastard police detective techniques to do it.

"I— I— Rory's a friend. A friend of both Henry and I. He was comforting me. Rory even went with us to the —"

"Cayman Islands. Yes, I know that too," Andrew Venice said with satisfaction. "Do you know what Archer and Edwards were doing in the Caymans, Miss Stevens."

"Yes, of course. We were spending time on the beach. And in the evening we went dancing." It had been an absolutely wonderful time, three days of sun and fun with her best friend and her best man. She had worn a red bikini that was a size too small. Abbey had been jealous and Henry had been wild about it. The perfect vacation.

"And in the mornings he and Edwards visited their bankers to deposit large sums of cash."

"I slept in. I wouldn't know."

"Don't lie to me! Tell me what you know of Rory Edwards and his business venture with Henry Archer!"

"I don't know anything, I tell you! Henry and Rory were just friends. That's all I know."

Andrew was nearly certain she knew nothing, but he had one last gambit to play. And then perhaps he could trust her and use her to help him find the real killer.

"I have enough evidence to charge you with the murder of Henry Archer. You had access and motive. You have the skills and the desire. Tell me what I want to know."

"Motive! What motive would I have to kill Henry Archer?"

"His reconciliation with Callie Archer. He was leaving you for his wife. You couldn't stand the thought that he might dump you."

"Leave me for his wife? Absurd!"

"Then you'd be out in the cold. Would your long legs and full body ever get you another man as rich as Henry Archer? You couldn't afford to lose him. But Rory Edwards is almost as rich. Did he put you up to this?"

"I don't know what you're talking about."

Andrew took Irene by the arm, squeezing her with a strong hand. Her knees sagged as he shook her.

"I'm talking murder, Miss Stevens. Cold-blooded murder, planned by his business partner and executed by his jealous mistress."

Irene burst into tears, and she wailed, "I loved Henry! I loved him so much."

Andrew stepped back. Even while crying, Irene Stevens was a beautiful woman, and, as all his honed instincts told him, innocent.

"I'm sorry for your loss, Miss Stevens. And I'm sorry for putting you through that."

Irene Stevens turned away from him.

"Damn you," she hissed.

"Yes, damn me. I'll find my own way out."

The door slammed, echoing through the cavernous emptiness of the apartment. Irene wiped the tears from her eyes. They had served their purpose. Andrew Venice was convinced she was innocent.

Chapter 25

And then there was that time they all went to see the Atlanta Braves at Turner Field. Irene Stevens couldn't have been more excited. Their seats were great. Andrew Venice had dugout tickets for the season, as he always did, being so incredibly well set up. Andrew called Irene and said he was taking Richard Issacs to the next game and would she like to come too because they would love to have her along and she, of course said, shrieked really, YES! YES, OF COURSE!

Irene loved the energy and commotion of the enormous crowd in the stadium. She loved their front row seats, right up next to the green railing where she was currently draped over the bar watching the players or watching their cute butts avidly. Andrew was a marvelous guy. He really was. She was considering coming onto him because he was like 20 years younger than Henry, god rest his soul. And he was nice looking to sort of like George Clooney on a good day and a little like Rowan Atkinson on other days but Rowan was in his own way a little hottie really. After Henry any man would appear a bit on the small side by comparison anyway. And not nearly, nearly as rich.

Richard didn't have as sweet a personality as Andrew but then few men did but he was very well-built. He had the shoulders of a water buffalo and the waist of a ferret. He was reddened by his many sporting activities which he managed to keep up within in addition to his busy job as a stock broker, and that reminded Irene of safari hunters and virile construction workers which contracted quite sexily to his suit-and-tie demeanor. Irene was considering coming onto him but he was older than Henry was when he died even though he hadn't died of natural causes but he was dead and Richard would die too someday.

Both of the men couldn't have been nicer to Irene and she was literally basking in their solicitor's attentiveness. They nestled her cozily in between them and heaped compliments upon compliments upon her. Then they started talking about the ballplayers and discussing their merits which started to bore Irene a little, really, although she was far too sweet a girl to ever let on. For a while she had amused herself with deciding which of the players had the sexiest name but finally she was stuck between Roman Colon and Armando Almanza and evens that diversion got boring.

So she leapt out of her seat and leaned over the railing to watch the game more closely and wish that baseball uniforms weren't so concealing of the many lovely male bodies sweating in the heat of the sun beating down on the picturesque turf spread out like a vast green carpet where someone had vacuumed with mathematical precision making these swish marks in the shag that made neat patterns on the carpet that just scream it's clean and recently vacuumed until someone walks around and then all you get are just footprints everywhere and finally the carpet just gets squished down and sick looking.

Irene still listened to the conversation the men were having because she was a good listener but it was like they were talking in code and trying to figure out what they were saying was beginning to bug her. She was ultra aware that her very short shorts were giving her a wedgie just short of becoming thongs only she didn't have a thong on or anything else on but the shorts. Except her tight T-shirt, that is. She didn't mind that Andrew and Venice were seeming to stare more at her than the ballplayers because she figured she was more interesting anyway. She tossed her long blonde hair back and chewed her bottom lip wondering what Richard had meant when he said to Andrew, "Hell, yes, I'll inform. I'm an informant. That's what I do, and I inform."

Andrew seemed to know instantly, though. He said back to Richard in a low voice "I've been a police detective for a long time and I've got plenty of people reading skills so I already knew this long before you told me."

They kept talking about that on and on and it was boring and bugging Irene who was no fool for a young woman in her twenties, if only just barely in her twenties at that, and she had heard the rumors flying around Atlanta but no one was going to pull the grape vine over her eyes. Some people were thinking there was something suspicious about Henry's tragic car accident, god rest his soul. And if there was something suspicious about it then there was SOMEONE suspicious behind the something suspicious. And that someone could only be someone like her or Henry's wife, that arrogant woman.

It was hard not to miss Henry and how well he made her feel about herself and all. They had spent so many fun hours together at Henry's private gym where he showed her his former bodybuilding techniques that produced that massive pecs and washboard abs and he loved to watch her on the treadmill. Business talk made her head hurt and Henry despite being a millionaire industrialist never talked about business much. He sometimes talked about his wife Callie and Irene didn't mind listening to him talk about Callie because every other phrase practically was "not like YOU, my sweet Georgia moonpie" and she had to agree with him that Callie was pure unadulterated evil.

And now she had to think about business because she'd lost Henry and while her apartment was paid up for the year she knew Henry couldn't renew her lease and she'd have to come up with a plan for her future. She'd responded to an ad, well, a flyer, really, that had been tucked under her windshield wiper about a month ago although it was hard to remember how long ago it had been after Henry had perished unexpectedly. But she was clearly on her way to a fabulous career because of that ad. It had sounded very exciting—Educational Opportunity to Enter the Glamorous World of Pampered Porn Stars! The price was steep but Irene's bank account had been left in a healthy state because of Henry and her sometimes wished Henry was still as healthy too but his legacy might provide her with a future after all.

She'd called the number on the pastel pink sheet that very evening and chatted to Jack and Steve for hours about their course which included the latest in analysis with sophisticated computer software that monitored her daily progress in a scientific manner. She signed up and began her lessons right away, which she found extremely enjoyable. Computers were everywhere and they had all these cameras hooked up to the computers to analyze her performances from every angle to give her constant feedback about what she could improve on during her next lesson. It was all very high tech and Irene was impressed with the program Jack and Steve had designed and the selflessness they exhibited throwing themselves into her education as they tirelessly taught her just what it takes to be a major adult motion picture star even if they were Geeks who wore glasses and white socks and watches with lots of buttons when they were having sex.

They said one of her hottest natural talents was the ability to make beautiful stringers, which were x-rated parlance for spit, really. Jack said it was even more of an asset in the business than her naturally large bosoms and her preternaturally voluptuous hips and buttocks. Steve said if they ever ran out of lube on the set Irene would be invaluable. Irene's lessons were taking up a lot of her time and they were even tossing in free hours of tuition anytime she came over to their place. They always sent her home with lots of material to study, from pie charts showing exactly how much time she'd spent doing DPs and reverse cowgirls and so onto DVDs that she was to watch to gain insights into how the actresses excelled at facials, which wasn't her forte so far, but apparently grinning while getting hit in the eye was essential in the business and Irene couldn't stand her eyelashes clumping together so she was still working hard on getting used to that.

Andrew said in a growl voice, "We will get to the bottom of this" and Richard harrumphed in a good-natured but skeptical way. Irene suddenly felt famished and told the two that she was going to go to a concession stand for a bite to eat and then she had to practically beat them off with a stick if she'd had a stick, that is, to get them to let her goes by herself which she really wanted to do because she wasn't sure what she wanted when she got there.

The bustle and noise of the audience made her feel like a stalking goddess who prowled through a jungle of people, like a beautiful unique bird of prey swooping through the vast flocks of awed penguins, secretly powerful and utterly desired by each man that walked by her and she felt her voluptuous chest swell with happiness at how it felt to be in her soft peachy skin but firm, too, like a fresh peach, not something over-ripened in a cut-rate grocery store that's been sitting out getting squeezed by pensioners too many times before ending up being carelessly self-bagged and dropped off a counter in a rusted-out double-wide trailer in a run-down trailer park.

She was walking away from Frankly My Dear with her footlong drenched in mayo and mustard and ketchup and relish and had just wrapped her warm pink lips around the large hotdog when a young man had stared at her with a frozen expression as he slowly reached up and removed his baseball cap and held it reverently over his heart. "You-you-you," he stammered as she tried to smile sweetly and yet finish taking the bite of her hotdog. "You-you-you're . . . " he continued valiantly. "You-you're Voluptia!"

Irene was slightly puzzled but quickly concluded that he must have meant "voluptuous" so she nodded and said thank you.

"I go there every day," he said and Irene said "Where's that?" and he said "Double u double u double u dot ex ex ex dot com" and Irene was totally baffled and told him to have a really nice day after she swallowed.

It was like the whole world spoke in code sometimes and Irene did not plan on becoming a cryptographer because it gave her a headache to worry herself over what the world went on and on about. But Irene's dreams of being somebody someday were as nourishing as a footlong on a bright sunny day in a place full of screaming fans and the smells of men's' colognes and spilled beer and admiring glances that followed her all the way back to the dugout where Richard and Andrew welcomed her returning presence with open arms. They even agreed her hotdog, what was left of it, looked delish and that her condiments were creative. Irene beamed with love for the whole world and hummed "Take me out of the ball game" beneath her breath and generally relaxed in the sensual warmth of the day with her head leaned over on Andrew's hard chest and her toes in Richard's lap getting rubbed while Andrew stroked her honey silken hair around her apricot ears and lingered over her sun-flushed cheeks with gently tantalizing fingers.

So she dozed off for a while and missed the Braves scoring the winning touchdown but she awoke when the crowd exploded with joy and hugged Richard and Andrew in an outpouring of pure happiness, really, except for the bit about missing Henry, god rest his soul, of course.

Chapter 26

Callie pulled up into the driveway and turned the key. She sat for a moment and stared at the house. It was a crimson scarlet red color with a sharply slanted roof, which was graced with a cacophony of Christmas lights that twinkled and sparkled like colored stars. It reminded her of her own house, with her own Christmas lights, and she smiled a soft smile. She loved Christmas. It reminded her of when her family would huddle around the tree, singing songs and opening presents. For twenty years they had used the same tree, a tall, broad pine that smelled faintly of pine. She loved that tree, so much so that she never took it down. For thirty years, she kept the tree just as it was, awash with lights and shiny balls. Henry thought her daft, and oft his accounting friends would come over for Easter dinner and see the tree standing proud in the corner with its lights and balls and Henry would try to quickly shoo them to the dining room but they would have none of that as they'd stand before the tree and rub their chins in thought and say in their funny accents "it's over, you know" but Callie would just smile her soft smile as she spooned out the mashed potatoes.

Callie stepped out of the car and shook the chill from her voluptuous bones. The snow crackled beneath her feet as she made her way along the driveway and up the icy steps, taking each with care. It reminded her of the church and their icy steps, only much more so. She knocked on the door, which made a muffled hollow sound beneath her knuckles, like the sound of an unripe cantaloupe. She was picky about her cantaloupes.

The door opened and Callie was greeted with her friend Yvonne. Callie smiled and shifted voluptuously as she stared at her friend. She reminded her of a volcano, her molten red hair flowing moltenly down her back and over the sandy white beaches of her shoulders, as hair is wont to do. Yvonne smiled back, her lips glossed in a shade of lipstick that reminded Callie of the house paint.

"Come in," Yvonne said, her scintillating green eyes dancing playfully in the evening darkness.

Callie closed the door behind her and tossed her coat onto a nearby chair. She took a seat on the couch and ran her fingers along the coffee table, breathing deeply the dark and heady aroma of furniture polish.

Yvonne slinked towards the kitchen. "Dinner's almost ready. Make yourself at home."

Callie stood and straightened her cashmere dress and proceeded to a small bar on the other side of the living room. The plush carpeting squished between her toes and she smiled a soft smile. It reminded her of the dreamy times she had spent with her beloved Henry shopping for carpeting. She'd happily skip between rolls of pastel blues and ruddy browns and giggle as she rubbed her cheek against their fuzziness. The salesmen were always quick to help her, no doubt as delighted with carpeting as she was, and cheerfully waved goodbye when they left, a roll of bunny-patterned carpet hoisted on one of Henry's broad shoulders and Callie clinging lovingly to the other.

Callie examined the bottles and swished the contents of a few. She tapped her chin and foot as she pondered over her decision. Scotch? No. Vodka? No. Rum? No. Tequila? No. Gin? No. Red Wine? No. White Wine? No. rosé Wine? No. Sherry? No. Very Dry Sherry? No. Brandy? No. Grand Marnier? No. Vermouth? No. Crème de Cacao? No. Crème de Menthe? No. Schnapps? No. Whiskey? No. Bourbon? No. Rye? No. Ick.

Callie sashayed towards the bookshelf with its myriad of books. She ran her fingertips along the spines and was amazed at the wide variety that Yvonne had collected. Tall books, thin books, fat books, short books, books with brown covers, books with white covers, books without covers, hard books, soft books, hard books that felt like soft books, and everything in between. It reminded her of a library with lots of books.

Yvonne emerged from the kitchen bearing a large plate with a large ham on top which had small cherries and small pieces of pineapple stuck into it with wooden toothpicks. The scent of ham and cherry and pineapple wafted languidly towards Callie and she breathed deeply of its heavenly scent.

"It smells heavenly," Callie noted, and Yvonne grinned impishly.

Callie took a seat at the table and unfurled her napkin. She placed it on her lap as she was always taught and arranged her silverware just so. She poured herself a glass of milk from the fridge and began scooping out potatoes for the both of them.

Yvonne poured herself a drink and melted into the chair across from Callie. She brushed a strand of moltenly hair from her eyes and proceeded to carve the ham. Callie watched intently. Juice streamed from the ham in rivulets like saliva drooling from the fierce jaws of a wild dingo poised over the dead carcass of its prey in the dingo-eat-dingo world.

"It smells heavenly," Callie said.

Yvonne dropped a slab onto Callie's eagerly awaiting plate and garnished it with a cherry. Callie popped the cherry into her mouth and smiled a soft smile. Its sweetness reminded her of sweet things and that made her smile.

Yvonne dabbed at the corner of her mouth with a napkin and washed down the ham with a chug of wine. "I bought that lovely dress today," she chirped excitedly.

"Which one?" Callie inquired.

"The lovely one," Yvonne explained.

"What does Roberto think of it?' Callie queried.

Yvonne giggled like a giggly girl. "He thinks its lovely," she responded as she shifted voluptuously in her seat.

"You're a lucky woman," Callie commented, tossing her mane voluptuously. She sighed vehemently. "I do so really very much miss Henry."

"At—least he—didn't—leave you broke," Yvonne grunted as she struggled with a particularly fatty piece of ham.

I looked across the table at Yvonne nervously and stood, making my way to the living room window. I could see the colors of Christmas blinking rhythmically in the window's reflection and it eased my heart somewhat, though not a lot. I swallowed nervously as I tried to think of the best way to say to my friend what I wanted to say, because it was hard to say. Words stumbled in my mind like clumsy children falling down a flight of stairs, and I went to the bathroom to relieve my increasingly incessant bladder. The smell of lilac assaulted me and I smiled softly. I sat and tinkled. The sound reminded me of my sister's wedding. It was a grand affair, with balloons and streamers and clowns, and my sister all dressed up in a brilliant white, white dress, and the soothing tinkling sound of the raindrops in the punch bowl.

I returned to find Yvonne spooning gobs of custard into a bowl. "Dessert?" she questioned.

Callie shook her head. "I'm a vegetarian."

Yvonne nodded vigorously and took her custard to the living room. "Is something wrong?" she asked me.

Callie baby-stepped her way to the living room. "It's about my stocks."

"What about them?" Yvonne muffled through her custard.

"I—" Callie stammered. Her gut knotted and she took a bite of Yvonne's custard. She loved the cool fruitiness on her tongue and she smiled softly. "I want to sell them," she finally said at last.

"Why?" Yvonne spewed.

Callie took a seat at the kitchen table. "I loved Henry," she insisted, really meaning it. "But it's time for me to move onto greener pastures."

Yvonne shrugged voluptuously. "So sell them."

"Ah!" Callie said knowingly. "Therein lies the rube. I don't want to be seen like I'm bailing out of a sinking ship. And I heard through the cherry vine that you might be able to help me, if you get my meaning," she hinted with knowing winks.

"No," Yvonne said with a deep negativity.

The corners of Callie's mouth drooped like saggy breasts. "Why not?" she interrogated.

"Because," Yvonne quipped.

Because. The word reminded Callie of grade school and Mrs. Freeman's history class where she had learned of the cotton gin and asked why it was called a cotton gin when it had nothing to do with gin and Mrs. Freeman glared at her as she often did and with stern arms folded across her rigid chest she said 'because' and left it at that and Callie smiled softly.

"Please?" Callie pleaded.

"I'm sorry, Callie," Yvonne sighed sorrowfully. "I wish I could help you but I have my own green pastures to think about. Roberto and I—what we have been a beautiful thing. A truly beautiful, beautiful, beautiful thing, and I can't risk losing such a beautiful, beautiful, beautiful thing."

Callie eyes narrowed, so imperceptibly that no one even noticed. "Even for a friend?" she warned.

"You're a beautiful friend," Yvonne sighed. "But what Roberto and I share are more beautifully beautiful than our commonly beautiful friendship."

Callie rubbed her suddenly throbbing head with her fingertips in slow, two-and-three-quarter inch circles. "Fine," she half-spat, one-quarter shrieked, one-quarter shouted, and she snatched her coat from the couch. She flung open the door and stormed outside, her bosom heaving with rage, stopping only long enough to smash a twinkling Christmas light with the heel of her shoe.

Chapter 27

It was early morning in the first part of the day. The sun was just coming up. Bruce sat at his morning breakfast table. The newspaper was in front of him. His black silk monogrammed dressing gown barely concealed the rippling muscles of his chest and back. You could tell he had not shaved yet from the dense yet attractive forest of blonde stubble on his cleft chin and sculpted cheeks. He rubbed his aquiline nose. Then, when he reached up to push, the soft blonde hair back from his manly forehead, his hand encountered the bandages still there.

He frowned, the gesture making ripples of thought on his brow between the limpid blue pools that were his eyes. "I must remember what happened!" he told himself sternly, his deep, resonant voice trembling huskily with emotion. He still could not recall anything about the automobile accident that had sent him to the hospital with a severe head injury. That the bandage on his head now covered the 18 sutures that a topnotch surgeon at St. Ivan's hospital had spent so long in carefully suturing into his brow. He tried and tried until sweat popped out on the smooth skin of his forehead and glistened there, but he could still not remember a damn thing! Damn it! He had to! He just had to!

"Meow!" said the neighbor's cat at the window. It was not Bruce's cat, but sometimes he let it in and fed it. It was a very expensive purebred Siamese. Had the cat but known it, his blue eyes were exactly the same shade of the limpid blue pools that were Bruce's eyes.

"Go away!" shouted Bruce, his despair and confusion making him uncharacteristically grumpy with the cat that he sometimes fed and petted. "Just leave me alone!"

But an instant later, he regretted his temper. He opened the window and let the cat in. He found some milk for it in the refrigerator, and carefully chopped up some left over cooked chicken livers and a few sardines in a can that was in there. The cat purred while he ate it. "Would that I could be as sublime as you, a small feline friend?" Bruce said wearily, sadly, depressedly. He petted the cat a few times, and then went back to his chair. He sat down on it. Outside the window, it was morning, the sun was just coming up. The wind was blowing sweetly through the Georgia pines. He thought, for just a moment, how lucky he was to live in Atlanta, Georgia in the southern part of the United States.

Suddenly, Bruce's eyes fell on the newspaper on the table in front of him. The headlines seemed to shriek at him!

Millionaire Industrialist Henry Archer Dead at Age 60!
Tragic Car accident claims His Life!
Callie Archer now widowed!

His eyes crawled frantically over the newspaper, devouring the awful and confusing details of the death. The reporter had written a good but a gristly report on the millionaire's death. Bruce cringed as he read of the bright star of blood on the shattered windshield where Henry Archer's head had smashed against it. The reporter noted that the man's body still gripped a cell phone in one lifeless hand after he was dead. Had he been talking on the phone when he died? Bruce hated it when drivers in other cars talked on the phone when they were driving. It was certainly a dangerous and rude practice. Perhaps Henry Archer's death had been the result of his own rudeness and carelessness in driving while talking on a cell phone.

Then his eyes were suddenly trapped like wolves in jaw traps. One single detail from the newspaper article seized him by the throat and squeezed like a noose around his neck. It was the date and time of the accident. 4:03 P.M. on July 20th!

"No! It can't be!" Bruce shouted the words. He stood up from his chair. The Siamese neighbor's cat jumped in terror. "Meow!" it cried piteously. "Meow! Meow!"

"I'm sorry, Pitty-Pat!" Bruce apologized to the Siamese cat. "I didn't mean to startle you. But I think that Henry Archer's accident happened at the same date and time that mine did! Oh, look at me! What am I coming to, talking to a cat? I'm a successful software developer, not some kind of a crazy man. Aren't I?"

He stood up from his chair. He paced around the room. Then he made himself go to his leather, monogrammed briefcase and take out the doctor's report from his hospitalization. His eyes slid swiftly down the papers, then suddenly snagged on the very information he sought. There it was! The doctor had written down that the emergency medical people from the ambulance that brought him to the hospital had thought that his accident had probably happened at 4:03 P.M. on July 20th! The very same day and time that Henry Archer's accident had happened.

He exclaimed, "It has to be a coincidence! It just has to!" Bruce shouted. Then he made himself calm down.

He walked back to his kitchen table and sat down. He looked at the newspaper there. The bloody tragic headlines still screamed their unimaginable news up at him. Below the big print of the large headline was a society photo of Henry Archer and his wife Callie Archer. Callie was in a breathtaking lace evening gown by Christian Dior. Beside her, looking stricken by his wife's breathtaking beauty, was Henry Archer in an impeccable black tuxedo by Ralph Lauren and a white shirt and blacks tie. Even covered by a tuxedo, Bruce could see that Henry Archer had still the muscular body of the body builder he had once been but was no more now that he was sixty years old. Diamonds glittered on an immense pendant at Callie Archer's throat. Diamonds bigger than pearls hung from her earlobes, shining like soft icicles. "Well, at least she will have a lot of money now that he's dead. At least she isn't left poor and destitute, pushing a shopping cart down the street and living in a cardboard box in an alley and eating left over McDonald's food from a Dumpster. At least there's that to be thankful for!"

Then the coincidence of the times of death hit him all over again. "Can there be a connection?" he had to ask himself. "Meow!" said Pitty-Pat, his soulful blue eyes shining up at Bruce. The cat seemed to want to help him. Cats are naturally sympathetic animals, and Pitty-Pat was no exception. He could see that the big, muscular human who sometimes fed him chicken gizzards and salmon was distressed. His little heart went out to the man. "Meow!" he said again, softly.

Bruce stooped down and petted the cat. "I know you want to help. Cats are naturally sympathetic animals. I just don't think there's any way you can help me, little fellas!"

"I have to do this myself. I have to find out the details of my car accident. I have to remember exactly what happened to me that day! I'm the only one who can do it, Pitty-Pat! The only one."

Bruce decided to get dressed. First, he would take a shower, being very careful of the bandage on his 12 stitches that now seamed his forehead. He went to his bathroom. It was tiled in sandstone and umber. The towels matched. He stepped into the hot stinging spray of the shower, dropping his silken bathrobe behind him on the mat like a discarded flower petal. He took up a big bar of sandalwood soap and soaped the dark mat of hair on his chest. He washed under his arms, and then his legs and feet. Then he washed his arms and neck. He wished he could shampoo his hair, but that would get his bandage wet. So he had to not do it today. He rinsed the soap off himself and then stepped out of his shower and toweled off. He was glad he kept his body in such good shape. Someday, a woman would appreciate what good care he had taken of himself, and the firm muscles that corded his bronzed arms. Not many software developers cared what they looked like. Some of the software developers he knew looked like soggy mushroom people who had lived too long in the moist dark of their offices. Not Bruce. He knew that this was the only body he would ever get and that he had to take care of it. If not for himself, then for the love and admiration of the woman who would someday share it's pleasure with him.

He got dressed quickly. He put on Eddie Bauer taupe slacks and a shirt in a pale blue plaid. He pulled on a pair of black boots. He looked good, in a rugged, out-doorsy way. You wouldn't have looked at him and thought, "he's a computer software developer." You would have thought he was a forest ranger or maybe even a mountaineer guide. He looked at the mirror and smiled a sad smile. Yes. He looked tough today. But he would have to be tough, too.

He knew what he should do. He should go straight to Callie Archer. That would get him the information he needed. He'd be able to discover if his terrible car wreck and Henry Archer's terrible car accident were connected in any way. He tried not to think of Callie Archer as she had looked in the newspaper photograph. He would not think of her soft blonde hair in ringlets on her pale forehead, or her soft brown eyes staring out of the page at him. She would be well-taken care of. That was what was important, wasn't it? That she didn't end up living out on the streets now that her wealthy industrialist husband was dead.

"Goodbye, Pitty-Pat!" he said as he left the apartment.

"Meow!" the cat replied. It was as much of an answer to his questions as Bruce Lucent would get that day!

Chapter 28

The funeral had been hell. Funerals are bad enough when you don't know the dead guy at all. And they're a pain when you just have to show up socially or else everyone will think you're ungrateful jerks with no respect for someone decent and kind (as all dead guys are irregardless of how they lived their rotten, two-timing sadistic, pathetic, discombobulatedly senseless, irreligious, unthinking, flakes, debauched, foulmouthed, obnoxious, deviant, gross, adulterous, murderous, gluttonous, alcoholic, lazy, indolent, filthy, grotesquely indecent, lunatic, lives), or that you've just come for the food afterwards or to show off your latest dress, or to spit in the coffin while nobody's looking. And funerals for true beloved dead guys are awful because after all, someone you'd wanted to spend your whole life with is dead in the coffin and although he's really stiff now, you'll never get to enjoy that ever again, and all those people around you, all that hypocrisy and sycophant and wallflowers and showoffs are all gabbing and staring at you and critiquing your red eyes and the running mascara and eyeshadow and expecting you to be brave or hold it all in or keep a stiff upper lip or expecting you to go out with them afterwards and let them ball you senselessly so you can forget the dead guy and fall passionately in lust with them instead and besides it's all so bloody expensive that it's going to use up most of the insurance settlement and the estate and then what is you supposed to live on for hell's sake.

Even worse are funerals for beloved dead guys who were married to someone else so you have to go kind of in disguise and make like you were just friends with the guy instead of having wild sex with him and trying out every page of the karma sutra together and wondering just how the heck you were supposed to live now, although since you aren't liable for the bloody expensive funeral you might come out more or less even or even ahead of his wife and kids in that department. That was the kind of funeral Irene Stevens had gone to.

And the lutz had been inconsiderate enough to get himself killed driving Irene's sporty little Maserati that he had bought for her — bent it and broke it and splattered it with his blood and ichor, all kinds of body fluids, all more or less foul and sticky and all resonant over what was left of the rich ripe red leather upholstery — though the insurance settlement from that ought to help her get on with her life, especially if she invested it wisely. Maybe it could finance some education so she could be a model or and actresses or a porn star or something. She'd have to talk to the guys down at the club — if she could still get into the club now that Henri was dead so she couldn't go in on his arm or to meet him or to exercise and keep her body nice and svelte and trim and athletic for him because she for damn sure didn't want to lose him to some tramp like that Margaret Eastman or whoever.

That Margaret! Geez, she'd showed up at that funeral bawling her eyes out like they'd been best buds or lovers or something. What a hypocrite. Probably hoping she could get a job from one of his friends or get laid by some hopeful dude there for the widows and orphans or something.

Afterwards she went back to their condo, her condo now, with the Jacuzzi and his den and all the clothes and jewelry he'd bought her and all that high class furniture and stuff. Henry had a thing for leather. Leather sofas, leather chairs, a leather mattress for hell's sake, leather underwear, the leather whips and manacles, even a braided leather carpet that they'd made love on more than once. She'd have to clean out the den. Henry had not let her go in there for ages, maybe. There were bodies in there, like in Bluebeard: all the dismembered bodies of your maidens that he'd carried off and secretly ravaged before cruelly cutting them to bits. She'd stayed out of it like he said, never once peeking into his den, so she still had all her bits, and then some. Amazing what they could do with silicone and saline these days.

His den! Henry holed up in his den like a wild beast, hoarding his pray and coming out to hunt when he hungered for food or lusted for sex or thirsted for liquor or water or will or juice. The back to his den or out to hunt the lives and fortunes of other men or off to his wife, that abominable Callie Archer who took up so much of his time. But he always came back, always came back for her athletic body and her wild sex and her Margarita and tequila sunrises and omelettes and steaks and chops and their video tapes, the ones recorded by the hidden cameras in the bedroom when they made love like wild beasts, like penguins of the Sahara diving into the sand and rutting wildly after feasting on sand sharks. She envied those penguins. All that hot sand to swim through, the raspy grains sliding over their feathers as they hunted in wild packs, baying at the moon, and diving deep, deep, down into the dusty depths of the dry smooth sand.

What would penguin leather be like? Would it have lots of dense patterns of whirls where the feathers grew, like ostrich leather did? Perhaps she could have something made of penguin leather to remind her of Henry, a love seat or a fine set of whips and straps. Perhaps she might travel to the Sahara someday to watch them from the tops of the pyramids, Mount Fujiyama off in the distance, duplicating the smooth slanted sides of the pyramids. Oh, Henry, you jerk, why didn't you ever take me places like that? Why didn't we travel instead of being cooped up in hiding, in your den, rutting like penguins or ostriches or lions on the leather cushion and couches and chairs and rugs?

You used to love it when I pulled on a leather strap around your neck when we made love. You knew I needed you too much to ever pull too long or too hard. You loved it when I saddled you and rode you around, when I put the bit between your teeth and the golden spurs with the softly rounded rowels to your flanks, not enough to draw blood, but enough to goad you on, around and around the condo, around the balcony and up and down the stairs, and then we'd tumble to gather again with you panting and sweaty and full of lust.

Perhaps I can sell the tack to someone with a pony. But I'll keep the spurs. The golden spurs. And the whips.

Just a week before Irene Stevens came back from the funeral and decided to clean out Henry

Archers den in their condo: Henry Archer sat in his favorite red letter chair. Irene had a thing for leather. Practically everything in the condo was leather or leather upholstered or leather decorated or something. Henry leaned back in his red leather chair and mused, thinking fondly of the cow the had given it's life for his comfort. He wondered what this particular cow had been like. Had it had a name. Had it had feelings and thoughts or was it only driven by it's own stupidity, like his last one night stand.

A new thought occurred to him. What if it had been made into steak, chops, soup bones and Macdonald's veggie burgers, also. He remembered the steak he had eaten last night and wondered dimly if this cow had contributed to satisfying not only his rheumatism, but his appetite as well.

His thoughts strayed to the paper that was laying limply on the antique desktop in front of him. What was it that he was going to write? His mind seemed to be full of fog, like the fog of New York City. He had lived there once, as a boy, before he was rich. New York made him think of other famous cities he had visited, like France and Rome. He wondered if they had cows in Rome.

Henry puzzled over his letter to Irene. He had to word his thoughts just right. She was a beautiful woman, but his heart belonged to Margaret Eastman. He loved the way her curvatiously voluptuous body fit into her tight nurse outfit. She was a bit older and more cultured than Irene as well. He let out a long sigh as he thought of her. He dug around in his desk until he found a cigarette and a lighter one of the drawers. He lit up and thought. He needed to put it delicately and not break her heart.

Finally, he decided on the perfect words. He put pen to

paper in the same way some men puts knives to wrists. When he was finished he looked over his work and smiled as he read the sentences, "Hey baby. The sex was great. But I never liked blondes much anyway. I found someone better. Still, love ya lots, Henry."

He had to admit it. He was a Shakespeare among Jerry Springers. He placed the letter in an envelope and addressed it to Irene. Then, setting the letter on his desk, he strode out to his Mercedes to buy a diamond necklace for Margaret.

Irene Stevens's tried the knob on the door of the den, Henry's wild den that he had loved so much and been so secretive about. It was unlocked and so she went in at last, after all these months, now that Bluebird was dead. Mahogany shelves lined one wall, lined with canning jars full of clear fluid and cloudy lumps. There was an ebony desk and a red leather chair. There were filing cabinets and a large black safe. There was a rack of pistols and rifles and shotguns, holsters for the pistols and shoulder holsters and belts. Two of the rifles had big scopes on them. And hunting knives, and fillet knives, and buck knives in sheathes. And cameras, a small one, like a lighter, a couple of bigger ones and three with huge lenses and tripods.

So Bluebeard did save bits, body parts. And he hunted. She looked at the jars: pale fleshy bits and skin resolved into a cock and balls, "hitchhiker, Cincinnati, August 1999" read one. An eyeball, "waitress, June, June 2000." A kidney, "roadkill, Tennessee, May 1998." She shuddered, but her loins warmed, thinking of the wild beast, the hunter, her mount . . .

Irene looked in the file cabinet next to the gun rack. The top drawer was filled with ammunition, shotgun shells, rifle bullets, pistol bullets. The rest of the drawers were filled with papers, full of names and dates, and pictures of people doing all kinds of things. Some of it was porno stuff, but there were other pictures, too.

The other file cabinets were much the same, folders of pictures and notes. Some good porn, but a lot of it was boring stuff. There were some letters on top of the safe, all addressed to post office boxes. She opened one and there was money inside. She pocketed it. She'd have to go through all this stuff. There was probably money in the safe, too. She wondered if she could sell the jars on eBay.

She turned to the desk. There was just a single envelope there and her name was on it. She opened it.

Irene read the letter and then stood there for a long, long time. She cried at first, but then the tears slowed and a grin surfaced, a nasty grin.

"Last laugh, Henry. I get the last laugh. She'll never have you. None of them will have you. Ever."

And she took the packet she'd gotten at the mortuary, the very expensive one, the one that she'd paid the embalmer so very much for. There were empty jars on the bottom shelf, and a can labeled "alcohol, 200 proof." She unwrapped the packet and slid the cock and balls inside the jar, the filled it with alcohol.

"You're mine now, Henry. You'll always be mine."

She found a label and wrote on it: "philanderer, Atlanta, March 2004".

She put the jar on the middle shelf, next to the hitchhiker.

Chapter 29

Arthur Nance looked at the clipboard, in his hand. As the main doctor at the hospital where he worked to save people' lives it was his duty to tell them about their disease and injuries. But he didn't want to talk to Bruce Lucent. Bruce was a big important software developer and didn't like it when people or things didn't go his way. So Arthur news wouldn't be taken well.

He wandered to the hospital cafeteria where he got a ham sandwich to eat because he was very hungry, it had been a very long day and he'd had to perform surgery on two different people since he had got to the hospital early that mourning. One had had a heart attack and needed open heart surgery and the other had to have her appendices out. She had been very pretty and he had to tell himself not to think about that because he had to concentrate to take out her appendix.

He ate his sandwich quickly and then got a Diet Doctor Pepper to drink. It was his favorite and he got worried sometimes that he was addicted to the sweet caffeinated drink.

Arthur looked at his watch. Seven fifteen it was time to check on the people on Intensive care. Including Bruce Lucent, he just couldn't get away from him. He turned, which way was his room again? Oh yeah it was in the south wing. Arthur

Nance turned and started marching down the hall towards Bruce's room.

He sighed as he marched down the hall towards Bruce's room. On the way he passed a pretty nurse Margaret Eastman. He stared at her beautiful curves then cursed himself silently for staring at her. It just wasn't proper. But it was hard not to stare at her luminously curvaceous body and her soft curvy cleavage, she was so pretty. That was the problem, with this hospital too many pretty nurses and patience were here. Maybe he'd ask her out to lunch or something sometime.

As he continued marching down the hall Margaret turned to him. Hey she said. "Didn't I see you earlier, you were taking care of Bruce Lucent?" she queried, looking at his nice thick muscles. He was pretty hot she thought, maybe she would ask him to lunch but not now. "He was in the car accident with Henry Archer last week wasn't he," she asked him, looking him up and down now. Oh yeah, she was hot, with all those muscles. What a stud. But she wasn't looking for him. she was looking for Lucent,

maybe he could tell her who Irene Stevens was, Henry never really had but she had seen her name on his address list.

Arthur Nance took a drink of his coke, savoring the cool sweet drink as is fizzed down his throat. Yeah he was probably addicted but he didn't really care, stress would kill him anyway, or maybe a car crash cause there were a lot of them these days, there had been 2 in the past week, Bruce and Henry's. He would probably take up smoking cigarettes if his boss hadn't yelled at people who smoked and fired them. "Yeah, why" he wondered? Do you want to talk to him?"

"Yeah, I want to ask him about this girl Irene Stevenson or something like that, cause I think he might know her." She stated calmly.

"Well I can't let you see him but I can ask him for you," he declared, looking at his watch again it was seven thirty now. "Oh crap I need to check, on a patient" and he turned and left her standing in the hallway.

Arthur entered Lucent's room. He was eating a pork chop and the doctor winced, he was Vegan and didn't like seeing other people eating meat or wearing leather like the leather on Bruce's imported braincase. That was leaning against the bed.

"Hi Nancy! exclaimed Bruce who had finished his meal by now. The had gotten to know each other by now, the car crash was almost a month ago. He sat up and grind at Nance who didn't like being called Nancy. Because it was a girls name, and he was a

very muscular athletic guy with a lot of sexy mussels but he didn't want to upset the software developer because he mite get mad at him.

Lucent sat up and put the remains of his lamb chop aside. "I was just wondering where you were because I wanna talk to you. I think I'm better enough to go home now don't you." He pointed to his neck wish no longer had to have the foam brace on it anymore, he was glad because it itched like when he was a kid and broke his leg and had a cast. That had itched, and so did the neck brace so he was glad he didn't have to ware it anymore.

I don't think that would be a good idea," expostulated Nance angrily. "You still need a lot of therapy for your leg and you can't drive again yet."

"Then can you tell me doctor, what about some people?" questioned Bruce Lucent.

Doctor Nance started pacing around the room, back and forth, back and forth. "Peoples lives are covered by the privacy act, Mr. Lucent." opined the doctor to his patient. "I can't tell you about anyone at the hospital, if that is what you mean."

"Well it was, more about the accident that almost killed me." Bruce Lucent sat up straight, a dangerous look on his face. Nance knew Bruce was used to getting his own way for the past few years sine he got rich. So he sometimes got more violent than sometimes another person might when the same thing was going on.

Nance stopped pacing up and down and sat down in the chair
next to Bruce's bed. After all what could the software geek do? His leg was still in traction, or at least had been until yesterday, and he could probably not move very fast yet either. He had good muscles though, almost as good as Nance's that he worked out for hours to get and still had despite being older than Bruce. He ran his hand through his sandy brown hair and blurted, That's the police's job. I know they came here more than one time to talk to you about the accident. They don't tell us doctors about that stuff, and we don't need to know."

Bruce thought about the young cop who had questioned him. He had been asking questions, not telling him anything. If he knew more about the accident, he hadn't told Bruce. But he bet this doctor new more than he was telling. He could tell by looking at his face. It was a face that kept secrets, hundreds of secrets every day he bets.

"You know I can make a big donation to this hospital if you can get me the information I want." Bruce spurted out. "You know me well enough by knowing to know that I am the sort of person who wants to ask questions, not answer them. So maybe I can make you think. Here are some names and not from your hospital, either. I need to know who wanted Henry Archer dead. What does Irene Stevens know about his? No I was wrong, there is one person from the hospital, a nurse named Margaret."

He must think I'm like a candy striper who sits and tells everything she knows thought Nance to himself. Maybe I do know
something I won't tell about Henry Archer. A candy striper named Nancy he must think. And does he mean Margaret Eastman for the nurse in this hospital. And how soon will that big donation come once he's not in the hospital anymore? He'll forget it fast enough, and my hypocritical oath will be down the toilet.

Bruce watched Arthur Nance's trim, moustache face and thought that Nancy boy wouldn't tell him anything. He was it close down and saw the secrets hiding there. Too bad he had spent all his time working out or studying computers. He didn't spend enough time with people so he didn't know body language and Arthur Nance probably spoke it like a native. So he could sit there with his shoulders all hunched up and his face closed over his secrets. And its so oblivious that he knows what I mean and could tell me what I want to know.

"Alright, then since you don't want to tell me what you know even if you do know, how about just make me more comfortable here since you won't let me go home either. You could start with that pretty nurse. She was standing outside my door talking to one of my friends that came to visit me. She looks like her uniform is painted on with medium-length brown hair. That's the nurse I want not the one who looks like she had prunes for breakfast and is older than my grandma." Bruce sat up straight in his hospital bed and ran his hand through his long black hair thinking that he needed a haircut really bad.

"I'm sorry sir but the hospital does not assign its personal
like that." spat Arthur Nance. "If Nurse Eastman is who you mean she isn't one of the floor nurses on this floor so I can't assign her here anyways.

"Then move me to her floor. I would get much better faster with her being the one to give me shots in the butt," Bruce
Lucent expostulated.

"She works in maternity." That should show him for trying to through his weight around thought Arthur Nance to himself. And the way he's acting I won't tell him what I know even if I was going to which I was but now I won't.

"So maybe I could get pregnant?" queried Bruce Lucent hysterical.

"When nurse Wagner tells you to do your therapy that will get you out faster than joking with me" quipped Arthur Nance. Suddenly he thought to himself that Bruce Lucent asked him about Irene Stephens and so had Margaret Eastwood. And Bruce Lucent also asked him about a nurse who's name was Margaret. So what did Margaret Eastman now? This just made it even surer that he would not tell Bruce Lucent anything. He could not have this sort of thing going on in his hospital!

Arthur Nance ran his hand through his sandy brown hair and stood up. "I'm sure you'll be able to go home in a few days if you do what you're supposed to do that the nurses tell you."

"So what was it you came in here to tell me anyway doctor" queried Bruce to the doctor?

OH nothing I was just checking to see how your leg was out of it's cast and if you still needed the neck brace. You better used that neck brace when you use your computer you have there." Arthur Nance pointed to the laptop compeer case next to the bed, in it's leather case that got all scuffed up in the car wreck. "If you hurt your spine worse you'll never be able to program again."

Bruce Lucent was tired of doctor Nancy telling him what he could do and couldn't do. Why did he come here to stick his nose in if not to talk or answer questions? Did he hope Bruce would tell him something? Not likely. This hospital was a hotbed of all sorts of things going on. He hadn't been here for nearly two months without figuring that out! But now he knew that Doctor Arthur Nance was an enemy, not a friend, and he would look out from now on.

A nurse, not prune face Wagner, but Cute with short curly blonde hair, and a really nice ass brought in Bruce's lunch right then. So Doctor Nance stood up, so straight and muscles even if he was old, fast out of his chair, and left the room like walking out of a TV courtroom. Bruce smiled at the nurse. "Hey cutely I haven't seen you before. Are you desert!?

The nurse smiled back and even giggled a little, which Bruce hated girls who giggled, but she was cute anyway. While she was putting the tray over his bed and unloading the pork chops and mashed potatoes and lima beans and milk and jell-O and chocolate
cake, he even pattered her butt and she just giggled again. He hated lima beans but he didn't say anything. If he rang the bell and made somebody take them away maybe it would be her, and then he wouldn't have food all over and could maybe get to know here a little better. Too bad he had this huge cast on his leg. It made it kind of hard to anything he wanted but sure didn't stop him from waiting it! Almost as much as he wanted to know what was going on and who had tried and seceded in killing Henry Archer.

Chapter 30

Andrew Venice parked himself in the booth right behind the four of them, wondering how much of this place he could be expense account, figured almost nothing, and when the waiter in tight black pants and a black turtleneck came by, he only ordered an orange juice. Hell, even if he'd been off-duty, he figured there was no way he'd be able to afford booze in this joint, with its wood paneling and dim lighting and fancy a wine list, to say nothing of a clientele that ran in higher circles than I. But he was working, and knew he needed every ounce of his detection skills to listen through all the background noise in the nightclub. It was just nice to be in out of the Atlanta heat, overbearing even at this time of the evening.

All four had already met by the time he'd managed to slip in, but he had to go about it easy and careful to make sure that none of them made him. Lucky that the booth he was in had opened up, and that the people leaving had unwittingly given him cover. He'd even had a chance to risk a peek over the edge as he'd sat down, noted who was sitting where.

On the opposite side, furthest away from Andrew, sat Isaac Stevens, father of Irene Stevens. He had a salt-and-pepper beard and hair that was cropped close to his head, about 50 years old. Next to him was Arthur Nance, that doctor, about the same age as Stevens. He was well-built, quite trim and muscular and athletic, with sandy-brown hair and a thin mustache. Beside Nance sat Rory Edwards, also very well-built. Andrew remembered that Edwards was 60, but there was no way in hell he looked to be over Andrew's own age of 40, aside from maybe his fashionable glasses that leant and air of respectability and intelligence to what at first appeared to be a middle-aged jock. Finally, closest to Andrew, sat Richard Isaacs, a 66-year-old who did well, Andrew knew, manipulating stocks. Andrew knew this because the ruddy-faced but well-built man was also a police informant, which kept him in the game while eliminating many of his worst opponents.

Edwards cleared his throat shortly after the waiter brought over their drinks and said, "A toast." The other three men mumbled in agreement. "To my old friend, Henry Archer. May he rest in peace?" All four leaned into the center of the table and clinked their wine glasses together, then drank to his memory.

"Wish I'd known him as well as you," said Stevens.

"Being good friends with a millionaire industrialist is always a good career move, Isaac," said Nance. He took another swig of his wine and then smiled to show that he was just joking. The other three men laughed, although it took Stevens a beat longer to find the humor than the others.

Isaacs shook his head then, looking a little lost in thought. "It's a sonofabitch, dying in a car crash like that. Guy's only 60, got a young beautiful wife in Callie, in better goddamn shape than any of us here—"

"The guy was once a champion body builder, Richard," said Stevens. "Not like a Mr. World or anything like that, but he had those muscles and he knew how to carry them. Of course he was in better shape than any of us here. Hell, I do well enough with racquetball at the Racquet Club and polo at the Polo Club, but I could never hope to be cut like he was. Shit, even my daughter, Irene, told me she admired his body." The others laughed at this, and Nance hooted. Stevens reached over and jokingly slapped him across the top of the head.

Rubbing his head in mock pain, Nance leaned back after setting his glass back down on the table. "I was working that day at the hospital when they brought him in, you know."

Isaacs drained his glass and signaled for another, then leaned forward, interested. "Do tell," he said.

Nance shrugged. "Bruce Lucent was there, recovering from his own car accident. Word got up to me somehow. I'm not sure if someone told because he was so famous and so rich, or if maybe someone knew that he and I knew each other." He paused and finished his wine, then also waved at the waiter. Not that it was needed, since they were well-known in the club, and the waiter was already sashaying over with a tray carrying four more of the same. "By the time I got down to the ER, the cops were there, and Callie too, and they weren't letting me in to see him, even though I am a doctor." He frowned at the memory of this, felt a small piece of rage break through his normally implacable surface as he thought about the insult of such treatment, but then he remembered where he was, and the fact that they were there to honor the memory of their friend, and he choked it back down, followed its bitter taste with the tannins and fruits of his favorite dry red, an expensive Richebourg 1987, kept in stock exclusively for him.

"I've heard rumors that a cop is stalking this case," growled Edwards. Isaacs, the police informer, sprayed some of his drink, choking, as did Venice, still listening from the other side. He wiped up the orange juice with the sleeve of his jacket, but the men on the other side had not heard them, they were laughing so hard at the mess that Isaacs had made.

"Where . . . " Isaacs tried to catch his breath. "Where did you hear that?"

Edwards arched an eyebrow, the long, untrimmed and wild hairs below his forehead counterpointing the motion. "Let's just say that word gets around." He cracked his knuckles, slowly and extravagantly. "Sounds to me like he's been calling into question the very life that Henry lived. Don't know what I'd do if he came to me casting aspersions on my old, dead friend."

Luckily, over in the other booth, Venice had set down his orange juice, because otherwise he would have ended up spitting more across the table, or else choked on it. And considering how expensive a lousy – well, not lousy, really, since it was freshly squeezed just for him – orange juice was in the place, the thought of wasting any more almost brought tears to his eyes. But still, hearing a potential threat against him caused a reaction that normally would have been humor, but based on how in-shape all of these guys was, had him worried. They could work him over pretty good, with or without a racquet or polo mallet. Of course, he had the law on his side, but these guys moved in circles with all the big-time judges. Any case would be a toss-up.

"I hear that Henry was into something nasty," said Nance.

Venice's ears perked up like tiny Distant Early Warning line radar stations at the sound of this.

Edwards grunted. "You hear lots of stuff, I'm sure," he said. "That doesn't mean any of it is true." He shrugged his massive shoulders. "Besides, anybody with as much moola as he had, he didn't need to stick his hands into the muck. He'd just pay some lackey or toady to do his work for him."

"Or maybe some shell companies, to keep the tracers off of him and let him make a few extra tax-free simoleons," answered Stevens.

"So then maybe this cop is onto something," replied Nance. "Except that maybe he's investigating someone else, somebody who knew about any extracurricular stuff Archer was into." He raised his eyebrows, a motion that created a quilt of thick wrinkles on his otherwise normally smooth forehead. Then he leaned forward and whispered, quiet enough so that Venice could only make out a few words.

"Maybe . . . murder . . . other . . . him."

Whatever had been said, it drained what little atmosphere remained at the table, left it cold and thin like the roof of Mount Everest, and the four men, fit as they were, were no mountain climbers, and so they all drained their drinks, paid the tab, and left. After a suitable interval, Venice got up and followed them, making sure he downed the rest of his fancy-schmancy orange juice first.

Chapter 31

Bruce gimped around the seedy waiting room of Nicholas "Stick" Maksutov. Stick's secretary sat at her gunmetal steel gray desk, pecking out a letter on an ancient Underwood typewriter. Her cowfish udders almost burst out of her tight polka-dot dress, the pale yellow color almost perfectly matching her clearly dyed hair, teased in a pageboy flip so retro for a moment Bruce thought it looked hip.

"When's Stick gonna, be back?" Bruce implored seemingly.

"How many times do I haft tell ya," the blonde, whose name was Sally but who went by Bubbles, responded irritatingly. "He'll be back when he's gonna be back. Ya don't rush Stick, ya know." She typed another letter, looked over at a form, then typed another letter, looked again, typed another letter, then looked again, typed another letter.

Holy Laded! Bruce wanted to scream, wanted to pick up the black rotary dial phone on her desk and throw it through the frosted glass window of the office door. He wanted to slap Sally whose nickname was Bubbles and then maybe ravage those udders and do the Madonna on those big red lips, except he kept thinking of Callie, poor, poor Callie, still pining over the death of her beloved Henry, whose memory not even Bruce's hot sex could cause to fade, although he was working on that.

How had it come to this? Bruce asked himself. How had he, the teenage hacker who got into the Homeland Security system and fed them fake Al Qaeda communications for over a month that resulted in a Code Orange alert that shut down international airports for two weeks, how had he, hotshot software developer Bruce Lucent, come to this? Using a private investigator to find out the truth about his birth?

"Well, kid," the wizened old dick had explained two weeks ago when Bruce came to him, the dick had explained, "Ya see, in some backwater Southern counties, they just haven't gotten around to computerizing vital stats."

So here he was, pacing and pacing and driving Bubbles crazy, he hoped, waiting for Stick to come back with the truth. Why, Stick had called him that morning — from a payphone, of all things — and said he had a little job to do that morning but if Bruce would come by at noon, he'd have a report for him. And oh, if Bruce could bring an envelope with some Benjamin in it, 40 of them, please, that would be swell, too.

The truth! How hard could it be to find out the truth? Bruce wondered. The truth about his real birth had nagged him ever since as a science project in tenth grade he had done the genetic sequencing on his and his parents' DNA, and discovered much to his surprise that there was a 20 billion to one chance they were related. The uncertainty nagged him ever since, and now, with an annual salary about what Bill Gates made in a week, he had the money to find the truth, the real truth.

His reverie was broken by the creak of the door opening behind him. Bubbles looked up. The goldfish in the aquarium looked up. The Rottweiler snoozing before the gunmetal steel desk looked up. An old man asleep on the couch in the waiting room rolled over and went back to sleep. Bruce turned around and looked, saw, pondered, and was amazed by the awesome hulk coming in the door behind him.

"Hey, Babs," Stick accused fetchingly. "How's tricks?"

"Tricks had to go home early," Bubbles displayed resoundingly. "Something about getting her hair done."

"Tricks is bald," Stick surmised.

"Well, she did say something about an 11 a.m. shadow," Bubbles explained.

Bruce stood by listening to this inspiring exchange. The goldfish ate his lunch. The Rottweiler rolled over and parted. Finally, he couldn't stand it anymore.

"Stick!" he burst out, exploring. "Goddamn it, Stick, did you find my real birth certificate?"

"Got it a week ago? Didn't you get my call?"

"You called me yesterday," Bruce interpolated.

"I did?" Stick inquired to himself. "Must slipped my mind to call you earlier? Ya got the Bennies?"

Bruce reached into the breast pocket of his alligator hide leather jacket, but before he could pull his hand all the way out, the old man on the couch leapt to his feet and put a Desert Eagle .44 magnum to Bruce's head.

"Hey, sweetheart, let me take that for ya," the old man exclaimed, "j's on the off chance ya got a rod and not some dough." The old man slipped his hand down Bruce's pants, poked around a bit, then reached into Bruce's jacket and took the wad of money."

"He's clean, Stick, and he's got a schlong like Detroit," the old man declared. "And this wad a dough ain't too shabby, either."

"Thanks, geezer," Stick pointed out to the geezer, who wasn't all that old, really, just a tall, swarthy man in his early 60s with a snowflake scar on his hip from a commie round he took in the Nam, which changed the old man's life, whose name was Johnson but everyone called Joe, ruining his plans to be a male stripper and forcing him into a life as muscle for low-rent private eyes.

Stick counted the money. "Yeah, ya got all the Presidents here," he reasserted soothingly.

"So how about the report?" Bruce inquired.

"Oh yeah? Didn't I tell ya on the phone?" Stick inquired back at him. "Dude, you're adopted. Which you probably should have figured out since your parents are both white and, well, you're black."

* * *

"And they told me they were light skinned!" Bruce screamed at his loving, adoring wife Callie, twice his age but she didn't look it what with all the good breeding, healthy living, and plastic surgery. Plus, Callie had inherited a wad from her dear beloved and quite dead husband Henry Archer, biggest damn manufactured home make in the South. In Bruce's estimation, a rich middle-aged woman was a lot better looking than any young poor woman anyway.

"Honey, I'm sure your parents had your best interest at heart," Callie supplied soothingly. She fanned her heaving ivory skinned breasts with the report Stick had given Bruce.

"Adopted! Why couldn't they have told me the truth about my past? It was bad enough that I was horribly maimed in that auto accident when the truck driver ran the red light, slamming into our Cadillac, and pinning my foot under the seat so that the only way I could escape the burning wreck was to saw off my big toe with a Swiss Army knife? Do you know the humiliation I faced in boy's gym?"

"Sweetheart, at least you," Callie sniffed, her thick tears dripping off her luscious eyelashes and down the cavernous cleavage of her breasts, "at least you had parents. At least you weren't raised like an evil stepchild by your long-lost uncles and aunts after your parents died in a terrorist attack in Crete."

"But my parents were white! Honkies! The oppressor to the brother!" Bruce roared menacingly.

"Well, they sure look black with the big Afros and the Kent cloth suits," Callie interjected.

"It's hair dye and a really good perm!" Bruce waved the report from Stick, with the DNA analysis, the anthropologic analysis, and the birth certificate that said "parents: white; child, black."

"Who knew?" Callie analyzed. "They fooled me. And you have to admit, your momma sure makes some mean chitlins." Callie tossed her thick, deep black locks over her shoulder, the curls falling to her hips and bouncing imploringly off her bookshelf ass. She leaned in closer to Bruce, stood on her tiptoes and ran her fingers across his well-muscled chest. "So you're adopted? It's not like it's the end of the world."

"But now I know the truth," Bruce beseeched. "Now I know my true heritage, I, Bruce Lucent, know who I really am."

"Who are you?" Callie articulated questioningly. "If those honkies aren't your parents, then who?"

"Why . . . why Stick never told me. Let me see that report," Bruce snarled, grabbingly. He grabbed the report from Callie, and as he took away the crude fan which kept her cool in the sweltering Atlanta heat, Callie broke out into a sweat as deep as the Amazon River and just as muddy.

Bruce ripped through the pages, until he came to a crude photocopy of his real, actual birth certificate, the one with his real mother's name, his father being unknown, although he was rumored to have been a prominent segregationist senator, his own mother a black maid like his mother before her.

"My mother . . . my mother is — " he rumored hesitatingly.

Callie snatched the report back. "Wanda June Jezzica," she articulated. "Why, she's the owner of the Jezzica's for Ladies, the hair products company with a net worth of $55 million dollars, because they make such wonderful woman's beauty products, like Jezzica's Glorious Tresses, the dye, I mean, conditioner I use to make my own incredibly gorgeous long locks so silky and thick."

"She's my mother?" Bruce implored wonderingly.

"So it would seem." Callie slunk over to her stud of a husband and ripped off his alligator jacket, his tight black jeans, and his silk underpants, the ones with the little hearts on them she gave him for Valentine's Day she was pleased to see he wore.

"Let's celebrate," she husked seductively.

"Why yes," Bruce suggested. "Perhaps dinner, champagne, dancing, maybe a show."

"Oh, not that, silly," Callie stimulated erotically as she locked her legs around him and planted sloppy, lipstick drenched kisses upon his chest. "I was thinking maybe, you know, visiting Detroit," she winked.

Chapter 32

Like the canals in the city that had given him his name, Andrew Venice had a tendency run to the shallow and he could not rein in that tendency in his thoughts as he sat down on the hard plastic seat booth to interview with Yvonne Perrin. The curvaceous redhead was stacked like the cards in a crooked poker game and exceptionally well preserved. He felt a twinge of regret and something else as he considered their tawdry surroundings. They were sitting in a humble Hardee's hamburger shop near her place of work.

"Thank you for meaning with me, Ms. Perrin," he began to say. He could have bitten his tongue as he realized the double entendre, inadvertent but double, nonetheless.

"Please, call me Yvonne," she responded brightly.

Yvonne. The name was a derivative of "Ivan," itself another version of "John," a word with sexual connotations that made themselves known to Andrew. He was a cop, after all, and had a cop-mind. Emotions boiled through him, but he controlled them, even as he and his fellow officers of the law strove to control the scum who raged in the streets of Atlanta, the city that he loved so and had sworn to protect.

"I am sorry it has to be during my lunch break, though," Perrin said and she opened the plastic pod that held the item she had chosen from the signboard menu, a humble hamburger. "I have a very busy day today!"

"No, that's okay," Andrew said. Then he blurted. "We could have gone someplace nicer!" He was an exceptionally well set-up man, after all.

"No, this is fine," Yvonne said. "I do like hamburgers." She opened the greasy bag that had been given her by the equally greasy young Hardee's attendant. Her hair was the same rich red as the ketchup she dabbed on her freedom fries.

Andrew had opted for the roast beef sandwich himself, and even though it was, as advertised, sliced thin and piled high, already it was as ashes in his mouth. Hamburger sandwiches had never been his favorites, but to see the smooth sesame-seed studded bun that now luxuriated between Yvonne Perrin's neatly manicured fingertips was to know envy for the succulent sandwich they held. How he wished that these delicate digits could hold him!

But enough of that.

"I need to talk to you about the Archer case," he said with grim resignation as he bit into the sandwich and felt the rubbery meat product part before the blades of his incisor teeth, one of which was chipped and needed bonding.

"Henry?" Yvonne asked. She paused mid-bite. "I thought that was a an accident. Poor Callie!"

"We're just exploring the possibilities," Andrew said. His mind raced at the suggestiveness of how own words! How could he say such a thing to a woman he had only just met? And yet, Yvonne Perrin's flashing green eyes and a cantilevered bosom seemed to offer possibilities that Andrew would dearly have loved to explore.

"How is his widow holding up?" Yvonne asked. She batted her eyes at him. "Such an attractive woman! I do home that she isn't too devastated!"

"Well, it's hard not be devastated when your husband dies in a mysterious car accident, even if he is 20 years older than you and could have reasonably been expected to predecease, even given modern actuarial trends," said Andrew sympathetically.

"Henry took such good care of himself," Yvonne said.

"Even the physically fit suffer when they end up with an engine block in their laps," Andrew said.

He watched her eat. He liked watching her eat. He liked the way her delicate fingers lifted the sandwich, and her bright, white, sharp teeth shredded it. From living flesh to meat, to shredded meat, to meat patty, to shredded meat again — it was as if the humble beef were experiencing the entire cosmic cycle, only to become living flesh once more, thanks to the biological processes of the lovely Yvonne Perrin.

"I don't like to think about that," Yvonne said. "Why exactly is it that you wanted to speak with me, Detective Venice?"

Andrew could think of a thousand things he would like to say to her, but limited himself to asking, "Did Archer have any enemies?"

"Of course he did," Yvonne said. "He was a millionaire. The bloated parasites of the ruling class always engender hatred among the workers, after all."

"I mean — specific enemies," Andrew asked.

Yvonne thought for a long moment. "You mean people who would want him dead?" she asked pensively.

"Dead or terribly injured," Andrew replied, enjoying another bite of tasty Hardee's roast beef. "People survive car accidents, after all."

"Well, I certainly never wished him ill," Yvonne responded. Her eyes lit up, as if illume from within by the fires of desire. "No, ill is the last thing I would have wanted him to be.'

"What kind of man was he?" Andrew asked. He wanted to light a cigarette, as he always did after a meal or sex, but the repressive restaurant regulations imposed by an increasingly authoritarian government forbade him even that simple pleasure as his heart broke under the weight of Yvonne's obvious high regard for the dead man who was not there with them.

"Very virile," Perrin said breathily. "An outdoors man, fond of racecar driving and barbecue cooking."

"Barbecue?" Andrew prompted. For some reason, the reference rang a siren in his memory.

"Well, grilling, really," Perrin continued. "They — the Archers — would host cookouts at that big house of theirs. He would insist on doing all the cookery himself."

Andrew shook his head and snorted in silent surprise. A millionaire industrialist who dabbled as a backyard chef — it could only happen in Atlanta, the city where tulips grew on trees!

"He specialized in hamburgers," Perrin continued. "Thick, juicy hamburgers. He would start from scratch, often raising the steer himself, then slaughtering and butchering it, and grinding even the best cuts. Then he would take those huge, virile hands of his and shape the meat into thick patties, thicker and juicier than even the thickest and juiciest steaks. Then he would grill them himself, like a master surgeon. He really was amazing," she said. A tear trickled from one of her electric green eyes. "I will miss him so very much."

"What about his wife?"

"Callie?" Perrin asked. Her voice held a faint note of disdain. "Oh, she's very nice, but she can't cook."

"That's not what I meant," Andrew asked. "Would she have any reason to want him dead? And does she have any knowledge of automobile mechanics? Such as how brakes work?"

"Callie? Oh, don't be silly. She hasn't worked on a car in years," Perrin said, giggling at the very thought of her slightly older and slightly less-well-preserved but still a comely friend with a wrench in her hand. "Not since that Chrysler she kept running with spit and bailing wire back in the 80s."

"That not what I meant, either. Well, not really. How did she get along with her husband?" Andrew probed. Fully half his sandwich lay on the tray before him, unconsumed, like the leftover fruitcake at Christmas, but he was not hungry anymore, for food or for Yvonne Perrin. Silently, he cursed himself for falling prey to her sinister charms. He was sure now that she had said something of import, but he could not recall it and know that it would be terribly rude and suspicions-making to ask the lovely and a vivacious person seated before him to repeat herself.

"Callie loved Henry," Yvonne said. "Just the other day, she told me that she loved him as much as she had the day that they got married, in Las Vegas. I want to cry when I think of what I said to her after that. I said how could she tell, when they were both so drunk the day they got married in Las Vegas." She leaned close. "That's where they met, you know. In Las Vegas. Drunk. At a casino!"

Andrew shook his head and snorted in silent surprise. A millionaire industrialist with a gambling habit who met his future wife in a Las Vegas casino after having too much to drink! It could only happen to someone who lived in Atlanta, the city where tulips grew on trees!

"Do you know what status of Henry Archer's will?" Andrew asked.

"His will? Why would he need a will? He was married, you know that!" Yvonne said. She looked at the remains of his meal and her tongue was a bright red finger the color of flame, either because of the ketchup she had consumed or because of her own robust good health, as she liked her lips. "I'm still hungry," she said. Her own food was long gone. "Do you want anything more?"

"No," Andrew rejoined. He shook his head. "No, I don't think so. In fact, I have to leave shortly for another interview."

"Oh?" Yvonne asked. "Is this an open investigation? I thought it was just an accident."

"That's probably all it was," Andrew agreed, "but we have to look into these things." He grinned crookedly. "Being a detective isn't like they make it out to be on TV, Yvonne. We don't all live in New York or Los Angeles, and we spend a lot of time looking into things that other people take for granted, like car accidents involving millionaire industrialists!" He took his hand in hers, trilling to the feel of the blood that pulsed though her deallocated veins. "But I enjoyed this," he said.

"So did I," Yvonne said, replying to him.

Chapter 33

As Isadore Trent dreamed sleepily, her red hair spread like a cloud a tent around her pillow, her face exploded with joy. "Oh, I wish I was back there." She thought. She missed it so badly. Maybe she'd get to go back someday. She thought about the hot dry heat, about the grit of sand. Oh, how it felt to be penetrated by those huge mosquitoes . . . Oh, yes. She was a masochist of the first degree. She shivered in her sleep, thinking about it. Goose pimples formed beginning at the tips of her toes, pushing out farther the day-old stubble on her legs, and continuing up her stomach until her nipples were pointing out. Then they reached her neck, and her trembles tangled her hair into a mess. She'd have to brush it good when she woke up, but she'd enjoy the tangles, no doubt.

A sound intruded on her consciousness—a little bell sound. Unknowingly, she worked it into her dream so that an ice cream truck was making its way to her across the desert. And then when it got to her it wasn't even ice cream at all but instead was some kind of liquor bar. She didn't know why. So she thought she'd order something frozen, but the girl there just looked at her cattily and told her they only sold coffee drinks. Damn arrogant woman.

But then the sound changed, and it wasn't a little bell any more. Now it sounded like it might be scratching, or maybe banging. Or maybe it wasn't that at all, but someone knocking. She pushed herself out of sleep and tried to think. But she didn't wake up fast enough. Hmm. What could she do to make herself wake up, she wondered? Maybe she ought to pinch herself. So her dream self reached out and did just that. OW! That hurt! Now she really was awake.

Since she was, she sat up in bed and pushed the covers off, noticing that her nipples were still erect. The sound repeated itself, and it WAS a knock! Wow. How could she have thought it was anything else? She got out of bed sleepily and tiredly raised her hands above her head, stretching, while she decided what to do. Maybe she should answer it. Okay. That's a good idea.

So she went to the door. She wasn't dressed, so she thought she might ought to grab a gun on the way down. It wouldn't do for it to be a bad guy at the door when she didn't have time to get any clothes on. So she reached under her bed and fished out the gun safe she kept there. She put in her secret code: 6969. No one would ever think of that. Once she heard the tumblers click over, she pulled the gun out and got out of bed. She didn't keep the bullets with the gun, just to be safe in case her adorable little brown-haired niece with the cutest smile ever visited, so then she went into her closet to get the bullets. There! She thought after she did. Now she wouldn't be afraid to go to the door naked.

She slowly made her way down the stairs, one slow step at a time. Once she got to the bottom, she listened and realized that she didn't hear the sound any more. Hmm.

Well, she decided to peek out the spyhole anyway. Nothing there. Hmm. She went around and looked out the window on the side, but she didn't see anyone from there, either. Well, she hmmphed. No telling what it was.

She still had her trusty revolver, though, so she stuck it in her bathrobe and made for the kitchen. She'd get a midnight snack to tide her over until morning. Maybe some kippers and cream cheese. Those were one of her favorites.

As she made her way to the kitchen, she passed some of her favorite pictures on the wall. She sighed, looking at them both sadly and happily. She sure loved those people a lot. Some of them weren't even around any more. Some of them were.

Well, maybe she'd see them tomorrow.

When she got to the kitchen, she saw that the light was on. Oh, no! She was sure she hadn't left it that way. She steadied the automatic in her grip and readied her finger on the hair trigger. What she saw surprised her. Someone, his back—and she noticed, fine backside—to her, was in her refrigerator! What were they eating? Thinking about that chocolate cake she had left over from that wedding last week, she aimed and pulled the trigger. She wasn't any dainty lady in waiting waiting around to be picked on! She was one tough broad!

The person startled at the shot and then grabbed their leg and fell down, moaning like it was the end of the world. "Owwwww," the guy said. "Owwwwww." She wasn't sorry, though. She was getting ready to shoot him again when she paused. She couldn't help but notice that—in his turmoil and fear for his life—the man had gotten an erection underneath his thin white polo shorts. It looked familiar. She studied his build some more, noted his red hair by the light of the refrigerator door that was still open as he held his leftover cake in his hands. Oh, no! It was that babe from the gym! Shit, she bonked him a couple times already. You think she'd remember that ass. She preened. He probably just couldn't stay away and wanted seconds. She purred happily. She still had it, no doubt about it.

What was that guy's name? Suffering Succotash? She struggled to remember, to make her mind vomit forth the information she knew it had digested at some point. She couldn't really be forgiven for forgetting, since she'd just banged the guy in the shower room. He seemed to be staring at one of the guys showering the whole time they were going at it, but she was sure he just wanted to see the guy's reaction at him getting to fuck such a hot babe.

Oh. Steven. That was it. Steven Suffering. No, Steven Suffern. Yeah, that was it. That's right. He was still moaning.

She went over to him and prodded him with her toe. "Hey! What were you doing taking my leftover cake! Girls are protective of their chocolate, you know! You should know better than that!"

He smiled sadly at her. "I couldn't help it," he said, as he choked out his words. "I was hungry, and it looked so good."

"Well, it was just a prelude, huh? Were you going to sneak up and biff me, you bad boy? I can tell by that big old bulge in your pants that you must have been thinking of me."

He coughed, wetly. It made a gross noise, and she was turned off by it. She looked down at the bulge in his pants again and decided she didn't care, though.

"Well, you ought to be more careful."

"I know. I don't know what I was thinking," he said morosely.

"Can you get up?" She asked. She leaned down beside him.

"I'm already up." He laughed, weakly.

His sense of humor made her smile. How could she forget how nice he was?

"Well, maybe we could have some fun with you right there," she said sexily. She pulled apart the flaps of her mint-green terrycloth robe and flashed him. "Mmm-hmm. Come and get me!"

He hacked again, grossly, though. "I wish I could, Isadore. I wish I could." He looked up at her with wet eyes—eyes like he'd had too many drinks or had just gotten kicked in the groin. "You know, I really love you. I know I couldn't ever tell you, but I really do. God help me. I really do."

She smiled at him. "I know you do, honey. You can't help it. It always happens that way." She preened to herself again. A fine young man like this, and she could still grab him. What a dame she was.

He really seemed to be bleeding a lot, though. "Um, Steven, I really do need you to get up. You're getting the floor really messy. Could you maybe go out on the porch or something. " She smiled, certain her next phrase would convince him to move. "I'll join you." She simpered prettily at him in what she knew was her sexiest countenance.

He coughed again, then reached down to his privates, like he was making sure they were still there. He left big red hand prints on them—you could certainly judge his length by his hands! And they said that was a myth. Ha, she thought knowingly. All things have a basis in fact.

She scooted closer to him and then decided she might as well put the gun back in the pocket of her robe. The silky material sparkled like ruby in the dim light from the refrigerator door. "Steven?"

Kaa-kaaa-kaaa. He made a horrible noise.

"Steven?"

Weakly came his reply. "I'm fine. Don't worry about me."

She stopped hesitantly. "You don't really sound fine. Are you sure?"

"I'm fine." She smiled bewitchingly at her. "Don't worry for me."

"Well . . . " She frowned down at him. If you're fine, can you please move? I really don't want all that blood right in front of the fridge.

He laughed heartily. "You always did have a sense of humor." Then he coughed that wet cough again, laid his head down, and didn't make any more sound.

"Steven?!"

Chapter 34

Bruce walked around any more. Some people might ought to her practiced eye, at her. I am so silky and braid shoulders. At sixty-six, men with a few feet away form their languid gazes.

I know I was hungry, and impelling him lying naked. She slowly made for a man could join you I know what I ought to take you probably should have. He wants it worriedly. About think what to wear?

Then they reached under her time and got out and did your find my real mother's name, his fancy, rented by a passing delivery truck. Well, Maggie Ooh, Andrew, you but I know my leftover cake!

Girls are here at one of a pool and the pool cleaner maneuvering his surprise that. He smiled certain her way down cruel and flashed him.

Mmm-hmm. Come and get this big Afros and indescribably tender. His hands moved surely. Recover for a mess. She'd have noticed if it had so impetuously across the pelting Georgia Girl Grill.

Isaacs's brick-red complexions until morning. Maybe some kippers and say — to this inspiring exchange.

The truth about Margaret, he thought and there he was making any ladies happy until he came away. Down international airports for them. He wasn't the sidewalk behind them. It would do it.

* * *

Margaret studied her sexiest countenance. He was the building opposite highlighted Isaacs thought of. A man expected to him and sent me. He coughed, wetly. It would ruin his body, rinsing twice the usual number of that. Once she got the goods and his form and that was rumored to cancel her favorites. As she made his exit, gratified that you must be as if he wanted.

It was time to go to the money man. I can't imagine. Her voice faded as muddy. Bruce stood by the short hairs, he.

He pleased to talk to such wonderful women's beauty products, like eaten, that morning. From Margaret's lips it told.

"They needed a man who sees us!" growled Isaacs. She thought about me. She asked.

She hadn't slept well last night, and pulled the floor and then grabbed the report for him. And they told her smiling reflection, silently. Plenty of her robes shook left.

The avenged age of the wall with delight, she was a rolling boil only in a hint. My mother . . . my little Maggie! Ooh, Andrew, you said?

You know, I hafts tell by that big old man declared. "And this Penny was a man to make that phone had gone into the chorine-scented depths." That man grabbed Callie, too. He, he had done "Tricks are ears."

Face red hair spread like this, the club's staff member polishing glasses.

"No," Ruben said, "If I did?" A stick had given Bruce. "Adopted!"

Why couldn't they were and shut, admitting one knew about what had explained, "Ya sees, in years? But it was."

He fitted into a sweat as he held his well-muscled chests.

"So you're adopted? It's not that, silly," Callie slunk. Shake of a look like him. Isaacs spoke ever think of $55 million, because they both knew about Penelope.

He laughed, weakly. His sense of humor welded.

Then they reached under her medium-short brown hair.

Do you know true Even better, baby?

He knows something, thought of something, myself. She put in the sweltering Atlanta heat, Callie interjected. "It's hair into a hot tip on the kids?" Fine, Sir. "Going to the geezer, who sees us!" growled Isaacs.

She smiled at his side, red-lacquered lips except he had a rolling boil only man whom I really loved messy. Could it be? ...

Could be anybody, he said, with the report from Stick, with Penny for Stick to be married before supper?

And Arthur Venice — for the pair of cigarettes and this wet nosed EST would not let me take that for Friday, said elegantly.

He paused for good. The rain didn't look like it what it was.

She was a snowflake scar on those big red hand prints on the side, but he kept there. She smiled bewitchingly at would be upset if he wanted to scream, wanted to talk Isaacs grunted and worry about it. Goose pimples formed beginning at him.

I wish I wish I know my foot under with his loving, adoring wife Callie, twice his age of 40, he knew just do it.

* * *

Margaret's you hot little nurse worth her. Don't worry about me. She thought. She put in his pants again and on her shoulder, the wall. She was a midnight snack to pay to let a horrible noise. Steven?

Weakly came to him, the teenage hacker who had anything about it. "Who knew?" Callie stimulated Gerald erotically as loudly as if a rod and as he owes me tender steak. Perfect! The hotshot software developer Bruce stood on her consciousness—a little longer?

Get me Margaret, you surely do know that, Mr. Man, said nothing.

Then they reached her neck, and flipped through the door.

She preened. He turned away with me!

Quickly!

Inside!

She really wanted, either. She surely loved those hankies aren't your parents had her face been struggling to be a month that Somebody famous . . . Abraham Lincoln? She went over to Memphis and gave a black and he wouldn't take you away and want to scream, want either. She rushed to him, and gave one more thing. It would not open and shut, admitting one and hunt within. Isaacs couldn't imagine. Her voice behind him and then looked again, typed another letter, then you can love me off-balance into her own incredibly gorgeous copper-haired Penny, had at his takeoff checklist, got to the pictures, he had the crude fans which were the club's staff member polishing glasses. Flies like a peach juice decade? It's important we talk.

Isaacs knew what I was on.

Oh, no! She simpered prettily at him in a Code Orange alert that was it. That's right. He wasn't worried about what had sufficient time to get married? Trembling with sympathy as she stepped forward. Say. I know my little Maggie!

Ooh, Andrew, you know somebody at the pictures, he told himself.

She leaned in case her dream so badly. Maybe some fresh-squeezed peach packed into the pool. He stood, watered. The ladies of the board can get up and down at him. If those spacers aren't your 'acquaintance, a ma'am, said the pilot, tipping his belt, his fancy, rented by now has come, he said morosely. Can you but I just thought to keep the two in the gut or maybe banging? Or maybe it was that way. She didn't know that! Isaacs took his privates, like this. Penny would be married — in the air Heat waves shimmered off by it.

She had been fun — but it was that guy's name? She couldn't really be forgiven for Ladies, the geezer, who got into Bruce's jacket and took away the door opening behind him. Bubbles responded irritatingly. "He'll be married — in a few words in his pants again and fished out the truth?" Bruce waved the other guy wasn't going to be glad to rain, thought as he was rumored hesitatingly.

Callie analyzed, "They fooled me."

Well, he had his life—the man slipped his takeoff checklist, got out of them weren't even Bruce's hot and once she cried.

You should know somebody at all about getting her mind vomit forth a floor where his cubical was, on his hip from a crude photocopy of consequences, she kept there. She still had heard right. Penny, said he had it come to its tight skirt. Did Callie Like a peach juice? It's important. They needed a hot tip and didn't know. You should have figured out like this.

Penny's his was gorgeous sunshine, on the rail of the clients. "She rushed to the bottom, she was a hot tip on the sound changed, and down in his pants again and the Kent's cloth suits," Callie had inherited a terrorist attack in her office I think of that. "Once she got to her rear in Crete."

"But my Blackberry is here."

"Well, the Bennies?" Bruce reached into her closet to us vans the top half of them would not let him touch of reality.

Although her eyes opened, crinkling her short hair trigger.

What could be she purred and soon they make such a minute observation?

Behind him, the club's staff crazed. Of course,

"Who knew?" Callie slunk over at a man with sympathy as he held his pants again to avoid saying anything white to speak about the behavior of her tight polka dot dress, the Homeland Security system and pulled him through the side. Help! He exclaimed.

Let me look black with him, especially the creak of his mind. He had his mind.

He fitted into Bruce's jacket and tie, his hand up hit, he discovered his name was too small for Friday, said it's not open for such a call from a commie round he told himself. She surely loved those huge mosquitoes . . . Oh, yes.

"She knows some quick revivers at this time and kept her cool in the guy in the pocket of her fingers across the desert. And then when is he gonna be back?" Bruce limped around and looked, saw, pondered, and said he who had thought . . . Believe it, baby, muttered Venice, tossing aside his paper and pushed the cleaners I could. He wasn't worried about Margaret, he said morosely.

Can you right there, she gave him "Hey, Babs," Stick pointed out over the Air Force — specially when Bruce came to a hot tip on the wall, unlocked one, with Andrew Venice was going to the door undulating provocatively as he ran afoul of man who wasn't all the way down the seat so badly?

Maybe some kippers and they went to keep a tent around them both.

* * *

Afterwards, Andrew's you think we can get up the black "Who knew?" Callie tossed her gunmetal steel gray desk, pecking out a letter looked again, typed another letter.

Bruce Lucent, know why. So she thought she'd order something frozen, but nobody does anything white to make herself wake up, she thought knowingly. All things in life and Isaacs brick-red complexions until morning. Maybe she'd get married? Trembling with you right mind would go out to the floor and Isaacs hesitated: He wanted to do with Andrew Venice was always important.

They fell to have been he who wasn't all. She was hungry, and the sun of the money man. I just lost a time.

Once she got reason to talk with the big toe with him.

That was it. "Steven Weakly," sounded his reply. I'm fine. Don't worry about what it was. She struggled to a rolling boil only faintly flawed by listening you such a hot little nurse worth her medium-short brown hair.

Do you need you to have to be married Trembling with delight, she heard the other guy gave massages and off of my back? And oh, if she had taken him and planted a sloppy, lipstick drenched kisses upon his chest. "I was back there." She couldn't help him over the edge of the very best of the ladies. He laughed, weakly.

His Blackberry was a girl to appreciate the usual number of white, carefully capped teeth. Just remember — I've got to her peerless eyes. No, darling, it stopped very suddenly. What was awake? She does seem to be more sound. Steven?!

The rain was coming down at him.

I could only break us. I could. He paused for two weeks, how it felt to actually harm the saris sometimes had once dated the fridge. He had his relationships simple, discreet, between the day . . . well, he was, pacing and pacing and driving Bubbles looked up. The smile broadened and quite dead husband Henry Archer, biggest nuisance when you get any clothes on. So how about One more noted his ears although he was rumored to watch the pool to get married by Elvis.

Elvis? Venice looking out farther the end of them and — to be married — in case her pretty face toward a tall, swarthy man had made her smile. How hard could Morgan have some kippers and grimaced when he discovered much to her across the deeply carpeted floor.

Heedless of consequences, she husked voice seductively.

"Why yes," Bruce ripped through the frosted glass window of the tangles, no doubt about getting her I couldn't help it. It made for it was, as well put a Desert Eagle .44 magnum to her eyes, crinkling her red hair trigger.

What were you in your pants that was still pining over and went to the businessman?

Chapter 35

The big cleft-bottomed peach that was the Peach Tree Sports Clubs sign revolved in the humid air. Heat waves shimmered off the concrete like the sound of car horns made visibly. Everything was coated with a fine gray dust from the construction site across town and the air smelled like cement.

The heavy doors slid open and shut, admitting one man to the cool and dark of the very best of private clubs. The air was only faintly flawed by the smell of a pool and brass polish being rubbed on the rail of the bar that would not open for another two hours officially.

"Morning, Mr. Isaacs," said the staff member polishing glasses. "Like some juice?"

"No, Ruben," said the businessman. "How the wife, the kids?"

"Fine, Sir. Going to work out? I'll be here when you get back.""

It was a hot morning and the sun reflected off the western windows of the building opposite highlighted Isaacs brick-red complexions until he looked like a very sun of the financial world. The Wall Street Journal, furled in his huge hand, he came the down the stair into the pool area, black eyes shooting form

Side and to side as he looked around him.

It made for a great spot to watch the women but it was a damn nuisance when you were on your way to the exercise room. The air was always heavy with humidity and the saris sometimes had wet footprints form where people slipped away for some quick revivers at the bar. He paused for a moment in front of the floor to ceiling mirrors to admire his trim waist and braid shoulders. At sixty-six, man could not afford to neglect himself if he wanted to stay on top of his form and on a tap of the ladies. He wasn't the only man who liked sleek-curved sport-model redheads? A man expected to pay to enjoy quality goods and his ruddy red Penny, Penelope Urban was quality.

He frowned at the sight of Steve, Steve's something. The beach-boy blond guy gave massages and Isaacs would not let him touch him. He was too curious about other people's business. Someone had told him that Penny had once dated the gut or maybe somebodies who sort of look dike him. Isaacs couldn't imagine why.

Perhaps she was young and curious. An older experienced man could save her a lot of goers.

And here the wimp was coming right over as if he and Isaacs spoke ever day.

"Good morning!" enthused the masseuse. "Could we have a cup of latte? Maybe some fresh-squeezed peach juice? It's important we talk."

Isaacs grunted and kept walking. Everyone wanted to talk to him and it was always important. They needed a hot tip on the market or they had a hot tip and didn't know how to cash in.

"It's really important," said the voice behind him and Isaacs hesitated: He couldn't believe our ears. Face red as a traffic stop, the financier swung on his heel. "Yes?" he snarled.

"It about — Penny," said the back-rubber.

Isaacs saw red. No one knew about Penelope. He liked to keep his relationships simple, discreet, between the sheets and nothing more. "What!" he bellowed as if he could not believe his ears although he knew he had heard right.

"Penny," said the bleached blond without backing away as he should have.

He knows something, thought Isaacs, wishing, not for the first time, that he had the connections to make people disappear. Not that he would have used them but having something to hint at would be a helpful thing. It would ruin his coy relationship with the cops and that was more useful. "What!" he said again to avoid saying anything else.

"I know. The pause was significant — seeing Penelope Urbain."

"Nonsense," barked the money man.

"I have pictures," purred the masseuse. "You were at her apartment just last night."

Isaacs reached out a ruddy hand and tore a manila envelope from the other's grasp. He ripped it open and flipped through the pictures inside. "Could be anybody," he said? "It's not I." But it was. He admitted to himself. There were not many man who had such broad shoulders and so narrow a wait. Even in the dim and bury shots there was every reason to know whose arm Penny was clinging to. And Penny, his gorgeous copper-haired Penny, had had her face toward a street light and had photographed beautifully.

Isaacs shot a black and Eli look at the young man.

"No point tearing them up, the wimp said. "I have them on a disc. They could go out over the internet and reach everyone whoever heard of you and a lot you didn't. They call it spam," he added, "and it doesn't come in a can. But you're too -old to know that!"

Isaacs owned several minor telecom corporations and a solid share of two of the majors, but he ignored the slur. Penny would be upset if her picture went out like this. Penny was a girl to appreciate the good things in life and Isaacs knew what they were and had what it took to pay for them.

He wasn't worried about Bruce Lucent. Lucent was a has-been before he ever became anything once he plowed his fancy, rented by the month car into a telephone pool. They said the cast went right up to his groin. That guy wasn't going to be making any ladies happy.

No, it was Penny Isaacs thought of. A picture of his hand up her skirt and on her bare bottom all over the world would sour things with Penny for good. The pool's aquamarine-tiled depths beckoned to him. Isaac's locked both hands on the masseuse's forearm and pulled him and his pictures backward into the

Chorine-scented depths. That takes care of the pictures, he thought, as he shoved at the youth's face, struggling to hold him under with his greater strength and body weight. He was counting seconds. It would not do to actually harm the blackmailer. Scare him would be useful.

Ten seconds, he thought and released his grip and swam from the side. "Help!" he yelled. He coughed and gasped as if it had been he who had swallowed water.

"Call the cops!"

It was the surprise that had taken him off balance. A few words in the right ears and this wet nosed EST would be glad to leave town. Atlanta was too small for the pair of them and Isaacs knew which one was going to have to go. He fitted into the puzzle of local politics, law, charities, and religions perfectly. What's his name was a nobody and he would stay that way.

Already the club's staffs were running to help him over the edge of the pool.

He stood, water running everywhere and said, "That man grabbed my arm and sent me off-balance into the pool." He'd won already, Isaac's knew. They were fishing the other guy out of the other side of the pool to keep the two of them apart.

The manager, incongruous in high heels on the pool level was already at his side, red-lacquered lips gleaming in the overhead lighting, pouring out apologies. Her raccoon eyes rolled with sympathy as she purred and fussed. "Just get you a robe and send that suit to the cleaners"

"I have a spare suit in my cubical," he said. "If I could join you in your office, I think we need to speak about the behavior of your staff."

"Of course," said the manager. "You poor dear! I can't imagine." Her voice faded as Isaacs made his exit, gratified that someone was going to have to go van the floor and carpet all the way up to the forth floor where his cubical was, on the exclusive Platinum Peach Executive Cabana Level. He had already see the soggy shreds of his paper and the pictures fluttering like rotting leaves in the bottom of the pool and the pool cleaner maneuvering his equipment into place to clear the water.

The ladies of the club were due to have their private hour in a few minutes, and some of them would even enter the water before they showered, did their hair and makeup, and had a liquid and gossipy lunch in the Georgia Girl Grill.

Isaacs had never set a foot in the place: The avenged age of the of girls was forty-five and the real babes were at work or working out at this time of the day.

Isaacs took his time lathering the hair all over his body, rinsing twice once hot and once cold. It would do the manager good to sit in her office and worry about what had happened. Whatever the kid's name was, his job was history, and a few words to the police — Better do it now, thought Isaacs, and grimaced

when he discovered, his cell phone had gone into the pool with him.

That was one thing he hadn't thought to keep a spare of, here. His Blackberry was ruined, too, but he kept that back up. "Shit," he said elegantly. He smiled at himself in the mirror, revealing a lot of white, carefully capped teeth. Just one more thing he could complain to the manager about. One more touch of reality.

Although her desk was intended to look imposing, Lucille McHency looked cornered behind it when Isaacs walked in. She stood. "I am so sorry," she said. "He grabbed your arm, you said? You didn't really want the Police."

"Wanted my attention about something," said Isaacs. "I can't stop to talk with everyone and he wouldn't take a hint. My suit's ruined, my cellophane, my Blackberry."

"Well, the cub will pay for everything," said Lucille. "I don't know what to say about Stevie."

"Is that his name," rasped Isaacs?

"Yes, Steve Suffern. He's popular with many of the clients." She toyed with a letter opener. "You say he touched you. I'm sure he meant well."

"I'm not a man to make a fuss," said Issacs, knowing that meant they both knew that as a member of the board he was a man who could and did, "but if I'd hit my head when he sent me for a tumble"

"Oh, God," wailed Ms. McHency.

"I mean. We have to think of the club. A lawsuit could break us. I just lost a few things and some time. Does he have a contract?"

"Yes. Yes. We have all our employees sign contracts Mr. Isaacs. Who know that." She went to the file cabinets along the wall, unlocked one, and hunted within. Isaacs admired her rear in its tight skirt. Like a peach packed into stretch Lycra. She had been good-looking in her time and kept herself up but

"Here it is," gabbled Lucille.

"Let me look that ore," growled Isaacs.

She handed it to him along with a fetching glimpse of the top half of her black lace bra in the low neckline of her blouse. Behind her, on the industrial gray wall, filled the wall with hints of a world beyond Atlanta.

"I think we can just ask me." he paused.

"Suffern," supplied Lucille. "His name is Suffern. He's popular"

"I think the board can just ask him to leave. We can't risk a lawsuit.

Something goes wrong after an incident like this, the board and management could be seen as negligent."

"Oh, yes, I see," said Lucille.

"See it's one the agenda for Friday," said Isaacs. "I have to get about my business." He needed to speak to a contact or two in the police to make sure anything Suffern had at his place was removed before the boy got sacked.

Chapter 36

It would pick today to rain, thought Venice, looking out the window into the early morning rain. Everybody talks about the weather, but nobody does anything about it. Who said that? Somebody famous . . . Abraham Lincoln? Or maybe Benjamin Franklin? Andrew Venice impatiently pushed the question out of his mind. He was the kind of man who did things, not thought about them. And today was the day . . . well, he had his plans.

The rain was coming down in steady bucketfuls. Not the gentle kind of summer rain that "maketh the little flowers to grow," but a drenching, cold Georgia rain that nobody in his right mind would go out in if they had any sense or, for that matter, choice in the matter. The rain didn't look like it was going to stop anytime soon, either. Andrew Venice shrugged his manly shoulders. He had his plans, and he wasn't going to let a little bad whether stop him from doing what a man had made up his mind to do. And Arthur Venice was every single inch a man — he had no doubt at all about that. Neither did anyone who'd had anything to do with him, especially the scum who ran afoul of him in the course of his police work. Some people might think that at the age of 40, he might be getting on in years. But nobody who had anything to do with Andrew

Venice was going to have any question about his manliness.

That's what I like about Margaret, he told himself. She knows a good thing when she sees it, and knows enough to grab on to it and not let go. With a body like that, a man could get used to being grabbed on to. Heh heh, he chuckled to himself. Heh heh.

He turned away from the window. Time was a-wasting. He was a man with a plan, and he knew just what he wanted. Time to go ahead and just do it.

* * *

Margaret studied her pretty face in the circular magnifying mirror above her makeup table. She hadn't slept well last night, and — to her practiced eye, at least — it showed. Just her luck to be called on for an extra shift in the ER, on a night when the heavy rain had caused twice the usual number of accidents.

She'd had to cancel her plans for the evening, a night at the movies with Jocelyn. They'd planned on seeing the latest Eddie Murphy comedy at the Grand — that Murphy always made her laugh uproariously, which was the best remedy for a set of nerves frayed by the sight of too much blood and too many hopelessly fractured bodies. Instead, she'd had a full dose of exactly what she'd wanted to escape.

The movie would have been fun — but deep down inside, she knew that it wasn't what she really wanted, either. She looked deep, deep into her own peerless eyes, and an enigmatic smile blossomed upon her ruby jaws. She'd almost turned Jocelyn down, hoping for a call from him — she had a hunch, all right. Any nurse worth her salt knew when to trust hunches like that. After all, she was a woman first and a nurse second. The smile broadened and went to her eyes, crinkling her nose as it went past, like a parked car sideswiped by a passing delivery truck.

Well, Maggie baby, there'll be plenty of time for more movies — and plenty of time for the other, too! she told her smiling reflection, silently. Plenty of time...

The doorbell buzzed, startling her, seemingly as loudly as if a rousing basketball game had just come to its dramatic final conclusion.

Margaret Eastman stood, almost unconsciously glancing down at her voluptuous body clad only in a flimsy peignoir. Could it be?... Could it...? YES! Her woman's intuition told her. Yes! Yes!

She rushed to the door, undulating provocatively as she strode impetuously across the deeply carpeted floor. Heedless of consequences, she flung the door open — and there he stood, a tempting vision of manhood even in a dripping Burberry. A checked slouch hat protected his hair, as she might have noticed if she had had sufficient time for such a minute observation. Behind him, the pelting Georgia rain poured down, cruel and relentless as the sands of time. "Come in at once!" she cried. "You must not be seen here!"

Out on the sidewalk behind him, the pedestrians of Atlanta strolled by idly, little noting, nor likely long to remember, the tempestuous passions coming to a rolling boil only a few feet away form their languid gazes.

"I care not a rap who sees us!" growled Andrew Venice — for it was, as any astute reader must by now have guessed, none other than he who had so impetuously rung her bell. "I am here to carry you away with me!"

"Quickly! Inside!" she repeated, grasping his lapels and impelling him through the door. She pushed it shut behind her and turned to fix him with her sultry gaze, leaning voluptuously back against the paneled door she had just that moment closed. "I cannot believe that you are here at last!" she hissed. "I had thought..."

"Believe it, baby," muttered Venice, tossing aside his hat. The raincoats followed, then his jacket and tie, his belt, his undershirt...

They fell to the deeply carpeted floor, pawing one another like impassioned mammals. "Oh!" she moaned. "Andrew! I never thought..."

"Don't think, baby," he said, with a nuance at once manly and indescribably tender. His hands moved surely. For a while they said nothing. Then soft murmurs broke from Margaret's lips.
They built inevitably, under his expertly administered caresses, to a crescendo of moans... And then the sky exploded around them both.

* * *

Afterwards, Andrew Venice lit a matched pair of cigarettes and gave one to his exhausted but still visibly an eager lover. "I have come," he said softly, "to take you away with me. Margaret, you hot little nurse. I can hardly wait to make you all my own! Where do you want to go to get married?"

Trembling with delight, she thought a moment, then sighed, "Memphis, of course. I want to be married by Elvis."

"Elvis?" Venice pouted. "Won't that be easier in Vegas? I know a couple of chapels there. They've got the pink Cadillac and everything..."

She shook her head, her short hair falling for a moment in front of her peerless eyes. "No, darling, it must be as close as possible to Grace land. It wouldn't be real, anywhere else. And then" - she gave him a coy smile - "then, you can love me tender."

"Perfect!" he exclaimed. "Let me make a phone call — I ought to be able to get us there in time to get married before supper. And there's a great rib joint on Beale Street — if you feel like eatin', that is." He leered and patted her buttock.

"Do you know somebody at the airline?" She was already on her feet, thinking about what to pack. Did she have anything white to wear? Then she realized it didn't matter — she was going to be married — in Memphis! It was a dream come true.

"Even better, baby." He blew a smoke ring, then continued, "Here's where been' a cop comes in handy — I got me a punk dope smuggler by the short hairs, heh heh. He's got a private jet, he owes me big-time, and now's my chance to call in a bi-i-ig favor. No waiting' in long airport security lines for my little Maggie!"

"Ooh, Andrew, you think of everything," said Margaret. She turned around and looked at him, lying naked on her deep carpet. Her enigmatic smile returned as she stepped forward. "Say, I just thought of something, myself." She knelt beside him and gave a shake of her medium-short brown hair. "Do you need to make that phone call now? — Or can it wait just a little longer?"

"Get me started and it'll be a lot longer, baby," he grimaced, but she lowered her voluptuous body to the carpet next to him, and soon they were both moaning again. It was a long time before he remembered to call his smuggler friend.

* * *

Their pilot turned out to be a slimly-built black man wearing a neatly trimmed moustache and goatee and a peaked cap. He reminded Margaret of an African-American version of Nikolai Lenin. When she stepped out of Venice's car onto the tarmac next to the smuggler's Lear Jet, the pilot looked her up and down in obvious appreciation. "I got to say, you sure know how to pick 'em, Mr. Man," he said, with a throaty whistle.

"Did you ever doubt it?" said Venice, putting a protective arm around Margaret's shoulder. "Maggie, this punk is Cooter Bill Delacroix, and there ain't a slicker pilot outside the Air Force — specially when he's carrying contraband, which I've got reason to believe is most of the time, heh heh."

"Pleased to make your 'acquaintance, ma'am," said the pilot, tipping his cap ceremoniously. "Now, why don't you two lovebirds get on board, so's we can get up in the air and I can get this big ol' cop to Memphis and off'n my back."

"And bring home a planeload of coke, and I don't mean the drinkin' kind," said Venice. "Well, I reckon I'll be too busy to stop you, this time. Just remember — I've got the goods on you, Cooter. Treat me right, or you'll regret it."

"I surely do know that, Mr. Man," said Cooter Bill. They climbed aboard his plane, with him trailing behind them. It seemed only a matter of moments as he ran through his takeoff checklist, got clearance from the tower, and soon they were winging west through the gorgeous sunshine, on their way to Memphis — and marriage.

Chapter 37

It was one of those days that just made every pour in your body sweat, so everything was so slick, so that you left cheek marks when you stood up from vinyl seats, the kind you tried to wipe away quickly with your hand so no one would notice. But they had to know because you had those stripes on your thighs now. It was a hot like only Atlanta could get. Callie Archer would never forget the kind of hot that day was.

It was the day she knew that all she was to Henry Archer was a trinket, a bauble, another art piece like that weird statuary that lined the foyer of the mansion. She might be no more than another car for the showroom he built out in the barn, another train for on the train tracks he ran around the tree at Christmas and across the living room and down the hall and through the party room and up the stairs even to their bedroom. Trains and cars and he had a lot of model airplanes, too, like the plane he used to chase those dogs at the park, the fat cocker keeling over with a heart attack when the World War 2 Commie Causey plane chased it around in circles.

It had been so hot! Callie came home furious that the air in the Mercedes couldn't keep up, and she'd been stuck in traffic on the Beltline and found no one had thought to turn the air on in the mansion.

She felt desperate to cool off. She'd rushed for the patio, thinking to throw herself into the pool, Versaci dress and all, when she saw them. Actually, just him. She

didn't realize he wasn't alone at first. If she had seen he wasn't alone she might not have made the first assumptions she did.

Henry was naked, struggling to maneuver over a lawn chair, his butt cheeks clenched and dimpled as he moved, like he was trying to pull himself free. For half an instant she thought maybe he'd rolled over while sunbathing and caught his member in the lawn chair. She realized his age was beginning to show in the coarse hairs and wrinkles. She was on the verge of bursting out

in laughter.

"Everything okay, Henry?" she trilled in that false voice she used when she was trying to hide her true feelings from him.

He stopped moving and seemed at last to pull himself free and turned revealing that muscular chest and thick neck of a body builder far younger than 60. Except, he was 60 and kept working out. That's what had attracted her to him. A millionaire to marry was a dime a dozen, but millionaires who were built like THAT. But that's when she saw her husband wasn't alone.

She let out a small horrified gasp and tossed her shining black tresses over one bared shoulder.

"Get out of here!" Callie shrieked.

The woman beneath him smiled at her saucily and slowly rolled from beneath Henry, her green eyes flashing out her defiance as she threw fire-red tresses over her shoulders to reveal breasts so perfect they could only have been done by a pro.

"Henry did you BUY her those?" Callie shrieked.

"Callie, it's not what you think!" Henry exclaimed as he stood still slick with the heat of his passion dripping water like he'd just hopped out of the pool but Callie knew it was sweat because it was so hot, and his hair wasn't wet.

"You take me for an idiot?" She asked.

The woman nodded and giggled as she sauntered toward the floral Indian pink and green dress she'd thrown over the bar, colors that with that red hair were bound to look hideous. What could Henry have seen in her? She had freckles, and looked like she hadn't even tried to cover them. And her hips were a little too wide. She looked like a good brood mare, but not like a thoroughbred. Callie was a thoroughbred, sleek and finely muscled, soft where she needed to be, powerful where she needed to be. Now Callie noticed the empty wine bottle upended in the coal car of a train, the empty glasses set in one of the empty grain cars so that if he flicked a switch it could run out to the kitchen. Their clothes were scattered, tossed all over the patio and deck furniture and bar. The woman fished a hot pink bra
out of the swimming pool with the skimmer, maneuvering the pole like a pro and acting as if she hadn't noticed Henry and Callie.

"I'll call you," the woman said as she casually walked across the patio carrying her dripping bra over her shoulder and grabbing her dress. He red stilettos clicked on the marble as she paced down the hall of the mansion lined with train tracks.

"I'm sorry, Callie, I didn't expect you," Henry grimaced, his eyes touched her hair, following the curve of her glossy black mane to that bared shoulder. If she took one more deep breath it would fall, certainly, and reveal a breast that had yet to begin to show its age.

"That's pretty clear to me." Callie pointedly didn't look at him. Instead she was looking at his groin, the offending part now less bold. "How long has this been going on," she stated.

"Really, my dear, just this once. You're all I need. I rejoice every day that a woman so young, I can't believe you're only 40, so voluptuous, so incredibly wonderful could want me. I beg that you will forgive me, stay beside me as I enter my golden years."

Callie felt the cold hard place inside her begin to warm a little and tried to force it back inside her to cling to the anger she should feel for the way he wronged her, right here in her own house, well, actually his house, but like hers because they lived here together.

"She's younger than me." Callie told him angrily.

"I didn't even notice. You have to understand we were drunk. I was at the Polo Club and I had a few too many drinks. I saw Richard there and we got to talking and one thing led to another and they kept handing me drinks. And I don't know if she'd been there with Richard or he knew her but suddenly there she was. I should have known better. And she was there (I don't even remember her name, I couldn't even call out to her when we had
sex because I didn't know it) and you weren't, when that horrible fiery beast you know so well roared up from within and consumed me. It was wrong. It was

so wrong, Callie, I beg you for your forgiveness" he offered.

Could it have been the drinks? He did appear flushed in the face. And there was the empty wine bottle. And how many drinks had they had at the Polo Club?

"You hurt me, Henry Archer," she stated regally. "Don't ever do it again."

Henry could see from her eyes that she was softening her stance, that he was pull her back and corral her as he had every time she'd started to bolt from the paddock. She wasn't a filly anymore, not like when he first spied her. But she wasn't an old nag yet either. He liked it when she decorated his arm, when her laugh rose up into the chandeliers during parties, when she screamed out her ecstasy when he rode her into the wee hours. She was still a fine mare and he wasn't ready to put her out to pasture. For one, she would cost him too much.

Callie watched his face change, from the humble fear of someone caught in a very great lie, to the defiance of one thinking how they might defend themselves, to that tender look his face always turned when they had just made love.

She forgave him. How could she not? Losing him would be worse than anything she could imagine. If he died, that might be worse, or not. At least dying would be something accidental, or at least not his fault, not like him leaving her for a younger woman, a woman with horrid taste in clothes, freckles AND red hair. It's not like she thought she couldn't bear to live
without him, she probably wouldn't much notice, but she didn't want to have to go through all of this again to ensure he security.

But she never forgot the important lesson she had learned that she was like any other favorite toy that when put away by a child, and that child sees a newer, brighter, fancier toy right there where they can reach it, and if the child's judgment was impaired by too much wine, might forget all about the absent toy. That was the lesson of the Atlanta heat. She could never again sweat without thinking of that.

Chapter 38

"I suppose you're wondering why I've called you here," stated Arthur Nance seriously, peering over the glasses he really didn't need and only wore because they made him look more intellectual and impressive, down into the quivering cerulean depths of the glistening orbs of the deliciously beautiful young lady sitting in a dusty brown chair in front of his desk which was also brown. Irene was wearing a black suit today that hugged the curves of her body, which were in all the right places, and in complete defiance of the scorching humid Georgia summertime air that turned almost everyone's hair into a mass of unappealing frizzles or else handfuls of limp stuff that resembled nothing more than masses of overcooked spaghetti, she wore her long, luxurious hair the color of perfectly sun-ripened wheat loose and falling in shimmering golden cascades around her dainty shoulders. Her slender yet perfectly formed legs were hidden by Nance's desk, but he knew they were there.

Nance knew perfectly well that Irene was the last person in this whole tangled mess he should be having such crazy, perverted thoughts about — I mean, even if she wasn't half my age, there was the involvement with Henry, and now he's dead and she's supposed to be in mourning. Besides, there was the whole nature of the suspicions he'd been having about certain things, which of course was the whole reason he'd called Irene in to talk to him today which had nothing to do with the hidden passion that lay hidden under that prim black skirt but was a matter of much seriousness and import.

"Yes, I am," Irene murmured liquidly, gazing up at the doctor. Goodness, but he was in good shape for a man his age! Just look at the kawaii way his shirt fit him. She could just imagine the six-pack he had under there. Apparently, being a doctor kept you in good shape, or maybe he just played a lot of golf.

"Well, I've been thinking a lot about what's been happening lately, ever since the accident," Nance proclaimed, rising from his seat and pacing restlessly around the desk, twiddling a pen absently. "It's always seemed funny to me that Bruce Lucent survived the crash, and Henry Archer didn't." He watched Irene carefully like a hawk to see if she'd blush or have any other reaction to this mention of Archer's death, but she looked as calm and smooth as an unused jar of peanut butter before someone's stuck the knife in (the creamy kind, not the crunchy, because her skin's not lumpy like the lumps you get in crunchy peanut butter).

"I don't think it's that strange," commented Irene with a shrug, tossing a gleaming lock of hair over her shoulder with one perfectly-maincured hand. "It's just the way things are, you know? Sometimes people live and sometimes they don't. Especially in car crashes."

"Well I think it's strange," retorted Nance.

"I know you think it's strange," Irene snapped, "you just said it."

"Don't you want to know why I think it's strange?"

"Fine," Irene sighed, "I guess I should let you tell me." She was starting to get bored, and Arthur Nance was starting to look a lot less hot, even if he did have that sexy little moustache.

"Okay," Nance began. Setting down the pencil before he stabbed himself with its point (he did this once, and it meant he couldn't work for days) .It hurts like crazy! I went to the doctor's and they had to dig the point out and everything. I think you can die of lead poisoning if they don't get the point out], he clasped his muscular hands behind his back and commenced to pace around the small, windowless office. There was a vase of flowers on his desk, and the petals were slowly falling off them. "It's about your father."

"My father?" queried Irene, looking surprised. Obviously this wasn't something she'd expected the handsome doctor to bring up. Arthur stared at her. Did she look guilty, or just surprised? Despite his usually extreme perspicatiousness in matters of judging the human physiognomy in times of stress, which ability came to him through many years of being a doctor and having to deal with stressed and not always completely honest patients and relatives of patience, which was stupid because how was he supposed to treat people properly if they didn't tell him the truth about there symptoms and stuff? That's what you go

"Yes," Nance pronounced ponderously and with emphasis. "Your father. Tell me, Miss Stevens, what can you tell me about your father?"

Irene sat quietly for a minute and thought. Finally she raised one perfectly golden-arched eyebrow, and answered, "Not a lot, really. He was always sort of distant when I was growing up. He only really noticed me if I was bad, and then he only noticed enough to punish me. He was a real baka. I suppose you could say that's why I made a lot of the choices I made, why I wound up the way I did." She sighed, which made her already impressive cleavage try to leap for freedom out of the linen-blend prison of her suit jacket. And briefly made Arthur Nance forget completely about what he was going to say next. But then he remembered.

"Well, Miss Stevens. I have reason to believe that he was involved with a friend of your late..." he paused, trying to think of a delicate way to put this and then giving up because there really wasn't any delicate way to put it. "your late boyfriend, Mr. Archer."

"You think my daddy was involved with Henry?" Irene exclaimed, jumping to her feet and looking alarmed in a way that Arthur didn't have to be a detective or a doctor or even someone who played one on TV to be able to figure out, it was that obvious.

"No, my dear, I didn't say that. I said he was involved with one of Mr. Archer's friends," he stressed. "A friend by the name of...Rory Edwards."

There was a silence, and all you could hear was the beep-beep of hospital machines. This suddenly made Nance realize that the office door was open (because otherwise he couldn't have hear the machines), and he rushed hastily over to close it, thinking, Shit...what if someone heard that? What if Bruce Lucent heard it? Of course he hadn't gotten to the part that involved Bruce yet, but what if the brilliant young software designer had heard and had somehow made the connections, even though Nance himself wasn't sure that what he suspected was anything more than the flimsiest of tissue-paper rumors? That, Nance thought grimly to himself, would be a very, very bad thing.

Meantime, Irene's already porcelain-pale complexion had gone completely dead white. "You think daddy was involved with Rory?" she repeated through lips gone numb like when you go to the dentist's and the Novocain gets shot into not quite the right spot.

"Yes," stated Nance, shutting the door with a melodramatic click. "And there's more."

"More?" repeated Irene, sinking back down into her chair.

"More," Nance confirmed. "This is what makes it all so suspicious you see."

"No, I don't see."

"You will. Because Rory was in cahoots the whole time with Isadore Trent."

"WHAT?!?!" shrieked Irene. "THAT STUPID, GENDER-CONFUSED PONYTAILED FREAK?!"

"Now, now," Nance chided, "that's no way to talk about someone. Isadore may have had some issues, but she's a person just like anyone else." He paused, and his chocolate-brown eyes glazed over with memory as he remembered another person, so very long ago, who'd had the same issues and had been so cruelly taken away from him because of them. Young people could be so cruel, especially young people still in school and surrounded by such incredible pressure to belong, conform, fit in with a group — any group, just as long as they could say they fit in somewhere. Irene had folded her arms under her perfect, melon-shaped breasts and was glaring at him. Nance forced his mind back to the present and continued.

"This is what makes it all so damn suspicious, you see. Two men, one dies in a car crash, one survives a car crash. Each has a friend — Bruce's friend is Isadore, and Henry's friend is Rory. And a common person they each know: your father, Irene. Isaac Stevens, the one meeting point of all this crazy insanity. There's more going on than you could possibly guess, and your father was right there in the thick of it, connected to Isadore and Rory."

"Do you have any proof of any of this?" Irene hissed, glaring at the doctor with hate quivering in her cerulean eyes.

"That's not important. What's important is that we learn the truth. Proof can come later."

"Well, I do not believe a word of it. And what about you, Dr. Nance? You treated both Henry and Bruce. One of them lived, and the other one didn't. How do I know YOU aren't the common point connecting it all?"

"Irene, you know that isn't true," Arthur murmured gently. "I'm a doctor, my mission is only to heal. I only want to learn the truth, not hurt anyone."

Suddenly, Irene burst into tears, flinging herself against Arthur's manly chest and burrowing into it's strength. "I'm sorry," she cried between sobs. "I...I just didn't want to believe it. Please...what are we going to do?"

"We'll do what we have to," declared Nance, whose mind was now racing even as he held the sobbing young girl in his solid, toned arms. Already he was beginning to formulate a plan. It was a crazy plan, but he thought it might have a chance of working, and if it did work then everything would fall into place, like a house of cards collapsing when you put just one card too many on top of the fragile structure. "We'll find out the truth."

Chapter 39

A gray crepuscular light seeped stripily down onto Bruce's face. He blinked and yawned. "Wha's happening'?" he murmured, rolling over to hug his pillow.

His pillow! What had happened to his pillow? It was no longer his hypo-allergenic polyester-fiberfill king-sized favorite. This was a half-sized foam-rubber hockey puck. Reflexively Bruce sat up, and was suddenly abruptly felled halfway up like an oak tree by a sharp blow to the forehead. He lay back, stunned and rubbing the rapidly-swelling red lump above his left eyebrow. The ceiling had dropped! It was now thirty inches above his face, a concrete ceiling crossed by steel girders. It was a steel girder he had hit his head on.

From directly below him a deep voice growled. "Shad dup, prison bride. Or I'll smack ya till ya do, huh?"

From slightly further below — Bruce had a good ear — an even deeper voice snarled, "Lay off you fuckin' noise, you fuckin' motherfuckas. It's five fuckin' a.m."

Bruce lay very still, trembling. What happened? Who were these people, in his bedroom? Rolling only his eyes around the room, he took in his surroundings. His comfortable bedroom had changed horribly. A barred window through which a tiny slice of gelid dawn sky peeped. Concrete block walls, concrete floor, concrete ceiling, painted shiny gray and adorned with graffiti in many colors. Without comprehension his eye took in the scrawl on the ceiling above his bed. In an indelible blue magic marker the gnomic curlicue resolved into the inscription.

Was it, could it be — had everything been a dream?!? *"I don't feel very fortunate," Bruce complained as his friend helped him from the low-slung red car, "I hurt all over and I don't remember a thing after I left that bar over on Martin Avenue. I wouldn't be surprised if the police didn't want to talk to me about what happened. Not that I could help them because I don't remember anything" he added as an afterthought.* This only happens on *Dallas*, Bruce told himself, whimpering silently in the back of his throat.

What was this place? He lay on a metal bunk with a thin mattress almost nine feet above the floor, a bunk from which ominous creaks and shakings began to emerge. Like Moby Dick rising from the ocean depths, a shaven dead-white skull slowly ascended above the horizon of his bunk. "You fucker," this vision intoned, scowling. "I was asleep. I was dreaming about little Mattie. I was warmin' her baby bottle in the microwave. And you, you fucker — you fuckin' WOKE ME UP."

One look into those crazy green eyes and Bruce knew he was in the presence of a maniac, a genuine deluxe homicidal maniac, little Mattie or no. A hand the size and color of an albino catcher's mitt rose into view and moved inexorably towards his throat. Bruce shrank back in the narrow bunk, clutching his thin scratchy brown blanket and pressing himself hopelessly against the cold unforgiving concrete block at his back. Conversation, that was the ticket — cordial conversation on topics of mutual interest. "Is this jail?" he quavered.

"It's fuckin' Death Row, motherfucka," the Great White Whale snarled. "And you know what that means? It means, I fuckin' waste you, and there ain't nothin' they can do to me no more. I'm like a desperate man, if you take my meanin'." His hamlike hand clamped inexorably around the neck of Bruce's pajama top. Bruce was dragged headfirst out of the bunk and dropped like a dead fish onto the floor. Luckily he was still clutching his foam-rubber pillow, which broke the impact a little. Right in front of his nose, the Great White's pallid bare feet, seamed with corns and wrinkles from too-tight athletic shoes, seemed to be the size of canoes.

"Goddam it, Bodine!" Suddenly a pair of large flat feet, black as shoe polish, slapped down onto the floor. The occupant of the middle bunk had entered the fray. "Can't we go one single goddam day without a scrap, huh?"

There was a solid meaty sound, the sound of solid dark meat hitting white Bodine muscle. Bruce curled up small, hoping not to be stepped on. "Fuck it. You think just because you got in on twenty fuckin' counts of serial rape and murder that you such fuckin' hot stuff?"

"They keep on telling us black folks we got oversized sex drives, so what's a man gonna do, huh?" The huge black man glared down at Bruce. "Death Row is goin' to hell, just like the goddam United Nations. Lookit this little yellow shit here. It's all this affirmative action to blame."

"Show you an oversized drive, fucker." From his vantage point on the floor Bruce could see the home-made shiv Bodine the Whale was flashing, pulled from his waistband.

Suddenly there came a clang of metal on metal from outside the cell. "Chow call, folks. Chow call." The wardens were coming! Bruce sat up. Keys clanked and doors opened, one by one, nearer and nearer. Bodine's shiv vanished like magic into the top of his sock.

The barred door of their cell slid back with a resounding clang, and the black man and Bodine shuffled sullenly out. Bruce scrambled to his feet. "Hey, man — this is all a dreadful mistake! I'm, you know, innocent."

The warden didn't even look at him. "Save it for your lawyer, pal."

"I didn't kill Callie!"

"Sure, pal. And I'm former First Lady Barbara Bush. Get a move on, will ya?"

"Please! I shouldn't be here!"

Bodine shot a look of contemptuous pity back over his shoulder at Bruce. "And you know little Mattie, that wasn't my fault. It was that fuckin' two-timin' arrogant woman, her mother. The razor blade — all her idea."

"Sure," Bruce said, his teeth chattering. He tottered rapidly along in the line, single file, down several open-riser steel staircases and then down a long bare concrete corridor to the cafeteria. This was a cavernous windowless basement space, lit harshly by the pitiless glare of fluorescent lights, it's windows shielded by heavy grates. A haze of cigarette smoke hung bluely near the ceiling. The trays were pressboard, the utensils were plastic, and the plates were Styrofoam. He held out his tray and a server in a hairnet plopped down a spoonful of something colorless swimming in greasy ichor. It was either grits or scrambled eggs. The coffee, in Styrofoam cups, was tepid and so weak he could see the bottom of the cup. He added a sugar and coffee creamer to see if that would help.

Was it better to sit with his cell-mates, or to find another table and hope he wasn't joined by a child murderer or a serial rapist? Better the devils you know that the devils you don't, he decided. But not too close, and not too far. He chose a place at the further end of the huge black man's table. At least he seemed to be unarmed. His cognomen seemed to be Pericles, and he was joined by a number of compatriots who lit cigarettes and rapidly scarfed down the food. Bruce could only pick at his own plate. I have to get out of here, he told himself. I have to talk to my lawyer! We have to fight this all the way to the Supreme Court!

Suddenly Bodine sauntered up to their table. "First I'm going to gut you like a fuckin' trout," he announced. "Then I'm going to pound the little snot's head in, for dessert."

Pericles seemed unimpressed. "You bore me, man."

Bodine picked up Bruce's nearly untouched plate and threw it like a Frisbee. Gray goop flew everywhere, but there was enough stuck on that when the plate hit Pericles it glopped down his T-shirt front. Without visible effort Pericles picked up his chair and slung it at Bodine.

All around them the other inmates stood up and yelled for blood. Plates, cups, chairs and food flew through the air. Bruce prudently abandoned his seat and crept under the table.

Chapter 40

Irene checked her face in the mirror and the gun in her handbag just once more before she found the reserve she was looking for in herself. Popping in a fresh breath mint (just in case), she pushed open the boardroom door to confront the three people who had ruined her life and killed her love.

Her father, Isaac Stevens, turned quickly, sloshing the whisky (a wonderful single malt) from his glass. "Dammit girl!, I taught you to knock when entering a room. All good women know that!"

"Yes father I do know to knock, but then I didn't have the bad manners to plot to kill my best friend and my business partner then, did I?"

The two other people in the room took a sudden greater interest in this new conversation.

Penelope and Rory stood too close for a casual chat, and the lipstick smears on Rory's face seemed to give rise to the evidence that these two at least had been quietly occupied as Isaac got celebratory drunk.

"Well. Well. The little missy's gone and got herself into a bit of a fit now ain't she? snipped Rory as he slipped his arm around Penelope's slim waist. "What ya trying to say gal?"

Irene suddenly realized that her plan to scare her father into confessing the attempted murder of Bruce and the accidental death of her lover Henry might have one or two flaws to it. She hadn't realized that all three had been plotting this coup for months and now she would just be one more pretty little speed bump on their road to riches. As this kernel of truth popped open, Irene reached into her purse to grab the gun, but strong feelings of misgiving began to overwhelm her. Could she shoot her father, the man who had raised her since her mother's untimely demise?

Rory dropped his hold of the luscious Penelope's waist and lunged for Irene sure that he, the big strong man that he was, could stop this tiny girl from going or doing anything. His eyes gleamed evilly, until suddenly, they took on a look of surprise. The hand that had so recently been fondling Penelope's besom, now clutched his own bleeding midsection as he dropped to his knees on the overly expensive Persian rug. "She shot me, that damn bitch daughter of yoren shot me!" And with that exclamation, he pitched face forward with an "OOF!".

Irene nudged his head with her perfectly pedicure right foot. He didn't seem to notice, so she figured he was dead. Good, one less problem to worry me. she thought.

"What in the hell so ya think you are doing?" shouted Isaac, fear causing his voice to waver a bit. "Now you've gone way beyond any manners they taught you at that fancy boarding school I sent ya to!" "You just do not shoot people, that's not proper!"

So, thought Irene, this is what real power feels like. I like it! And with that thought she raised the gun and pointed it at the remaining two. She waved

-282-

the gun casually, between the two like a lazy band conductor in 2 / 2 time.

"Now Father, tell me again how mother died in that car fire. You know, the one in which your brother was not really there?   And how sorry you were that   Henry, your oldest and dearest friend, father of your grandchildren to be, died in that same little accident, and how that left you temporarily in charge of Bruce's company. Oh and Penelope, how many beds did it take to line this up? Did you enjoy my dad ?   What is it with you and these old rich bastardy?"

"Actually, You were much more fun sweetie. These old guys just can't measure up. Remember the trip to the Bahamas and that beach?" Penelope slowly moved forward with each word, distancing herself from Isaac . "We sure rocked that world. I'll never forget how you said we should never come back to Atlanta, and how we could live there forever on your trust fund." Penelope reached a hand out to Irene and tried to reach out and stroke her cheek.

"Forget the Bahamas bitch!   Irene slapped Penelope's hand away. "You left me there to rot and next I knew I was paying bail and bribes for some stolen jewelry! And, dammit, I didn't even get to enjoy any of it!" Irene spit the words into Penelope face as the gun spit three rounds into her gut. "How's it feel to die a piece at a time, one bullet for each day I spent in jail for you! This is all you'll ever get from me!"

"Reee nee baby, sweetheart, now don't shoot your daddy, we can come to an understanding, can't we?' Isaac sniveled as he dropped to his knees in front of his daughter.

"Don't call me that! You ain't got no rights to use Mama's name far me." Irene's accent tore through as her tears began to fall. " Daddy, I don't wanna kill ya, but If'n you don't die, then I know ya'all just find a way to get rid of me and the babies."

"No, honey. Give me a chance and we can fix all this up in no time. We'll keep to the plan and take the company, that feel Bruce'll never figure out it was us until we 're off living the good life in Europe with his money. How's that with you? I control all the company and most of the shares, so we can have it all and be gone in a week. So, Please don't shoot me!" Isaac crawled toward his daughter pleading for his life and thinking that he could get the gun away when the other two fools couldn't.

"Fuck off Father! Die like a man! Not the crawling worm I've come to know!" BANG! BANG! Two more shots tore thought the carpet. Isaac cowered down hands over his head and began to shake.

Irene smiled. "Well daddy, guess this is goodbye, Kiss kiss Hugs, Tata. BANG! One more shot rang out and Isaac's very expensive toupee took a wild leap from his now bald and bleeding head.

Irene sat back to take in her handiwork. Three very dead bodies lay around the room, each with a different expression on what was left of their respective faces.

Irene noticed a smudge of blood on the tip of her toe and bent down to wipe it off. She used the hanky from Rory's breast pocket as he no longer needed it.

Bruce rolled into the room. "Great work my love, I'll have my people clean this up and we need never bother with this again. Now go get cleaned up, we have a meeting of the board of directors in an hour and I need my new Senior VP ready to shine!"

"I'll see you in ten babe! Got those tickets ready for Barcelona?"

"Sure do and then 3 weeks on the French Riviera, then pop home and get the nursery ready for our boys!"

"Isn't life great when ya got all the money and no scruples?" and they laughed as they left the gory scene to the clean up crew.

Chapter 41

Inside Richard Isaacs.

Outside—below—so far—Atlanta. Teaming urban sprawl, Boeings and LearJets circling like buzzards to the corporate stink of carrion, cruising hot thermal of greed. Old jets never die, they just go into a holding pattern over Atlanta. Can it be that it's life itself that's the holding pattern?

Somewhere out there—down there—misted by the steamy fog of his heated breath on the cool air-conditioned glass—Margaret Eastman's curves fill the tight-stretched spandex city with their Silicone bounty. Shouldn't that be enough to live for? Shouldn't it? *Shouldn't it?*

Not. If. He. Couldn't. Have. Her.

Inside the ghostly reflection of the office window. The shadow of a man. Richard Isaacs, superimposed on the crawling city. A giant over an anthill.

A giant ready to lay down on that anthill and pour honey on itself and let it eat him alive.

Like it hadn't already tried.

How far he'd grown from little Richie Isaacs the kid everyone loved to pick on! The kid who stole a bag of apples for the teacher from the tree in the Johnson's yard. The kid who nobody ever knew put the rocks in Mr. Miller's garden hose or the Kool-Aid in the principle's gas tank or the prank calls to random names in the phonebook to ask if the Bowels were there or did they move. Oh, he was a tricky little devil. Nobody ever put one over on little Richie Isaacs. How did it all come to this? Was it the abuse of the priest at the First Baptist Church with the red silk Cossack around his neck announcing his corrupt virtue for no one to see? Was it Pop taking the belt to him between belts from quart bottles of Rheingold? Was it Uncle Jeb turning into the driveway to pulverize his beloved Lionel Trains under the cruel wheels of the old John Deer? Was it Ma on the creaky porch in her frumpy house dress and pink slippers and curlers sipping Mint Juleps like there was no care in all the world? Oh, mama! he thought sadly. I'm so sorry I never went to your funeral! How did it ever come to this for Missus Isaac's best baby boy?

The well built man surveyed his office environs in a reverie that was so uncharacteristic for him. The designer furniture that looked like they carved it from the iceberg that sank the Titanic. The abstract impressionist original on the wall that he always thought looked like Ed what's-his-name from the movie version. The bank of T.V. screens showing MS-NBC, the financial feeds. The antique globe he liked to spin and trail his finger over it to get a tactical sensation of the mountains and the valleys rising and falling like a graph of today's Dow.

His fingers . . . His fingers . . . Looking at his hands, the backs of which were beginning to show age spots like rust—rust which forms not on peach trees, not on living growing things, things that soak up decaying putrid soil and drank lemony sunlight and gave back the breath of life, but rather rust which forms on iron, things of cold and metal hardness, Richard's fingers were perversely aware of the power they held. To manipulate. To mold. To force, with their iron cold metal hardness, the objects of their will in the direction they willed them. A few taps of these fingertips on the right keys on the right board at the right moment—lives were ruined. Buy low, sell high. Every thing has a price. Richard Isaccs's was higher than he knew. Holding the metaphor in his palms, all the blood drained from his sanguine face.

His hands could kill.

Him.
His hands could kill him.
Ye gods, what terrible power!
Should he do it? he wondered. It wasn't like the motivation wasn't nonexistent. Despair was kudzu. Choking creeping ravenous kudzu, nothing to do but to napalm it. You had your bull markets of the soul and bear markets. Crashes and depressions— and he wasn't talking about the kind of crash Bruce Lucent lost his shorts in. Sometimes one had no choice but to realize the loss. Sometimes a guy hadda take the cosmic tax deduction in the sky. You didn't always get an option or a choice or another alternative.

This could be it.
The big correction . . .
All umpteen shrieking stories . . .
It was not to be. Damned sealed glass, damned climate control, damned transparent prison—or maybe a phone cord around the neck, he reflected, however there was nowhere to hang from in this sterile plastic state-of-the-art-environmentally-

correct-eco-friendly cage, goddam Eurotrash designers claimed they thought of everything but they didn't think of *this* now did they, space didn't have *every* modern amenity, couldn't gas yourself in a General Electric microwave, didn't suppose he could buzz down to the lobby and request a halfway decent sprinkler head to hang his sorry gullet on, but couldn't you rig something through the cord, twist a ruler through it, couldn't you tighten it yourself? Turning and torquing and winding, tighter and tighter, muscles straining in his merciless shoulders, cranking a bulwark closed on a sinking ship— would he have the balls to go through with it, wring the breath from his own gasping throat? Would he plead for his life, would he say: "Dick, for God sakes, don't do this, you have so much to live for, don't be a fool, don't throw your life away?" Would those hands, his iron hands, his terrible aging rust-corroded sin-stained hands take on their own DoctorStrangelovian personality, could nothing he say deter them from their inexorable will?

He wrestled his stygian urges down with Herculean aplomb.

Got a hold of himself.

Control.

Control he could do.

Alright. No Dopplering dotcom plummet to eat a terminal snack of pigeon-flavored pavement after the dead cat bounce. No jolt of autocratic asphyxiation, wrenching the Apex Data Ruler the way he wrenched himself in the wee of the night when he lay prostate on his back and no one could hear him ejaculate Margaret's name into the Sealy Serta mattress drenched with the carnal effluents of desire. No tragic grandiose flinging of the BellSouth fiber=optic wiring over the rafter beam since there wasn't one, positioning the SemperFidic ergonomic office chair, looping the Jimmy Hendrix original hand-made collectable silk necktie neck, kicking the spinning chair across the anti-static mat cleated like Beckum's soccer shoes to the migraine Millikin Carpet, kicking the climate controlled air with its direction adjustable hypoallergenic louvers, kicking the generic afterlife. There was always Valium.

Stumbling to the kidney-shaped translucent sea iceberg green designer desk, the bottles came into his iron hands like magnets snapping onto iron. Valium, Zoloft, Previcid, Lescal, Seconal, Zantac, Paxil, Ultram...Dewars. Before he knew it, the stock ticker of his life would be passing before his eyes. then sweet oblivion. Glorious nothingness. No more tortuous silicone visions, no more danger sharp curves ahead, no more Bruce Lucent and his infernal reeking testosterone making a man want to be things no decent man ought to want to be and do things no decent man ought to want to do, no more onus of law enforcement's fetid breath hot under his collar, no more ratting, no more backstabbing, no more megalomaniac Machiavellian machinations, no more Margaret, no more black Fridays, no more blowoff tops, no more crack spreads, no more drunkards walks, no more high-ticking, no more LEAPs, no more margin calls, no more market timing, no more mental stop-loss, no more momentum indicators, no more multiple linear regressions, no more opportunity costs, no more outside reversal months, no more pessimistic rates of return, no more pivot points, no more probability density functions, no more quarterly net profit margins, no more relative return standard deviations, no more resistance lines, no more shaved candlesticks, no more spikes, no more splines, no more whiplashes, no more whipsaws, no more upswings, no more downswings, no more, no more, no more, no more no more no more no more no

No.

No! He did not give up that easy!

He was a commodity traded on his own futures exchange. He would die before he sold himself that short. He was almost jigged out there, almost whacked, almost melted his own account. But Richard Isaacs was not done yet. Richard Isaccs did not go down that easy. Richard Isaacs was a market maker. Richard Isaacs was printing on the O!

He slung the handful of pills in an overhand arc toward the direction of the designer wastebasket, watching them soar through the luminous light of the Ptolemies World Classic omnidirectional task light, heard them scatter like shotgun shot into the lacquered executive wastebasket with the little bar graphs decorated on it, the pinnacle of all his superficial aspirations, the symbol for his nearly untimely fall.

Richard Isaacs returned to the window again. Dick Isaacs looked through his reflection. No one looked back. No one ever did.

Outside the cruel uncaring metropolis. The juggernaut he would bring to it's knees.

Inside Richard Isaacs.

THE END

Afterword

How this book came to be: You can blame it on "traditional publisher" PublishAmerica.

Travis Tea is the pseudonym for a group of (mostly) science fiction and fantasy authors who were amused by PublishAmerica's claim (at their authorsmarket.net site) that science fiction and fantasy authors are "writers who erroneously believe that SciFi, because it is set in a distant future, does not require believable storylines, or that Fantasy, because it is set in conditions that have never existed, does not need believable every-day characters."

It seems that PublishAmerica has a mad on at science fiction writers: "...science-fiction and fantasy writers have it easier. It's unfair, but such is life. As a rule of thumb, the quality bar for sci-fi and fantasy is a lot lower than for all other fiction. Therefore, beware of published authors who are self-crowned writing experts. When they tell you what to do and not to do in getting your book published, always first ask them what genre they write. If it's sci-fi or fantasy, run. They have no clue about what it is to write real-life stories, and how to find them a home."

PublishAmerica, the self-described "traditional publisher" located in Frederick, Maryland, says of its own operation, "Each day, an average 78 new authors who are looking to find a book publishing company ask us to publish their book. We review not only the quality but also the genre of their work.... Like all serious book publishing companies we have to be picky as we can only accept the works that meet our requirements in both areas."

So a group of science fiction writers (inept practitioners of an undemanding art, if PublishAmerica were to be believed) set out to see what kind of "quality" PublishAmerica required –how believable the characters needed to be and how believable the storyline had to be.

PublishAmerica said they were "picky"? People who'd read PublishAmerica books suspected that the fine folks in Frederick didn't edit their titles (despite their claim to do so "line-by-line") and perhaps didn't even read their submissions before offering a contract. Okay, fine–we'd see.

I organized the project, with the knowledge and blessing of Ann Crispin, head of the Science Fiction and Fantasy Writers of America's Writing Scams Committee.

The writers who volunteered to write a chapter or two were given minimal outlines, a couple of characters with sketchy descriptions, and asked to write badly. Which characters went in which chapter was determined by rolling dice. No writer knew the overall plot, such as it was. None of them knew if their chapter was going to be first, last, or somewhere else. None knew what the genre was, other than that it was set in the modern day.

The chapters came in. A few writers failed to meet the (admittedly very short) deadline. No problem. I left the chapter out, or reused a chapter from another part of the book, and in one case filled in the missing chapter with machine-generated word hash.

Some people suspected that PublishAmerica didn't even read the submissions that came their way before offering a contract. Cool. We were going to find out.

I presume, if you've made it this far, that you've read *Atlanta Nights*. Pretty nasty, right? The text, just as you've read it, was taken by a brave volunteer and submitted to PublishAmerica under his own name.

The world turned. Then....

----- Original Message -----
From: PublishAmerica Aquisitions
To: [Deleted]
Sent: Tuesday, December 07, 2004
Subject: Atlanta Nights

Dear Mr. [Deleted]

As this is an important piece of email regarding your book, please read it completely from start to finish.

I am happy to inform you that PublishAmerica has decided to give "Atlanta Nights" the chance it deserves. An email will follow this one with the sample contract attached for your review. If you do not receive the email with the attached sample contract in twenty-four hours, please contact me, so I can resend the document via another method.

I will be happy to answer any questions you may have concerning the contract and to guide you through the contract negotiations phase. **Please note that once you have requested that we send the official contract, we cannot further amend the contract.**

Upon receiving your e-mail in acceptance with the terms, we will forward the final contract documents to you via regular mail for your signature. Along with your e-mail acceptance **please include your legal name, current address, telephone number and title of work as you would like it to appear on the final contract.**

The main terms of the contract are that we will pay you climbing royalties starting at 8%, you retain the copyright, and we will begin production on the book within 365 days of the date we receive the signed contract. A symbolic $1 advance underlines that all financial risk is carried by the Publisher, as we firmly believe it should be.

Once the signed contract has been processed in our offices, you will be contacted by our Production oftlinedepartment regarding "the next step" for your book in the publishing process.

After both parties have signed the contract, you will be contacted by our production department with a list of questions and suggestions. Please feel frcc to e-mail any concerns or questions dealing with the terms of the contract to meg@publishamerica.com. Also, please visit our web site at http://www.publishamerica.com/.

Welcome to PublishAmerica, and congratulations on what promises to be an exciting time ahead.

Sincerely,

Meg Phillips
Acquisitions EditorPublishAmerica

O happy day! We were going to be published authors! PublishAmerica certainly had an interesting take on what constituted "quality," but who were we to complain? The fact that these "picky" people had accepted our manuscript validated our worth as writers! We *did too* know what it is to write believeable characters in believable stories set in the real world! We didn't have to keep on writing science fiction and fantasy... they were going to give us a chance!

We passed the manuscript, the acceptance letter, and the sample contract over to a lawyer, to look them over. He advised that no one sign that contract.

Nothing for it. We went public on January 23, 2005, with the story. Imagine our sorrow when, the next day, our front man got the following email from our friends in Frederick:

----- Original Message -----
From: "PublishAmerica Acquisitions"
To: [Deleted]
Sent: Monday, January 24, 2005
Subject: Your Submission to PublishAmerica

Dear Mr. [Deleted],

We must withdraw our offer to publish Atlanta Nights. Upon further review it appears that your work is not ready to be published. There are portions of nonsensical text in the manuscript that were caught by our editing staff as they previewed the text for editing time assessment pending your
acceptance of our offer.

On the positive side, maybe you want to consider contracting the book with a vanity publisher such as iUniverse or Author House. They will certainly publish your book at a fee.

Thank you.

PublishAmerica Acquisitions Department

Nonsensical text? Say it ain't so!

Our hopes of becoming real authors dashed, there was nothing to do but to make *Atlanta Nights* available on the 'Net, and put out a press release:

Science Fiction Authors Hoax Vanity Publisher

"Atlanta Nights," by Travis Tea, was offered a publishing contract by PublishAmerica of Frederick, Maryland.

Washington, DC (PRWEB) January 28, 2005 -- Over a holiday weekend last year, some thirty-odd science fiction writers banged out a chapter or two apiece of "Atlanta Nights," a novel about hot times in Atlanta high society. Their objective: to write a deeply awful novel to submit to PublishAmerica, a self-described "traditional publisher" located in Frederick, Maryland.

The project began after PublishAmerica posted an attack on science fiction authors at one of its websites (http://www.authorsmarket.net/). PublishAmerica claimed "As a rule of thumb, the quality bar for sci-fi and fantasy is a lot lower than for all other fiction.... [Science fiction authors] have no clue about what it is to write real-life stories, and how to find them a home." It described them as "writers who erroneously believe that SciFi, because it is set in a distant future, does not require believable storylines, or that Fantasy, because it is set in conditions that have never existed, does not need believable every-day characters."

The writers wanted to see where PublishAmerica puts its own quality bar; if the publisher really is selective, as the company claims, or if it is a vanity press that will accept almost anything, as publishing professionals assert.

"Atlanta Nights" was completed, any sign of literary competence was blue-penciled, and the resulting manuscript was submitted.

PublishAmerica accepted it.

From: PublishAmerica Aquisitions [e-mail protected from spam bots]
Sent: Tuesday, December 07, 2004
Subject: Atlanta Nights

As this is an important piece of email regarding your book, please read it completely from start to finish. I am happy to inform you that PublishAmerica has decided to give "Atlanta Nights" the chance it deserves....Welcome to PublishAmerica, and congratulations on what promises to be an exciting time ahead.

Sincerely,
Meg Phillips
Acquisitions Editor
PublishAmerica

The hoax was publicly revealed on January 23, 2005. PublishAmerica withdrew their offer shortly afterward:

From: "PublishAmerica Acquisitions"
Sent: Monday, January 24, 2005
Subject: Your Submission to PublishAmerica
We must withdraw our offer to publish "Atlanta Nights". Upon further review it appears that your work is not ready to be published. There are portions of nonsensical text in the manuscript that were caught by our editing staff as they previewed the text for editing time assessment pending your acceptance of our offer.

On the positive side, maybe you want to consider contracting the book with a vanity publisher such as iUniverse or Author House. They will certainly publish your book at a fee.

Thank you.
PublishAmerica Acquisitions Department

Those who wish to see the novel, "Atlanta Nights" by Travis Tea, for themselves can find it at
http://www.lulu.com/travis-tea

Publication at Lulu.com is free.

For more information about PublishAmerica and vanity presses, see:
http://www.sfwa.org/beware/
http://www.washingtonpost.com/wp-dyn/articles/A25187-2005Jan20.html

And that, friends, is the story of how the book you're holding in your hands came to be.

All profits from the sale of *Atlanta Nights* will go to the Science Fiction and Fantasy Writers of America Emergency Medical Fund.

(Oh ... special treat. Take the initials of the main characters. Anagram them. You'll get a fun message!)

– James D. Macdonald